I
STOP
SOME-
WHERE

TE CARTER

Feiwel and Friends
New York

A FEIWEL AND FRIENDS BOOK
An imprint of Macmillan Publishing Group, LLC
175 Fifth Avenue, New York, NY 10010

Our books may be purchased in bulk for promotional, educational, or business use. Please contact your local bookseller or the Macmillan Corporate and Premium Sales Department at (800) 221-7945 ext. 5442 or by e-mail at MacmillanSpecialMarkets@macmillan.com.

Library of Congress Cataloging-in-Publication Data is available.

ISBN 978-1-250-12464-7 (hardcover) / ISBN 978-1-250-12465-4 (ebook)

Book design by Eileen Savage

Feiwel and Friends logo designed by Filomena Tuosto

First edition, 2018

10 9 8 7 6 5 4 3 2 1

fiercereads.com

To the girls who survive,
To the girls who are found too late,
To the girls who are never found . . .
You are beautiful.
You are loved.
You are **believed**.

I bequeath myself to the dirt to grow from
    the grass I love,
If you want me again look for me under your
    boot-soles.
You will hardly know who I am or what
    I mean...

Failing to fetch me at first keep encouraged,
Missing me one place search another,
I stop somewhere waiting for you.

        —Walt Whitman, "Song of Myself"

They call the houses "zombies," and our town is full of them. Empty places where people used to live, where there were memories until life and all its broken parts happened.

Homes caught between the living and the dead. People can't afford them and the banks don't want them. So they rot, turning into something ugly. It feels like there are hundreds of them in Hollow Oaks, even if that's probably impossible. And there are even more in the towns beyond us.

So many places for a girl to disappear.

I suppose this is a fitting place for a girl like me. I disappeared before I actually did. And now, I'm trapped here. Forgotten.

This whole town is full of ghosts.

chapter one

S
he came in here with her brand-new shoes. Happy. I don't know her, but I'd seen her at school.

I think her name's Rebecca. Maybe Rachel. Something with an *R*. She was a freshman. A year younger than me. Maybe she's still a freshman. I don't know how much time has passed; I don't know how long I've been here.

"Please," she begs, but he doesn't stop hurting her.

It never stops.

I wish I felt more for her. I almost wish I could feel it the way I used to. Could suffer her fear alongside her, but I can't anymore. I can't let myself feel it.

There have been seven girls since the night I came here. To this room. This forgotten place for forgotten girls.

The room is a box. There's nothing on the walls. No posters or pictures or even a tacky wreath. Nothing to make it more than a room. The walls are just place markers. Beige and boring and broken. The holes came later. With the damage that fills the room.

"Please," the girl says again.

There's gum on her shoe. That's what I look at, because

otherwise, I have to look at him. His familiar and confusing smile.

The gum's on her left shoe. They're brand-new, looking like they just came out of a box, but the soles don't care. There's a giant wad of gum smeared across the bottom. She would've been mortified if she'd realized it. I mean, before. I don't think gum's a priority now. Still, it bugs me. The way it got onto her new shoes. The way it took something good, something beautiful, and slowly ruined it without her knowing. I hate the way these unseen things damage us in secret.

It was pink, although most of it's grime now from being on the bottom of her shoe. In the cracks, though, in the places where the dirt couldn't reach, pink still sneaks through. I hope for the pink. I wish for it, because I have to focus on gum.

"Please."

She's so pretty. Of course she is. They're all pretty. I suppose it should be flattering, to be one of them. It means I'm pretty, too. That was all I thought I wanted. To be part of something. To be special.

I don't feel pretty. I don't feel special, either. I don't feel much.

Keep looking at the gum.

I don't want to look up. I don't want my eyes to travel to the tops of her shoes, to her blue-and-white socks, up her pale legs. I don't want to see it. I've seen it so many times now.

I can't let myself look at him. Don't want to remember how his hands felt. All the things he said to me. The way he touched me. The same way he's touching her. That invasion of something you don't know how to hold on to. I force myself to forget those things.

Just think about gum.

So I try, instead, to remember gum. I remember how it was,

even if I can't taste it. I remember the first day of school. How we carried it like a weapon. We walked into classrooms, challenged our teachers with the knowledge that we carried it. It took maybe a day to realize the teacher didn't care anyway. Why would they? It was only gum.

But every so often, there'd be one teacher who agonized over the residue stuck to the underside of the chair when they went to flip it over, as they put the classroom back into its evening state of waiting.

I miss the pettiness of it all. The way we think when the world still makes sense and spins altogether for us. When gum is nothing more than gum. When it doesn't cling to the shoes of a girl who's crying.

Oh, God, I need her to stop crying.

"Why are you doing this?" she asks.

He doesn't answer. He's a cliché. He looks for the young ones, the pretty ones.

The weak ones.

That's it, though, isn't it? He thinks we're all weak.

He takes off her shoes and there's nothing left to stare at. Nothing except him. With her. His hands are clean today, but they were so dirty that night. He hadn't even bothered to wash his hands for me.

Without the gum, without anything to distract me, I close my eyes and pretend not to know what he's doing. While she cries, I ignore her. Try not to hear. Try not to remember how he laughed. I try not to feel the way the carpet scratched my skin.

I wonder about the people who lived here before. They left furniture, boxes. Most of what made them a family. All the things that made this a home. When they left, they probably thought someone else would come along. That someone would make this house a part of their lives. Maybe exist like they had. I don't think they imagined this.

Would it have changed anything if they'd known? I've seen how some of them leave. Strangers forcing them to choose which things to keep. What to save. What parts of home aren't linked to that sense of place.

"You're hurting me," the girl cries, interrupting my thoughts.

Shut up, I think, dreaming about the ghosts. The ones who were here until it was forgotten. I wonder if they had kids.

I bet they cried when they left. Not for the reasons Rebecca/Rachel is crying. They cried because it was their home. Sure, maybe there was another house somewhere, but a house isn't the same as home. A house has walls and rooms and a roof. Home is the annoying rattle the pipes make in winter when you get up before school to brush your teeth. The rattle that you miss when you stay somewhere else. Home is knowing exactly where the trash can is.

There was one time—several years ago now—I watched the people across the street as they lost whatever fight they were trying to win. We stood on our front lawn, like the rest of our neighbors. We were helpless while the sheriff's department dragged them from the house. Changed the locks as they watched. Separated them from everything they were. Because the bank said they were out of time.

When I was younger, I didn't understand. It was sad and it bothered me, but I didn't feel it the way I do now. Seeing what someone's home becomes. What the banks were saving. This room is what they created.

Hollow Oaks, New York, is an impossible town. It's impossible for people to stay here, just like it's impossible for anyone to find me.

I wish I could remember when I came to this room. I remember gum, but not time. I don't know how many days or weeks or years have passed. I don't know how long ago the people who owned this place left. I don't know how long I've been here or how long it will take until they remember I'm missing.

But I do remember before. Vivid details and memories of even the smallest things. Gum. The smell of rose petals. The way it felt crawling into bed after the sheets had just been washed. Yet I can't remember how long it's been. I only remember after. A perpetual state of after.

"No," the girl says.

I just want her to be quiet. I don't want to be here, but I can't seem to get away. There's only folding myself into before.

There has to be an end to this. There has to be a finite number of girls. There has to be a limit to how many times I can hear the word no.

There has to be a limit to how many times this can happen.

chapter two

There's that nursery rhyme. You know it? All about what makes a girl. We're sugar and spice and everything nice, but that sounds like a cookie recipe. It doesn't sound like the composition of a person.

I wanted to be pretty. That's part of what makes a girl, I think. That inherent need to be pretty. Pretty is important. Pretty is good. Girls who are pretty are likable.

Pretty is power.

I didn't think I was pretty. I thought that was why people hated me. Early in middle school, it was awful. I grew up too fast. I stood in the bathroom outside my fifth-grade class and cried, because the boys thought it was funny to snap the back of my bra. The girls said I was a whore because I couldn't stop myself from growing up.

There was a book they passed around. They used to list each girl's defining features. Some were pretty. Some weren't, but they were funny. I wasn't those things. I was a slut. I was poor. I was dirty.

I was only eleven. I didn't want to be defined by these words.

It didn't last forever. Maybe a year. Eventually, other girls had boobs, too, and I was just someone else. They never said they were sorry, though. They never welcomed me. I was still on the edges of the world, but eventually, it wasn't constant. It was only a remark here or there. But I couldn't forget the names they'd used. Even if they'd stopped using them, I knew that, once, they'd thought those things of me and so, somewhere, it must have been true. It put me outside of them, even if they seemed to have moved on to other things.

I don't know if it would have been different if my mom had been there. There was only my dad because she'd left right after I was born. She tried on the name Mother, but she couldn't juxtapose it with being Sierra and so I was down a parent right away. She doesn't call. She sends birthday cards once a year. Sometimes even in the right month.

Dad and I used to go fishing in the summer. It was before the whispered comments about my body. Before they asked if I should really be eating that second piece of pizza at lunch given what I looked like. It was before I cared about being pretty.

We were like criminals, creeping out into the stealth of dawn, already on the water before the sun came up. We stole the day and it was beautiful.

I was only allowed to drink coffee on those mornings. Coffee wasn't something for kids, he'd say, but when we both found ourselves yawning, he'd pour a little into the top of his thermos and pass it over to me. A secret. A promise. I didn't like the taste of it but I loved it for being a part of us.

"Can we watch a movie tonight?" I asked as I sipped at the coffee, the acrid burning both terrible and sweet.

"Sure, Ellie, what do you want to watch?"

I never wanted to watch anything in particular. I simply wanted him to stay awake.

I loved my dad. I *love* my dad. Still.

These were our moments, and we'd make plans under the sun and we believed them. After dinner on those nights, we'd put in a movie, but he'd be asleep before the opening credits finished. He tried. He meant to stay awake; he just couldn't.

But on those mornings, he did. It was something for us.

I miss those moments the most.

It's not clear why we stopped going. Maybe he got too tired. Maybe the boat rental cost too much. I don't know. It just was, and then it wasn't. Like most of the things that happen in our lives.

Still, I wonder how much it has to do with what happened the last time.

We were out on the lake that morning, our lines cast. We never caught anything. It wasn't about actually catching a fish. It was about us, and about secret illicit coffee, and about the plans we made that we believed we'd follow through on.

"Look at these jerks," he said.

Their boat had a motor and shone brighter than the sun on the water. They owned it. They owned everything.

"They're going to kill the damn fish," my dad complained.

They were riding through the lake, the boat spearing the waves, and the guys were tossing bottles over the sides. They were barely older than me, also with their dad. Their music cut through the sounds of them taking the lake away from us. Because that's what they were doing. They took the lake from us. They reminded us that the mornings we had weren't ours, that they were only borrowed time.

"Why are they doing that?" I asked my father.

"They think they can do anything."

"But there are rules," I argued.

He shook his head and packed up the things in the boat, taking in the lines. "Be careful with people like that, Ellie. They have it all, but it's never good enough."

I tell myself that's why we stopped going. The fish were going to die anyway, with the bottles bobbing on the surface of the water. It was all ruined by someone else's noise and carelessness. Maybe they never would've come back, but it wouldn't have been the same.

It's poetic to frame my life with them. With the lake. If I walked to the end of the driveway from this house, kept going past the trees, I'd be able to see the ghost of that boat still on the water.

I told myself it was okay. I was getting older anyway. Pretty girls didn't wake before dawn and go fishing. I wanted to be pretty, so it was fine.

Later, I remember how my dad would stand in my doorway, watching me. Trying to reach me across so little space, yet so much. He stared at me like you look at a museum display or a creature in the zoo. I was the coelacanth, and he was awed by my strangeness.

"I brought you something," he said, holding a bag out across the threshold to my bedroom.

My room was an experiment. Posters and magazine pages and images covered the walls and the vanity and my dresser. All the people I wanted to be, wanted to look like. They were the people who mattered. I stared at myself in the mirror, hating how I looked. I hated how the curves made the boys poke me through the back of my chair in class, and how they made the girls call me fat. I hated how far the people in the magazines were from me. I thought I would never count, because I wasn't them.

"What is it?" I asked my dad, gesturing toward the bag he was holding.

"I thought you might like it."

It happened every few nights. He'd show up, presenting an offering in a plastic bag. Makeup. Clothes. Hair bands. He tried. He tried and so I tried, but the discount stickers said it all.

They were marked down, because the lipstick was too orange. The tank top wasn't cut right. The hairpins would have been perfect for a girl my age—ten years ago. But I wore them for him and he smiled, because he didn't know the difference.

"Thanks, Dad. I love it," I lied.

"You're beautiful, Ellie."

I was a markdown girl.

I did know the difference.

chapter three

Rachel or Rebecca is still crying.

That's another thing that makes a girl. We have an endless well of tears.

When I watched them come in, she was holding his hand. Smiling. She thought it was a date. She didn't know that they only bring certain girls here. There are other places, for the other kinds of girls. The ones they want people to know about. They don't have to hide with some girls. But here . . .

I think they like it here even better.

The other girls don't cry the same way.

"Please," Rachel/Rebecca says.

Such a futile word. She can say it forever and nobody's going to hear her. Nobody but me, and what can I do? I said it, too. I begged. It didn't change anything.

"Just be good," he says.

He brought music and he turns it up. Not loud enough that her cries are washed away, of course. The crying is his favorite part.

I wish there'd been music that night. I wish there'd been anything but the brown walls and the way he kissed me.

chapter four

K ate lived behind our house. The hill that ran from our backyard to hers was steep and it had rained the night before. She came outside, wearing headphones and a hoodie over her bathing suit, and headed right for the lawn chair. I'd been watching her for a few days, debating on asking for help. I knew her routine. She came out, went to sleep, and went back inside after she woke up again.

I tried to get to her quickly, to reach her before she fell asleep. I slipped while I was running, cutting the palm of my hand on a rock and smearing my shorts with mud.

"Hi," I said, a muddy, crumpled thing at the bottom of the hill in her backyard.

She took off her headphones. "Ellie, right?"

I didn't know how she knew, but I guess it was the same way I knew she was Kate. Like a census of your neighbors that's mailed to you when you're born, complete with names and a one-sentence description. Kate slept a lot and was older than me. I was Ellie, the weird girl covered in mud.

"Yeah. I . . . I go to Saint Elizabeth's. I mean, I did. Last year. Like last month. I just finished there is what I'm saying."

She nodded and sat down. I waited to see if she'd fall asleep.

"My church used to pay for it. For school, I mean. But they can't anymore," I said.

"That sucks."

"It does. But I'm not here about that."

"What's up, Ellie?" she asked.

I didn't know how to ask her. How to tell her what I needed. I don't know why—even now—I trusted her. I don't know what made me sure she wouldn't ridicule me for asking. But something about her seemed wise. Indifferent to the way people looked at her. Maybe it was because she was older. Maybe it was her purple hair. No one in the magazines or at my school had purple hair. She didn't look like everyone else, either, but she didn't seem to mind. Maybe that was what I needed. Someone who was okay with being her own version of okay.

"I have to start school—high school—in a few weeks. I don't know anyone," I said. "I didn't really have any friends at Saint Elizabeth's, but it doesn't matter now anyway, and I . . . I don't want to be a loser."

Kate looked at me in my muddy shorts and my markdown shirt. On it was a singing ear of corn. I don't know what that was supposed to mean. But I can promise it was marked down as soon as it arrived at the store. What girl wants to be identified by musical vegetables?

"Yeah, I'll help. That's what you're asking, right?"

I nodded.

"Okay."

"Why?" I had asked her, but I guess I was surprised it was easy. I guess I expected her to say no and when she didn't, I wasn't sure what to do with that.

"What do you mean?" Kate asked.

13

"Why do you want to help me?"

She looked bored, but she gestured to the other lawn chair. It was hard to tell with Kate; she wore boredom like an heirloom. It sat on her like something passed down through the years, something she'd forgotten she even wore, or wore out of obligation. Not a conscious choice, but a part of who she had to be.

She sighed and stared up at the sky. "I was supposed to go to college this year. I'm not. I'm taking a year off. Let's call it reinvention. You can be my partner in it. We can both be reinvented. Why not?"

I liked the word. *Reinvention* sounded interesting. It sounded a lot better than what it was—a favor from a stranger because I didn't have real friends.

"Clothes," Kate said, looking at my corn shirt. "You need to start with clothes." She leaned back into her chair and put her hood up, covering her face. I wasn't sure why she wore the bathing suit if she was just going to wrap herself up anyway.

"Can you take me?" I asked.

"Yeah, sure."

"Thanks. My dad . . . he's clueless, you know?"

"Is there a guy?" Kate asked. "There's always a guy."

"There's no guy," I said. There wasn't; I hadn't really considered it. I was so worried about being pretty, about being like everyone else. I wanted to be normal. To be good and to be noticed, but not in the ways they noticed me. I didn't want to look different, to have curves where other girls didn't, to be the kid with no mom. They said that was my problem. That I was trying to make up for missing my mom by being gross. Like my breasts somehow grew based on how many parents I did—or didn't—have.

"Really? No secret love interest? That's refreshing."

"I mean, there was one guy I thought was cute. Jeremy," I admitted. "He sat two desks up in English. But I never talked to him. And I won't now. He'll be at a different school."

"It's a big world out there. I'm sure you can find him online."

"Maybe," I said.

I didn't go online much. I'd joined Facebook the year before, after everyone else had moved on to other platforms. I only had one friend, though—a distant relative in Omaha. There were two girls in an anime group I joined who talked to me, but neither ever responded when I tried to add them. People basically accept anyone's friend requests, but never mine. It was more embarrassing to have one friend than not to have Facebook, so I deleted my profile.

"But it's not about that," I told Kate. "I just want to belong."

"Hollow Oaks isn't a place you want to belong," Kate said.

"I do."

She paused and looked at me. I couldn't see her expression because of her hood, but after a minute, she nodded. "Yeah, all right. I'll help. I'm going to sleep now, though. I'll come by tomorrow afternoon. We'll do some shopping."

She slipped her headphones on, and I was dismissed. I crawled back up the hill to my house, getting mud stuck in my fingernails. She was sound asleep when I turned back to wave.

---

chapter five

When he's finally done with her, the girl with the gum hurries to leave. She grabs the little bit of herself that's left and rushes out of the room, only to realize she has to wait for him for a ride home.

When they leave me alone, silence settles back in. The silence of the place when it's just me here hurts almost as bad. Almost.

I hate it. I hate that nothing indicates what kind of place this is. I hate that there's no sign, no warning. For me. For the ones who came after. For the girl who doesn't know there's gum on her shoe.

The door's closed, but he left the light on. Most of the time it's dark.

When I see the flicker of color, I turn my head to make sure it isn't a trick. My eyes making up stories in the light—after so much darkness. But I keep staring, and it's definitely there. A little bit of color amid the endless brown.

I don't actually know if it's hers. It could be anyone's. It could have been here for days. Maybe I just haven't seen it before. Either way, though, it's there. It's something.

I wish it was something important. I wish it mattered, because it aches too much to be what it is. It's a small tube, the cap dented with teeth marks. One of the things you hold on to while you're searching for something else in your bag, putting it between your teeth and biting down to make sure it doesn't fall. The letters are faded; I don't know what brand it is or what her preferences are. It could be spearmint or bubble gum or pomegranate. We put so much thought into it, into these details, and then it ends up here.

It's just lip balm. Just . . . life.

Ordinary and simple and necessary.

And tainted.

Something so common, a part of her everyday. Probably used almost by reflex at this point.

But now, it's a trigger. It will remind her every time. When she digs through another purse and finds a tube like it, she'll remember. She'll remember when she reaches for this one, and it's gone. She'll wonder if she left it here. And then she'll relive what happened here.

I want to save it for her. To save the one part of her they didn't take. Didn't steal in this room. I want to make remembering hurt less for her, but I'm not in the business of saving much these days.

chapter six

"Dad, Kate's going to take me shopping tomorrow. Can I have money for clothes?"

He was half asleep, John Wayne doing something or other on TV.

"Sure, Ellie. My wallet's on the counter."

I went to the kitchen to get the money, rifling through his wallet. It was next to the perpetual pile of bills. Almost every one of them had the red stamp on the front: PAST DUE. The pile was always the same size, and past due was the constant state of things.

"Bring me a soda," he yelled from the couch.

I saw his vest for work hanging on the back of one of the kitchen chairs and reminded myself I needed to iron it.

Our dog, Fred, woke up as I headed back to the living room. He beat me to the sofa. I squeezed in between him and my dad, handing my father the can.

"Are you working all weekend?" I asked.

"Of course. One of these days maybe I'll get to do a single shift. A man can dream, right?"

Imagine it. Imagine having dreams, and then, you can't. He was like my mom. They came here with a plan. He'd finished film school and she was a writer. They were going to memori- alize Hollow Oaks, to tell the world about this place. They had goals, and then they had me.

"We should watch a movie," I told him. When he'd stay awake, he would tell me a little about what he'd learned during film school. I always liked hearing his stories, but it was so hard for him to stay awake. Maybe he wasn't tired as much as he was weary. Weary of working double shifts at a job meant for a teenager, because that was what you got when you had a daughter in a place like this.

"Maybe later," he said. We wouldn't. He wouldn't make it through the Western he was watching.

"You can skip the commercials," I said. I didn't think he needed to know about bathtub scum.

"The remote's over there." He pointed toward the TV.

"Oh." I could have gotten up, but I was comfortable between him and Fred. I still liked the moments we could find.

Maybe it was some kind of omen. Wayne Breward placed television ads for his real estate firm, because he could. He ran his campaign as tax assessor with commercials, even though everyone else had signs, just because he could. Wayne Breward and the rest of the Breward family needed Hollow Oaks to wor- ship them. They'd saved the town from the edge of ruin, and they reminded us of it constantly.

"The number of these abandoned homes continues to rise," he said from the TV. "Every month, there are more. If they're not fixed, think about what that means for you, the homeowner who didn't run away."

My dad pushed me off him and moved to get the remote. He changed the channel and handed it to me before sitting down again.

"Well, I guess we're watching a movie. Anything but listening to that asshole."

"It's sad. All the houses," I said.

"What's sad is how nobody helps," my father argued. "It's easy to pitch in and support Wayne Breward, to make his little company the hero of this town, but I knew those people, Ellie. They were good people, a lot of them."

"From the factory?"

Hollow Oaks had always been a broken town, but it used to be full. The factories had closed first. People stopped buying the products they made, or the companies found ways to make them somewhere else cheaper. My dad had worked a second job, to make a little extra when I was a baby, and when the factories closed, the second job became his only job.

When the evictions in our neighborhood started, he'd go outside. Talk to people while strangers made them choose what they could take with them. Gave them a time limit for packing up their histories. My father would chat with people and try to help. Try to make it hurt a bit less, but over time, he stopped chatting. He'd watch them from our yard instead. No one spoke. It became too shameful to have to explain it. To have to tell your neighbors that it wasn't your fault. That your medical bills had gotten too high. That the interest rates changed. Whatever it was that caused it, it was humiliating to stand on the curb in front of what was your home and pretend there was anything left for you.

Sooner or later, my dad didn't watch, either. We only knew it kept happening because there were less people at the grocery store every time we went. We knew because of Wayne Breward and his ads. All his great successes at saving the poor houses from people like us.

"What are people supposed to do?" my dad asked in response to another of the ads. "You take their jobs, then you tell them it's going to cost more for them to stick around? We're all only human."

"Yeah," I said, because I didn't know what else to say. I was fourteen. I spent my afternoons watching YouTube and staring at girls online, trying to figure out what made them special. Trying to find all the ingredients that made up a girl, that made her pretty and worthwhile. I didn't understand mortgages and economic collapses and what it feels like to have your dreams die. I had yet to figure out my dreams.

My dad tried several times to talk to me about Wayne Breward, about corruption, about what power means for people who don't have it. He tried again that night, while I played with a wad of cash in my pocket and dreamed about paying full price for eyeliner.

I guess you can add selfish to the things that make a girl. At least this one.

chapter seven

I started school with the right clothes. My curves showed where they were supposed to but nowhere else, and Kate had helped me with my hair. We'd bleached two strips down the front and dyed them blue so the color framed my face. With my new T-shirts that were a testament to my apathy, I fit in by not caring about fitting in.

And it worked. No one said a word. They looked at me like I was just another girl. I didn't make fast friends on the first day of school, no, but there weren't comments made in gym class. I didn't have to change in the bathroom stall in the locker room, just to avoid the way they stared. There were no notes passed to me later, when they'd ask if I needed to whore myself out to pay for my implants. Since obviously my dad couldn't afford bread.

It was three days into school and my locker was stuck. I figured I had the combination wrong and tried again, but it wouldn't open. The late August day was too warm, and sweat was spilling down my new shirt. The school didn't want to spring for air-conditioning, so we finished the day with our clothes stuck to us.

"Having trouble?" He leaned against my locker with all the confidence in the world. I'd seen him a few times. We weren't in classes together, but he'd smiled at me every day because his math class was across the hall from mine. On the first day, he'd winked at me. On the second day, he'd commented on my shirt. It was self-deprecating—a shirt that mocked my introversion by claiming reading the shirt was enough social interaction for a day. We'd run into each other in the hall between classes and he'd laughed at it. And said I was too cute to be antisocial.

And now he stood at my locker, smiling at me while I tried to get it open.

"My locker's stuck," I told him. It was obvious, since I was pulling on it, but I told him anyway.

"You're new here." A statement, not a question.

"Sort of. I mean, I've lived here forever. But here, yeah. I went to Saint Elizabeth's."

He pushed me to the side. "Cool. I'm Caleb." Punching the bottom right of the metal door, he simultaneously spun the dial into place. It opened on the first try. "Sometimes you gotta rough 'em up a bit. They're tricky like that."

"Ellie. I mean, you didn't ask, but I'm Ellie."

He leaned back against the locker beside mine while I found my books. Three days and I already had a bag full of homework.

"Nice to officially meet you, Ellie. Elusive girl from the hallway."

"I'm not elusive. That's where my class is," I said.

He laughed as if I was the most hilarious person he'd ever met. "Yeah. So, Miss Not Elusive, what're you doing now?"

He wasn't exactly attractive. There was something wrong about the way he moved, the way he smiled. Everything about

Caleb was off somehow. He was tall, but he walked like he'd woken that morning into his tallness and now he couldn't figure out how to get his body to work the same way.

There was also the way he smiled. It was cute, but it had this way about it. Like he'd learned about smiling from a textbook. The idea of smiling came through, but it seemed like he just followed the directions rather than actually smiled.

"I . . . um, nothing really. I have to read."

We had a test Monday on summer reading, which I'd put off all summer to work on reinvention.

"What're you reading?" He took my bag from me and rummaged through it. *Great Expectations*? They're still teaching this crap, huh?"

"Aren't you, like, a junior?"

"Yeah. How'd you guess?"

I hadn't had to guess. It had been three days, but everyone knew Caleb and his older brother, Noah; you didn't need friends to know who they were. They walked through the school like the only people who'd ever mattered. It was probably true.

"I mean, they didn't exactly shake up the curriculum in the two years since you were a freshman. I think Dickens has some staying power."

He turned to me and brushed his fingers along my arm. "You're cute, Ellie."

It wasn't the kind of cute you want to be called as a girl; it was the kind of cute you call your puppy, or your brother when he eats paste.

"Thanks?"

"Really. I wasn't kidding yesterday. You're way too cute to be antisocial."

"Oh." I had nothing to say to that.

He didn't move, but he didn't say anything, and I wasn't sure what the natural steps were in a conversation like this. I closed my locker and reached for my bag. Caleb tossed the book in and slung the bag over his shoulder.

"Listen, Elusive Ellie. You're cute. It's Friday. You don't want to go home right away. Come out with me."

"Um, I don't know," I said.

"Why not? What's the worst that can happen? I'm a nice guy."

I didn't really have a why not. A part of me wanted to go out with him. Although he wasn't conventionally cute, he was talking to me. He'd noticed me for three days and he remembered my shirt. He was paying attention and I didn't have a reason to say no. But I didn't want to say yes, either. It felt too . . . sudden. It had only been three days.

Caleb smiled again and grabbed my hand. "Ellie, Ellie, Ellie. There are better things to do on a Friday than sitting around reading garbage."

I liked the way he said my name. It was effortless. I liked that he remembered it.

"Where are we going?" I asked, deciding he was right. What was the worst that could happen?

He wrapped his arm around my waist as he led me out of school. "Trust me, Ellie."

We drove to the river, to a house that sat right along the water. "It's not mine," he said as we pulled into the driveway. "We're fixing it. No one lives here anymore."

"Fixing it how?" I sat in his car, wondering if I should be sitting there. If there were unwritten rules about what you were supposed to do when a guy like Caleb asks you randomly to hang out in an abandoned house.

"My dad gets them from the banks or whatever and we keep

'em up. Then, eventually, we give them back. When they have their shit together, I guess."

"What about the people who own it, though?" I asked. "What happens to them?" I knew what happened to them. My dad still talked about it. I'd seen it. But I wanted to hear it from Caleb's point of view. What did they think happened to the lives they cleaned up?

He shrugged. "Not our problem. Besides, they left. This one here? They just walked out. There's stuff in the closets still."

I thought of my dad. Of the things he'd said about the people he'd known. I thought of watching our neighbors across the street. Of how their daughter, who was only a few years older than me, begged them to let her have more time. How she cried because she hadn't known and she hadn't had enough time to get her stuff.

I thought of the mornings my dad and I went fishing and of how we probably stopped going because of the Breward boys. Because they reminded us just how much they owned. I thought of all the things my father would say about me sitting in a car with Wayne Breward's youngest son, about how he'd feel about us trespassing in these people's home. Even if it wasn't really theirs anymore.

"What're you thinking about?" Caleb asked, and he smiled.

I wish I could say I told him all the things I thought about. That I shared those stories so he would know what he was really fixing up. I wish I was that kind of girl.

But I guess I was a sucker for a nice smile.

"Nothing," I said.

Inside, the house had been left in the middle of existing. The dining room table and chairs were dusty, but the place mats and dishes were still set. The overhead chandelier was off, since there was no electricity, but the sun came through the window and flickered off the glass.

I reached across one of the faded curtains. A spider crawled out from behind it, disturbed by our being there.

"It's weird," I said, walking into the kitchen and turning on the faucet, running my hand through the invisible water. "It's like they planned to come back."

Caleb came up behind me, wrapped his arms around my waist, and leaned into my ear. I didn't mind his closeness. He smelled like pine, for some reason, and he was warm. I liked the way he held on to me. How it felt like belonging when he wrapped himself around me that way. It felt like someone wanted me to be a part of them. Of their space.

But it was still a surprise. And I wasn't sure I was supposed to feel how I did, so I shrugged him off and leaned closer to the window over the sink, trying to see if there were signs of anyone left.

Caleb moved to my side and looked out the window with me. "People don't like letting go," he said. "They weren't coming back. They just didn't want to see it empty."

"It's so quiet."

Without the normal whirring sounds of daily life—the refrigerator, the electric lightbulbs and their strange almost inaudible buzz, the creaks of people moving in their chairs from another room—the house was a silent box of memory. A place that *was*. Outside, a squirrel ran across the porch, where leaves had gathered and died.

"Come on. We're almost done with the upstairs," Caleb said. "It's less depressing." This time, he didn't grab my hand. He simply waited and offered it. I looked out the window a bit longer, until the squirrel ran away, out of view, before turning to

Caleb. The afternoon sun shone in his eyes, steel sparkling when he smiled at me.

I took his hand and let him lead me upstairs. He was right. The rooms were painted and clean. They had the soulless feel of a furniture display in a department store, but at least it wasn't like having the ghosts of other people wait for us to stop invading their space.

We walked down the hall to the master bedroom. The bed was still there. Unmade because they'd taken the sheets but otherwise intact.

Caleb threw himself onto it and gestured for me to join him.

"I probably shouldn't," I said. I wasn't sure I was supposed to lie on a bed with any boy, especially one I'd just met, and worse, in a stranger's bed. I'd spent enough time in Catholic school to know that good girls didn't do those kinds of things.

With Caleb, I both liked the way he tried to make my choices for me and hated how he made me feel uncomfortable. But it was a strange feeling. I was drawn to him, even when I didn't want to be. Probably because I was at the point where I watched enough movies with my dad to see how people fell in love. To see how they kissed and held each other. To know I wanted someone to look at me that way.

"Ellie, come here," Caleb said from the bed, taking up most of it. "I won't do anything. I promise. I'll be good."

I shook my head and walked to the window again. From upstairs, I could see across the yard. A swing set of rotten wood and an aboveground pool with only three remaining sides stood between the house and the river. I lifted the window, letting the sound of water fill the room.

"Ellie."

"It doesn't feel real," I told him.

"What do you mean?"

"It's like being in a story. This house. It's someone else's story. I feel like we're intruding."

"Hey, turn around." I did and he sat up. "I'm allowed to be here. We're not doing anything wrong."

"Maybe," I said. I couldn't explain it. There was what was legally okay and what I felt. Someone had lived here. Someone had loved here, and we didn't belong in that.

The water was the only sound for a while. I leaned against the wall, the breeze tickling my elbows, while Caleb lay on the bed and stared at the ceiling. I started to take inventory of him. Who he was. What he looked like. How he moved.

"I really like this house," he said finally, still not looking at me. "This is my favorite we've done."

"Why's that?" I asked.

He moved onto his side. "There's so much still here. It's still real. I guess it's like pretending. It's like being someone else. Have you ever wanted to be someone else?"

I nodded, but it bugged me. I felt like he shouldn't be able to read me so easily in three days. Then again, I told myself, maybe that's how people are. Maybe that's how you find the right people. They're the ones who know what you feel in a moment, without ever needing to say the words aloud.

Caleb reached an arm out. "Come here, Ellie. Please? Come pretend with me."

It takes a lot of things to make a girl, but breaking her? It only takes a few pretty words and a crooked smile.

chapter eight

A nother night.
Another girl.
She's older. They usually like them young. She has hollow eyes, though. Hollow eyes in a hollow girl in a hollow town.

She's silent and it makes him angry. They expect them all to cry. They all do, except this one refuses.

His hands move so fast. I remember them. His rage running down his arms, gathering in his hands. They're clean and pretty hands. Manicured maybe. He goes to someone and pays them to clean off the girls he hurts.

"What's your problem?" he asks as he hits her again.

She only smiles. In other circumstances, I would admire her. I'd want to be her friend. I'd want that kind of strength in my life. But I don't admire her now. I hate her instead. I hate her for being strong. I hate her, because I should have been strong, too.

He fills the wall with more damage, because hitting her gets no response. Plaster dust settles on his manicured hands and he clenches his fists by his side.

"Fine. You want to play games?"

They never go for the face anymore. They prefer their damage to be hidden, to be in the places you need to protect. They want you to feel shame if you show anyone. They're careful to hurt you only in the places you've been told to keep private.

This girl is different, though. She fights back. Not physically, but she smiles instead of crying. Still, I see it all in her eyes. The pain. The fear. I know fear; it's present here in this room all the time. I live alongside it. It's all I have to keep me company.

"Bitch," he says, and he pushes her down.

My jeans cost $18 and my father had to work two hours to pay for them. They were weak. Like me. This girl's pants must have cost more, because he has to work harder.

What eventually breaks her isn't his fists. It's not what he does. Or what he plans to do.

He hurts her by saying her name.

"Gretchen." He says it like a lover says a name, but he doesn't touch her like a lover should. His face is so close to hers.

That night, his breath smelled like alcohol.

"Don't say my name," she pleads. There it is. The begging. The need. It's what he thrives on. It's not crying, but it'll have to do.

"Gretchen," he says again.

He asked me my name. But he never used it. He still doesn't use it. I wonder if he even remembers it.

"Fuck you," she replies, and I close my eyes. I hear the echo of his hands. The walls will remember tonight.

I'm scared. Both for her and for myself. I don't want him to continue. I want her to be allowed to leave. I don't want to share this space.

She's only so strong. She fights as much as she can, but

eventually he wins. She'll get to go home. She'll hide the bruises. She'll keep smiling, even though she'll forget how to mean it.

After.

That's what I know now. I only know the existence of after. That, and a mess of memories that don't make sense alongside each other.

Life happens in the strangest moments. It's a calendar of days, pages of time folding one over the other. The memories become stories, and they fill us up until we can't be filled anymore. That's all I was left with. Nothing to fill the space but my hurt and all the things I remember.

It's not all bad, though. There's as much beauty as there is pain. I keep my eyes closed and I surround myself with the memories of what was good. I fill after with before. With the memory of coming home from school and lying on my bed with Fred. While he chewed my textbooks and I worried about paying for them at the end of the year. I fill space with thoughts of stolen sips of coffee in the first golden streaks of morning. Memories of violins and candy canes and the funny way you look in the mirror when you run your hand through the misty residue after a shower.

I remember all those things, and I think of them instead. I try not to hear what's happening, try not to remember the parts I want to forget. I think of the good and I try to forget $18 jeans and the way I asked for it and knowing it was all going to happen anyway.

chapter nine

After the day by the river, Caleb didn't talk to me again. I saw him around school, but he didn't acknowledge I was there. He didn't even look at me when we ran into each other in the math hallway. I smiled at him, and he saw right through me. I tried not to let it hurt. I told myself it was only one day. One day means nothing. It wasn't personal. That's what I let myself believe. That it wasn't because I was the kind of girl no one would ever want more than one day with.

I want to say I made a lot of new friends, that I didn't look up every time I heard his voice in the hall, didn't feel like crying when I saw him flirting with someone else out of a line of girls.

He'd called it pretend. I should've known it was.

There were kids I talked to, sure. I asked Doug Martindale for notes when I got the flu. Sometimes I sat with Heather O'Neill at lunch. She was allergic to pretty much everything, so she had to have which days she came to lunch preapproved. During the rest of the week, I sat alone. But when I sat alone, no one pointed and laughed. I was no longer the girl forced to be by herself. I was just a girl who existed, nothing more. It was better than it had been, even if it still hurt that I could have disappeared and no one would have noticed.

I talked in class. When they called on me. And my words faded into the din of school. Nothing memorable. Boys weren't poking at me anymore, and girls didn't call me fat. I didn't find notes in my locker making fun of my clothes. They didn't call me names. Smelly Ellie or Ellie the Belly. They just didn't call me anything.

The thing was, Kate hadn't failed. I blended in. That's what I'd told her I wanted. And it had been. I'd thought it would be enough to fade into the wallpaper. But then, there was an afternoon by the river with a boy who called me cute and wanted to fill his day with me so badly that he wouldn't take no for an answer. And now, I wanted more.

But what I wanted didn't matter.

In the time that followed, I learned about plot diagrams and the Roman Empire and boiling points. I was filled with the things that made a person. Made a girl.

Holidays came and went. I stayed home and watched '50s monster movies with my dad on Halloween. We had turkey sandwiches from the deli at the store for Thanksgiving, before he went in to work overnight for the Black Friday sales. At Christmas, he gave me a pair of parrot earrings. I'd loved parrots when I was twelve. I gave him a new set of windshield wipers.

I told myself not to wonder what Caleb was doing. What kind of world existed for people like him. I tried not to think about it as the year changed into the next, tried not to wonder if I'd know what it was like to belong somewhere.

As life does, it went on until it was spring. My blue hair faded, although it didn't go away completely. The dark roots came in, but there were still pieces of matted blue at the ends. My head looked moldy.

I was at my locker again, trying to remember what homework I had that night. I didn't feel like digging out my planner to check, but I was afraid I'd forget something. I was a good student. I sort of liked school, but that wasn't why. I was a good student mainly because I didn't have anything else to do.

"Elusive Ellie, where the hell have you been?"

I turned around, quick-scanning the hallway. Maybe I'd heard him wrong. It had been months.

Caleb stood in the doorway to the science lab, filling the space between the hall and the room. I hated how he smiled and my heart hoped. It wasn't fair. It wasn't okay that he wasn't even someone I knew. He didn't want to be around me, and yet when he smiled and I saw his eyes crinkle up as he watched me, I couldn't help but wish there was an explanation.

"Um, here?" I said.

"I haven't seen you around."

He crossed the hall, oblivious to the people passing. Our school population had dropped, even in the year I was there. We'd lost twelve students since September. Soon, there'd be nobody left in Hollow Oaks.

The door to the science lab closed behind him as he approached. Sometimes it seemed like the entire world waited for him to possess it, then shut down when he was finished.

He stood in front of me, reaching out to close my locker. "What have you been up to?" he asked.

"I don't know," I said, leaning back against the neighboring locker, holding my books to my chest. Caleb put his arms on either side of me, his body closing the space between us.

"I've missed you." I could feel his breath when he spoke.

35

I looked to the side and his hands were only inches from me. There was no space left that was mine.

"You seem to be doing just fine without me."

"Don't be like that, Ellie," he said, reaching a hand up to grab the back of my head. "You never called. It's been months. I wondered if you forgot all about me."

My brain kept rationalizing. Reminding me I knew very little about Caleb Breward, and most of what I did know wasn't great. It tried to show me all the days he'd passed me in the hall and wouldn't look at me. My brain had a long list of amazing reasons I should have walked away, but Caleb's closeness did things inside of me I didn't know how to process. All the rational thoughts were there, but then I wondered what it would be like if he leaned just a little closer and kissed me.

I went to Catholic school. I had only my dad and my dog to keep me company. How I felt with Caleb inches from me, his mouth slightly open, was terrifying. But I didn't move. I kind of liked being terrified. I thought this was what it felt like to fall in love. I thought this was why they called it falling, because I couldn't seem to stay grounded when I just wanted him to kiss me.

I tried, though.

"You didn't give me your number," I reminded him.

He spun away from me, and I exhaled while he leaned against the locker beside me. I waited for him to tell me why today. Why he'd remembered me now.

"I'm so bored," he said. "This is boring."

"I'm sorry?"

"Not you. This." He swung his arm out to indicate . . . something. The school? Our town? Life?

"What are you doing Saturday night?" he asked and turned

back to me, but he didn't give me time to reply. Since my reply would have been something along the lines of eat a sandwich and watch a movie, it was probably best I was silent. "Gina Lynn's having a party."

I knew *of* Gina Lynn, but I didn't know her. She was the kind of girl Caleb would know. She was the kind of girl who expected people to call her Gina Lynn.

"Good to know."

He smiled. "I'm asking you to come with me, Ellie. I wasn't reciting a calendar."

"Oh. I mean, I'm not invited." Gina Lynn wasn't mean to me or anything. She didn't even know I was alive.

"I just invited you. So you'll come?" he asked.

I couldn't see myself there, but I wanted to picture it. I imagined being the kind of girl Gina Lynn and Caleb talked to at lunch. How would the world be different for that girl?

"Yeah. Okay," I said.

"Pick you up at eight?"

"Um . . . I mean, I'm going to be out. Can I just meet you there?" He'd dropped me off at school after that day by the river and now, I realized he didn't know where I lived. I realized I didn't want him to. I didn't want him to come to my house. Didn't want him to see the way we'd forgotten to take down the screens and how they'd torn in the winter. Or how my dad had gotten the Christmas lights stuck in the gutters, so they were still hanging there. I didn't want Caleb to know these things about me.

"All right, Elusive Ellie," he said. "Then give me your phone."

"Why?"

He held out his hand, waiting. "So I can put my number in it. And you can call me this time."

"You can call me, too," I said. I handed him my phone and he programmed his number in.

"You're cute. I'll see you around. Saturday. Don't forget," he said, giving back my phone.

I'd never missed having a mother. Not until Caleb. I'd had my dad and Fred and there were the few kids I talked to at school or church on Sundays. Besides, I didn't have much to compare my life to, so I didn't know to miss her.

The characters from books and movies and TV weren't like me. Some had moms and some didn't, but their stories weren't like mine. They didn't spend five nights a week making themselves macaroni and cheese from a box. Their lives were interesting and mine was . . . mine.

I sometimes thought being around Kate was like having a mom. She told me how to wear my hair and what to notice when people said things. She told me people lie. That's something a mom might have told me.

After Caleb, I started to wish my mom had stayed. Not that my dad had been the one who'd left, but that she'd been there. I wished for someone who could have explained what I felt with him. Could have told me about love and sex and all the things I needed to navigate alone.

Wishes grow inside of you. They attach themselves to your bones and make you ache when you try to ignore them. I hate everything about wishing. I hate how I look back at the moments that made me. I hate remembering, and I hate wishing it had been different. There were so many yeses that should have been nos and so many nos that should have been inferred.

A girl could drive herself crazy reliving the minutes she wishes hadn't happened, the things she needs to take back.

chapter ten

He's done with Gretchen now. Her smile was lost with the other parts of her he tore away. She's shaking as she tries to put herself back together.

The lightbulb flickers; it's dying.

When I was really little, when Dad was still at the factory, I'd been home with Mrs. Otis, the woman who lived down the street. I was sitting in her kitchen, trying to color. She'd decided to watch something on TV. It was either a soap opera or some police show; I don't know what it was, but I know I wasn't interested. It was something for old people.

Overhead, the light kept coming in and out. I stared up at it, watching it fight. Watching it gasp for life. Even light wants to live. Even light feels the heaviness of darkness when it's time.

The door opens, scraping the carpet. It's worn through. Stained. Brown like the walls.

Poor Gretchen. She thinks it's over.

"We need a new lightbulb," he says.

"So get one."

Gretchen watches them. They're a contrast; for all the

violence, one has clean hands. The other . . . he likes the way they cry. He likes watching them register it. He doesn't pretend here.

I won't give them their names. They don't deserve names. They don't deserve to be someone.

"There aren't any upstairs. I'll have to buy one."

To listen to the mundane, to hear them talk of lightbulbs while Gretchen watches, while she tries to figure out what comes next, it can make a person sick.

"So buy one," he says. The other one shrugs and leaves. He's done here now anyway.

The new one closes the door. Gretchen starts to cry.

"What's your name?" he asks.

"Fuck you," she says again, but it's quiet this time.

He laughs.

As always, I close my eyes, but it's never enough. The sound gets through. The memories get through.

There are things we know and then there are things we wish we didn't.

I tell myself that the way this happens, that it *can* happen, is because people prefer not to know. Our town needs what it needs, and there are sacrifices. It's only girls.

I can't hate people like I should, though. There's too much good left. It's the good that keeps me sane.

There is still music and there are paintings and snowstorms and backyard ice-skating and Christmas trees and then there's pizza and fairy tales and tulips and the way the sand on the beach squishes between your toes. I know those aren't all because of people, but we share these things because they're good. I think of those things and I try not to hear her crying. Try not to remember the carpet. How it burned my knees.

It's so cold here. The walls outside don't keep the chill from the room.

I want to be warm again. I want to curl up in bed with my dog and sip on soup while I pretend to be sick and my dad is off from work and my biggest fear is about finding a hypotenuse.

I want to live where there's good.

I want to live.

chapter eleven

didn't tell Kate about Caleb until the second time he talked to me. It's like I knew it might not last. But after he asked me to Gina Lynn's party, I went to Kate.

I hadn't seen her much since school started. We'd spent two months in the summer together. Mostly we went to the mall and she gave me directions for fading until no one made fun of me and then we went to her house and fell asleep on chairs in the backyard. We barely talked. I don't know what she got from spending time with me, but she was there for me and that was what I needed.

And now I needed her again. I went to her house and stood on her porch. When she opened the door, I told her I needed to be better than just enough now. I needed to be pretty.

We were in her room and I gave her the full rundown of the one day I'd had with Caleb. There wasn't much to tell, but I wanted her to know because if she knew, she could make me the right kind of girl.

"What kind of people remake other people's memories?" Kate asked, as she pushed a pile of clothes off her desk chair and patted the seat. "They just take these people's houses and try to pretend nothing ever happened? Like those people didn't exist? They're just erasing people."

"I don't know. It's weird, isn't it?"

She sighed. "This whole damn town is weird. Sit still." My hair needed to be fixed first. She grabbed her scissors and hacked off the moldy bits. The result was an asymmetrical mess, but at least I didn't look like a salad topping. "Is he nice at least?"

"I think so?" We'd only spoken the two times, unless you counted a rogue comment the first week of school.

"You don't know?" she asked, and she sat down across from me, pushing my bangs from my face.

"Not really. I like him, but I don't really know him. Do you think I'm being stupid?"

"What do you like about him?"

I leaned back in the chair and tried to answer her. I couldn't explain what I liked, but maybe she could help me find the words. Just like she helped me find the girl they wanted. "He's confident. I like that he's so sure of himself."

"I knew Noah, Caleb's brother. The older one. What is he? A senior now?"

I nodded. "Was he nice?"

Kate shook her head. "No, but he had that same confidence. I never really understood it. Girls adored him. He was . . . something. There was something about him."

"Good something?" I asked.

"I don't have time to take you to the mall before tomorrow," she said, not answering me. "Do you want to borrow something?"

"Will it fit?"

"Stop it," she said. "We're the same size."

I looked at her as she got up and went over to her closet to search for clothes. My dad couldn't afford to keep dressing me anyway, but I didn't want to tell her that.

We weren't the same size. Not really. We may have weighed the same and we were around the same height, but Kate's body was put together like it should have been. Mine always felt accidental. Some parts were too big and others too small and clothes either clung to my chest or hung on my hips because of it.

"I think Caleb has the same something," I told her. "I can't explain it. But I really want him to like me."

"He's not special. There are plenty of guys. If he doesn't like you, Ellie, it's not you, okay?"

"I don't know," I said. Because I didn't. I couldn't speak to what it was. Outside of physical responses because he invaded my space so easily.

Kate shrugged, flipping through hangers. "Look, people liked Noah. I never saw it. But there was always a group of girls who thought he was the reason they existed. Caleb wasn't really on my radar, but I can imagine it's partly the same thing. I don't know what it is about them."

I got up to help her, but she shooed me back to the chair, carrying a pile of clothes. "There are a lot of stories about the Brewards, though. Just be careful, okay?"

"What kind of stories?"

"You're not . . ." She paused. "You remember when I asked this summer? If there was a guy?"

"Yeah."

"You said this was for you," she said, tossing the clothes onto her bed and sitting down again. Waiting for me to start going through them. "You said there wasn't a guy."

"There was Jeremy. He just wasn't the reason," I reminded her.

"Have you ever had a boyfriend?" she asked.

I looked down at my shoes and shook my head.

"Just be careful. Guys like Noah and Caleb are going to have very different expectations," she said.

"You mean about sex and stuff?"

"Yeah, and stuff."

Kate's room looked like mine. Somewhat. Except all her magazines and posters and ideas weren't of the people she wanted to be but of the ones she felt like she was. It was a subtle difference, but she wasn't borrowing from other people's lives. She just lived her own. I think that's why I liked her. She let me borrow from her. Not just her clothes, but with Kate, I could borrow what it was like to be good enough.

Maybe that's what I liked about Caleb, too. That day, in the house, was borrowed. I sat in a borrowed house, making borrowed memories with a borrowed boy. He'd said we were only pretending that day, but I was always pretending.

"Try these on," Kate said, picking up a pair of jeans.

"You don't have to let me borrow these."

"I don't need them. Besides, I'm reinventing myself. You should take them. It'll give me a reason to start over. I can buy myself a new wardrobe, too. We'll both be entirely new people by the time summer comes around again."

Can you call someone a friend when they don't know a thing about you? And when you don't understand them, either?

Kate and I shared nothing except proximity, but she was the closest thing I had to a friend. There'd been a few kids I talked to at Saint Elizabeth's. They'd been there at school when no one else had been, but not beyond that. And after we went to different high schools, they hadn't stayed in touch. They forgot, because life went forward and I was part of them before.

Forgetting is the most human activity we have.

I tried on the clothes, even though Kate had stopped paying attention. She stared at the ceiling while I tried to show them off.

"I need out of this place," she said. I stood in front of her in her clothes, but she wasn't looking. She wasn't talking to me.

I didn't say anything. I never said anything. I just kept trying on clothes.

I have so many memories of moments like this. Not just with Kate. My memories are full of times when I quietly functioned, as if I was nothing but a part of the scenery.

Kate wasn't watching me. She'd said she wanted to leave Hollow Oaks. And I didn't know what to say or how to help. I didn't ask questions, either, because I was worried about Caleb and my clothes and everything I wanted. Everything I needed from Kate. Not what she needed in return.

"I like this one. Do you think he'll notice me in this?" I asked. I don't even remember what the outfit looked like. I didn't like it more than the others; I wanted to change the subject because I didn't know what else to do.

"Yeah, you look good," she said, even though she still wasn't looking.

After a while of me standing there in her clothes, she got up and picked up the rest. She threw them in a bag and put it down in front of her closet.

"This should be plenty." She leaned the bag against the door so it wouldn't topple over. "But if you need more, just let me know before I leave. When I go, I don't want to bring anything from here with me."

I know it was selfish. Kate had started to crack. Her sadness seeped into that day. She was vulnerable in that moment, and I could have asked. I could have tried to understand. I could have tried to know what she knew about our town. About the people in our town.

Memory is tricky. I don't remember anything else in particular about that day. I don't really know if what I remember is even true. Maybe I'm a liar and none of this is how it happened. I think that was the conversation we had. I think her sadness was part of that moment for me, but that's only my story. It's only my memory of what went on, and Kate may say the day was entirely different. She may remember only that I didn't ask why she was so sad.

Maybe it would've been different if I had. I wish I had, but what's the point of wishing? We're all just what we are. We can't go on wishing we weren't. Wishing is just as selfish in the end.

chapter twelve

Almost everyone was invited to Gina Lynn's party. Except me, of course, until Caleb invited me. It's the almost that hurts the most. Almost is like being half real.

People pulsed through her house when I arrived, but I didn't see her anywhere. I didn't see Caleb, either.

Hey, where are you? I texted him.

Porch.

Nobody noticed me as I cut through the room. I made my way outside, into the cold. Spring was playing games with us. Weeks earlier, it had snuck in overnight, erasing our memory of winter in a matter of hours. When we'd gone to bed, winter had lingered in the snowbanks and in the way the trees still hunched over from the weight of it. And then suddenly, spring. We woke to birds singing, birds who appeared to have been shipped overnight on a secret train, and we remembered music.

But now, winter was trying to force a comeback. Everyone outside stood looking at the pool, wondering what happened. I was shivering, wearing a skirt and thin shirt I'd borrowed from Kate when spring was still a promise.

I saw him from the periphery. From the in-between where the people inside faded into the background, but the people outside were only figures in the night. It made sense; I was a periphery girl.

"Hey," I said to his back.

When he turned to look at me, I swear the light from the porch surrounded him. But I think I made that up. I think I want to remember him that way. I want to believe there was something that made him special. I want to believe that loneliness doesn't just mess with our hearts.

"Ellie! You came," Caleb said.

"I said I would."

"I know. I wasn't sure, though. I worried. You're late."

I'd walked to the party, after telling my dad I was going to a friend's. He wouldn't have stopped me from going to Gina Lynn's. I didn't have other friends, so it wouldn't have made a difference if I'd said her name. But, for some reason, I lied. I lied and I don't know why I did.

"Yeah, well, I was doing things."

He laughed. "Mysterious things. Of course. I'd expect nothing less from my Elusive Ellie."

My. I heard it. The claim he laid on me. I smiled at the word.

He moved closer and I stepped back. It was automatic. Since earlier in the week, by my locker, I hadn't stopped thinking about the possibility. But now that he was close again, I was scared. I was afraid of the way I knew I'd hurt if he waited months to talk to me again. I didn't want to fall for a guy just because he'd smiled at me and said my name a few times. I was afraid of what would happen if there was more to it than that, but I was also afraid of how I'd feel if there wasn't.

"I don't think I'm supposed to be here," I said.

I'd always imagined being wanted. Of someone loving me. Choosing me. But here was this boy and if he kissed me, I knew I'd always worry about going back to not being wanted.

"Why not?"

He kept coming closer and I kept backing up, but then I was against the house itself and he was right there. I took a step forward, even while my mind told me to escape into the frame of the house.

Caleb put his hand on my arm and I hated how easy it was. I hated how he made me feel. I hated that I didn't want him to stop.

"Gina Lynn didn't invite me," I said, even though I didn't care at all about the party.

"So? I did. I want you here." He took a piece of my hair and twisted it around his finger. "I wanted to see you tonight, Ellie. I've thought about you every day."

"But it's not your party."

He smiled and leaned closer. "You're beautiful and sweet and I want you here, okay?"

I'd always imagined kissing. It was something that happened all the time to other people. I even saw my dad kiss someone once.

I don't remember her name. He didn't date much, but there was one woman. When I was six or so. I remember her hair. It was dark, but outside, it shone in the light. I loved how it told two stories. I didn't know how they'd met, but I watched when he went outside to meet her. She stood by her car and he went to her and they kissed. It was the way I imagined strangers realize they know each other across space. That you meet someone and suddenly there's a recognition that a place in your life belongs to someone else. It was like, when he kissed her, that place didn't feel empty anymore.

I'd always pictured experiencing it myself. I'd thought about it with Caleb. But none of that happened when he kissed me.

I hadn't seen it coming, even though I'd been thinking about it, and his mouth was open and his teeth scratched my bottom lip. But I smiled when he moved away, because I wanted it to be better. I wanted him to do it again.

"I really like you, Ellie."

"Why?" I asked. I almost tried to talk him out of it. Tried to tell him how little he knew about me, but he laughed and took my hand. He didn't answer.

Caleb led me into the party. He'd invited me because he could. He'd kissed me because he could. Just like his dad, Caleb lived in a world of could and we drifted from room to room on the privilege of it.

"What do you want to do?" he asked, grabbing drinks for us both.

"Whatever you want. I don't care."

"Would you feel better if I introduced you to Gina Lynn? If you had permission or whatever?" I knew he was mocking me, and I felt ridiculous for saying anything. I'd been a freshman for almost a year and I still felt like a little girl.

"It's fine. It doesn't matter," I said.

"No, I'll introduce you. Gina Lynn and I go way back. She's like my sister."

Gina Lynn wasn't the sort of girl most guys would view like a sister. She was a photograph. The kind of girl people make magazines for just to have excuses to look at them. Her hair cascaded. Naturally. It formed frills of gold that bounced, along with everything else on her that was supposed to bounce. Her eyes were brown, which she'd complained were ugly, but they were flecked with gold, too. Because that's what Gina Lynn was. The golden girl.

"Caleb Breward. You're a dick." She kissed him, and I wondered if he bit her lip, too.

"Oh, why's that?"

"You haven't even said hello."

"That's what I'm doing now. This is Ellie. I invited her."

She looked at me, taking in all the things that made us different, and she nodded. "Mike's outside. He's trying to open the pool. I told him it was too cold, but he's fucked up."

"We can go swimming," Caleb said. "It's not that cold. Fuck March anyway. What the hell happened to spring?"

"The same thing that always happens," she said. "It changes every day. But no swimming regardless. I told him we weren't doing the pool, even if it stayed warm. Not after last summer. It took weeks to clean that shit up."

"Mike's not gonna listen, you know."

"Yeah, I know. He's a tool. Do me a favor? Tell his ass to get back inside." Gina Lynn ran her hand along Caleb's arm, tapping her fingers on his elbow. "Please? I don't feel like fighting with him."

Caleb turned to me. "I'll be right back. Socialize or something."

He left me standing there, with a cup of warm beer I didn't want.

"So, what's your name again?" Gina Lynn asked. "Sally?"

"Ellie."

"Nice. Where are you from?"

"Here." It was a recurring question. It was strange to be from a place that didn't know you were a part of it.

"Oh, are you new?"

"I went to Saint Elizabeth's. Last year. I mean, I'm not new new. I've always lived here. But yeah, this year new, I guess."

"Weird. I've never seen you. Anyway, yeah, nice to meet you. I've gotta go mingle, though, okay? You know how it is, right? Gotta feed the troglodytes." She laughed, but I'm not sure she was kidding.

I went back to the porch. Nobody was by the pool anymore, including anyone named Mike. I didn't know anyone at the party except Caleb, and I didn't know how to find him, so I settled in on one of the pool chairs. It had a layer of frost on it, which seeped through my skirt.

When Caleb found me later, he didn't explain or apologize for leaving me alone outside for more than an hour. He was drunk and he spun me around, kissing me again. This time, my lip was unharmed. But I still didn't have those sparks. I didn't feel it in my toes or feel any of the other things I was supposed to. I just felt . . . nothing. Except happy he'd picked me.

"Come on," he said, pressing himself against me. "Gina Lynn said we can use her sister's room."

He took my hand, leading me to a pink room with unicorns on the walls. He tossed a stuffed bear onto the floor. Everything in the room sparkled.

"This is awkward," I said as he sat down on the bed.

"Awkward how?"

"Here, I mean. This is a little girl's room."

"Don't you like me?" he asked. "Why are you thinking about some little girl?"

"I don't know. I mean, it's just weird."

"So you don't like me?"

I sat down next to him. "No, I do. I'm sorry. Never mind."

He kissed me again, and I tried to feel it. I tried to put him into that space, the one that was waiting for someone. I did like him, so I didn't know why it felt so strange. I wanted to kiss him, and I wanted to be around him. But I also wanted it to feel different. My body reacted to his nearness, but it felt like responding to someone through a fog. It was disappointing. There were none of the fireworks you see in movies.

"You're really beautiful, Ellie," he said.

It wasn't horrible. I liked how he looked at me between kisses, how he tangled my hair in his fingers. I liked his steely gray eyes and the way they didn't blink, even when I tried to talk instead of kiss him. I even liked that he seemed more desperate the longer we were in the room. Like he couldn't get enough of me. I liked how badly he seemed to need me. His hands gripped my thighs and I remembered what Kate had said about how naïve I could be. But I liked it, too. I liked feeling wanted like that.

Maybe this is how we fall in love. Not because we can't stand to be apart from someone, but because a guy says you're beautiful and you don't really know about kissing him in a room full of pink unicorns, but you figure it's good enough. And then you find yourself falling for that need in him. The way he looks at you and whispers your name and almost seems to want to devour you. And it's both scary and somewhat exciting, because it means maybe you really are beautiful.

All of this unfolds and then suddenly, this person has carved their way into your life and it's strange that they weren't always there. You tell yourself that the movies and pop songs are wrong. That love isn't an explosion; it's a slow burn.

But hell. I don't know if that's what love is, either. I was fourteen.

This isn't a story of great romance or of true love. It's simply a story of being lonely and how comforting it is to be called beautiful.

chapter thirteen

He comes back with the lightbulb. Gretchen's crying and the bruises are already starting to blossom, but it's over now. They both wait for her, irritated it's taking her so long to get dressed, not understanding that collecting each piece of her takes time. They don't feel how strongly her shame shimmers in the room.

She's on her hands and knees gathering pieces of herself when she finds it. In the time that must have passed since the girl with the gum on her shoes was here, no one thought to clean. The lip balm cap falls off, and Gretchen reaches forward. Picks it up, holding it close.

"It was you, wasn't it?" she asks, keeping her back to them as she recognizes what it is. She quickly tucks the lip balm into her pocket.

"What the hell are you talking about?" He puts the lightbulb on the end table and goes to Gretchen, picking her up off the floor. "Hurry the fuck up. Jesus."

"It doesn't matter how long it's been, you know." Something in her changes. A stillness comes over her. They don't notice, because they don't notice anything, but as soon as Gretchen put the lip balm in her pocket, everything about her slowed.

She buttons her shirt, where she can. Two of the buttons are lost somewhere in the room. They don't matter, though. Not now.

"Someone's going to find out," she says. "You can't hide this forever. Maybe I'll even tell them."

"Nobody's going to believe you."

"Where is she?" Gretchen asks.

I try not to let it happen. The sparks, those last dying embers, kindle. I feel it blazing before I can tell it to stop. Hope refuses to die, even in a place like this. But I could be wrong. She may not be asking what I hope she is. I don't want to feel it for nothing.

"Get her out of here," he tells his brother. He takes out the lightbulb, leaving no light in the room except the faint streak from outside. "I don't want to look at her."

She stops in the doorway, while he drags her from the room. The new lightbulb bursts to life, and she smiles as she looks back. I almost think she's looking right at me. But that's impossible.

Once they're gone, I lie on the bed. It was nice once. I like the headboard. There are scratches in it and when they leave the light on, it reflects off the headboard and reminds me of sunlight. The ripples in the wood sparkle.

I remember sunlight. I remember the way it never stayed the same. It would sneak around branches and behind buildings, pretending to say good-bye. But just as you started to miss it, it came back and it warmed you.

Since I've been here, I haven't seen the sunlight much. It doesn't matter, though. Sunlight can't make me warm anymore.

chapter fourteen

After Gina Lynn's party, Caleb was my boyfriend. There was no official decision. Nothing happened to make it true. We'd had a borrowed day, and then he found me again months later, and after we'd kissed, we kept kissing. Like I said, it wasn't a romance. But it was something.

By late May—by my birthday—this something had become the biggest part of my life. I hadn't been a girl people noticed, unless it was to make me feel bad about myself, but now they did. They saw how Caleb held my hand as we walked down the hall. They watched him press himself against me outside my math class and kiss me way too passionately for school. They saw how he laughed when the teachers would ask him to stop. Sometimes I felt a little bad about that, especially when my math teacher would shake his head as I cut between him and Caleb to sneak into class. I wanted my teachers to like me, but I'd still have the taste of Caleb's lips on mine when I walked past them.

When my birthday came, I realized I didn't know how to take this part of my life and juxtapose it with the rest. I didn't want Caleb to come to my house. I didn't want to sit at the table with both him and my dad, Caleb totally unaware of how my father felt about his family, and my dad trying to see what I saw. Trying to give Caleb a chance just for me.

"I made reservations at Mario's," my dad said. Mario's was an Italian restaurant in St. Agatha. It wasn't fancy or anything, but it was better than the pizza place in Hollow Oaks. "I promise I won't ask them to sing to you again."

We went to Mario's every year for my birthday, and then we'd come home and eat cupcakes. It always felt like a waste to make a whole cake for only two of us. We'd each have one cupcake instead and we'd talk.

We'd talked less in the last few years about anything that counted, but we still had this one day. My birthday was special, even if my dad and I had drifted apart.

But this year, I wanted to spend the evening with Caleb, and I didn't know how to tell my father.

"Oh . . . I was . . . Well, um . . ."

I hadn't told him I had a boyfriend. I knew that would lead to him asking about him, and he'd find out who it was. I knew he'd do his best to see Caleb separately from his father, but I still didn't want to talk to him about it. I didn't want to defend how I felt. Mostly because I wasn't exactly sure why I did.

My dad watched me stumble over my words. "Do you want to invite that girl from down the hill?" he asked. He'd seen me going to Kate's more and more, because as I tried to make sense of Caleb, I went to her for help. For guidance on how to be.

"No, it's just that some kids at school were having a party, and I guess I figured I'd go. Can you change the reservation? Maybe we can go for lunch Sunday?" I asked.

He looked over my head and out my bedroom window. I don't know what he was looking for, because our town didn't have anything worth looking at. "I have to work," he said. "We can do it next weekend, if you don't mind. But I feel really terrible that—"

"Don't." I knew I wanted to spend my birthday with Caleb, but I didn't want my dad feeling guilty for my choices. "I should have said something. And I'm fine waiting. It'll be like an extra-special, extra-long birthday celebration."

"Should I still get cupcakes?" he asked.

I shook my head. "We'll get something at Mario's next week. Maybe splurge and split a cannoli?"

"It's your birthday, Ellie," he said. "Whatever you want. I'm going to go cancel. Have fun at your party."

I watched him walk away. I saw his shoulders start to sag. I saw how he waited until he was almost around the corner before he fully let the weight push down on him. And I wanted to tell him I was sorry. I wanted to explain. I even considered texting Caleb and asking him to forget it. But then I thought about what he'd said—that he had a really special surprise for me and he couldn't wait—and I wanted to know what it was. I wanted to spend the evening with him, and so I turned back to my mirror and worried about my makeup. I fixed my hair and I told myself my dad would be okay. That there were plenty more birthdays and that we'd have more time next weekend anyway. I told myself whatever I needed to believe so I didn't have to think about it too much.

When I met up with Caleb, he drove me back to the house where we'd first gone. They were getting rid of it soon. He set up a cake, grape juice instead of wine, and hamburgers he'd gotten on the way to meet me.

"I thought it might be nice to be here. It's not as nice as a restaurant, I know, but it's kind of like our house. Like it's just us. And this is our place," he said.

I ate my hamburger in silence. I didn't care about going any-where else. I didn't care about anything. He'd done this. For me. No one besides my dad had ever done anything for me. I guess Kate kind of had, too, but it wasn't the same. With her, it wasn't for me as much as it was for us both.

"You're disappointed."

"No," I replied. "I'm really not. I promise. It's just . . ."

We sat by the light of our phones. He didn't want to use can-dles because we weren't supposed to be there. The house was supposed to be done.

"I just thought this place was special," he explained. "It's where we started after all."

"Until you disappeared for months on end."

He looked at me, his eyes dark in the dim light. "I expected you to call me. I told you."

I didn't feel like reminding him. Not tonight. I didn't need to tell him again that he'd never given me his number. That we'd passed each other every single day at school in the hall by my math class. That he'd been with several other girls in the months between. I didn't want to ruin what he gave me, so I just nodded.

"You're right," I said. "But it's okay, because now I know."

"Now you know."

We didn't have much to talk about. Even when we went out, it was to a party or with his friends. And whenever we went somewhere alone—his car, another house, the lake—we spent way more time kissing than speaking.

"I have something else for you," he said after we'd finished our burgers. We didn't eat the cake, even though it was there, because he seemed anxious. He kept shifting in his seat, and he finished eating well before I did. I could sense he was waiting for whatever was next.

"Oh yeah?" I asked.

"I told you. I wanted to do something special."

"This is special."

He stood up and held out his hand. "Come with me, Ellie."

I followed him, holding his hand, up the stairs as he guided us with his phone.

We ended up in the master bedroom. He'd brought sheets and pillows and he'd made the bed. On one of the pillows, there was a small box wrapped in pink paper. I hated pink, but I didn't want to tell him that.

He went to the bed, lying down with his head on the other pillow. He patted the bed beside him. "Remember you wouldn't trust me that day? You wouldn't lie down with me?"

"I still shouldn't do that," I said. "There are all kinds of warnings about lying in strange beds with strange boys."

"Am I strange?" he asked.

"Maybe."

"Come here. Please?"

This time, I did. He was Caleb. He was my boyfriend. We'd spent enough time with each other that I trusted him. I knew it might be a bad idea, because I wasn't ready for being in a bed with him, but I also figured he'd understand that.

"Can I open it?" I asked, lifting the box from the pillow.

"Of course. Happy birthday, Ellie."

It wasn't big. Just a simple silver chain with a tiny diamond heart. Maybe it was fake, but I doubted it. Caleb wasn't the kind of guy who bought fake diamonds.

"This is so pretty," I said.

He leaned over and took the necklace from me, putting it back in the box, before dropping the box to the floor. "Just like you," he whispered, as he grabbed my wrists with his hands.

"You're so pretty, Ellie." He kissed me and held me down on the bed, my body under him as I tried to turn off what I felt. I wasn't at that point in our relationship, but it was really hard to tell myself that when I felt him on top of me.

"Ellie," he said, repeating my name as he kissed me. He moved his hands down. So far, we'd kissed plenty and he'd touched me, but always over my clothes. Now, his hands moved quickly as he pushed my shirt from my shoulder, kissing my bare skin along my neck and at the top of my chest.

I sighed. "I don't think I can," I said. "Not yet."

"Whatever you want. It's your birthday. Just tell me when to stop."

I eventually did—after he'd found his way under my skirt, his hands on the edges of my underwear. I had to say it three times, but he did stop.

We lay on the bed, my heart beating and my body agonizing over not continuing. "I'm sorry," I said. "I'm just not ready yet."

He leaned over and fixed my shirt, pulling it back up so only my arms were exposed. "Don't apologize. You don't need to be sorry. I'm sure you would be amazing, but I can wait for you."

We spent a few more hours there, never making it downstairs to finish the cake. I don't know what he ended up doing with it. If he threw it out later. If he left it there to rot. If he gave it to someone else. By the time it was after midnight, I figured I should go home and we didn't have time for cake.

"You should drop me off here," I said when we got close to my house. We were at a park and Caleb pulled up to the curb.

"Why won't you let me come over?" he asked.

"My dad's asleep," I told him.

He turned the car off and kissed me. "I wish we could have stayed."

"I can only imagine what kind of trouble we'd have gotten into."

"I doubt it. You can't even imagine the things I think about doing with you."

I walked home and I wondered what would happen if Caleb ever saw where I lived. I wondered if he'd turn to kiss me some night and see the way our lawn had more dirt than grass. I didn't want him to see the remnants of the broken fence that still formed an edge around the yard. I didn't want him to see the real me. I wanted him to see the girl in another girl's clothes. The one who pretended with him in borrowed houses.

When I got home, my dad was asleep. He'd left the kitchen light on, and in the middle of the table were two cupcakes and a card. It was of a hummingbird, with a prewritten silly "happy birthday" wish. He'd gotten me an iTunes gift card.

Under the gift card was a note.

Happy Birthday, Ellie. Fifteen. You're growing up so fast. I know you'll be late, but just in case you're hungry . . . Love, Dad.

chapter fifteen

T ime, when you're young, doesn't pass in the same way. It feels endless. It's hard to keep track of how seasons change, of when days become months, because we fill time until there's nothing left of it. We fill it with parties and bonfires and school and sports and relationships and people, but it's never enough. Because there's so much time, we need to fill it entirely. Boredom frightens us.

School was out for only a week and we were already bored. It was interminable time. Kate was getting ready to leave for school in Ohio, and my dad worked. And now, because of Caleb, I was part of other people.

Nearly a year had passed since that day I went to Kate and asked her to help me. In a year, a whole world had grown around me. We don't have timelines or memories of how we change. Not exactly. There's time and it moves, but then we seem to wake one day different. Like everything else, change just is.

We were all at Gina Lynn's, sitting by her pool. I'd been there a few more times for parties. They all generally went the same way. People pretended to want to have conversations, but eventually, we all ended up separated. Caleb and I spent a lot of time in Gina Lynn's sister's room. It turned out her sister lived with her only a few weekends a year, because most of the time she was with their dad. Gina Lynn hadn't told me. Caleb hadn't even told me. It was just something someone else knew and then I did and then it was truth.

Caleb and Gina Lynn were swimming. Everyone else sat around on the edges of the pool, watching time pass in slow ticking strokes. Boredom staring us down across three months of summer.

Caleb's brother, Noah, started the game. They called it loser baiting. He'd graduated and he wasn't spending time with us, but he'd started it and from him, it grew until everyone took part. Well, everyone who was at Gina Lynn's that summer.

The game was stupid, but we were stupid and we were bored. That's how these things happen, I guess. Someone says it and it grows from an idea into a part of us, until we can't remember life before it.

"Have you seen these, Ellie?" Jasmine asked. She gestured for me to lean closer, to see what was playing on Kyle's iPad.

"Seen what?"

"Noah started this thing. These videos are awesome."

When you're fifteen, it's easy. It's easy not to feel anything because it's not you. It's not your experience, and sure, it was mean, but the fiction of others is just that—it's fiction.

"This is my favorite," Jasmine said.

The woman was fat. Not curvy like me or even just plump. She was obscenely fat, and she wore tight pants that folded over themselves with the rolls on her body. Her shirt was too short, and skin came out below the fabric, over her pants.

It was Gina Lynn's voice in the video. "Hey, honey," she said. "You dropped something."

The fat woman turned, waiting in line at whatever fast-food place they'd filmed it, her hands full of ketchup packets. It was stereotype as entertainment, because they found people at their worst. Maybe she was going home with the ketchup after getting food to feed her family. Maybe she was picking up an order for her office. But she was fat and she was waiting in line for hamburgers and she was carrying ketchup, so she was a target.

Kyle ran onto the screen in the video, knocking the ketchup out of the woman's hands. "Oops. Sorry," he said, and then he disappeared.

Gina Lynn kept filming, zooming in on the woman's backside as she bent over to pick up the ketchup. "In its natural habitat, the fatty scavenges for sustenance," she whispered.

There were so many of them. An old man looking for directions to the train and getting confused when they told him he needed to travel to 1894 for the railroad. A woman getting angry at a pharmacist because she needed the generic but her prescription wouldn't allow for substitutions. Her poverty was the punch line. All people just trying to survive, turned into mockery and ridicule for us. Because we were bored and we had nothing to do with ourselves and they weren't us.

I should've said something then. Should've pointed it out that day, but I thought I was part of them. I was happy to be part of an us, and so I kept my mouth shut.

When the factory closed, my father was ashamed. He wasn't proud of working there, either, but it got worse later. When he ended up at the store, he stopped talking to his family, his friends. We still visited my grandparents before they died, but sooner or later, the world outside fades away if you don't make an effort to hold on to it.

Hollow Oaks was barely a town. We had a bank and a pizza place and a post office and a few random local stores. And we had the monolith on the hill. The big-box store that hovered over us all, the monster that it was. Before the store, my dad said the whole area had been trees and a field. It was the field where my mom had told him she was leaving. I guess it was poetic to have it torn away. To be where he had to remember, every single day, the life that wasn't.

Dad didn't wear a uniform. Just a vest over his clothes. I was supposed to iron it for him. He could've done it himself, sure, but I'd ironed it since I was ten. Every Friday. It was our routine. Once I started spending time with Caleb, though, I moved it to Thursday because I was out on Fridays. And then summer came and I was out all the time, and we walked into the store and I saw how wrinkled it was.

It didn't matter. Not really. It only mattered because there was one person I could rely on, and now, he couldn't rely on me.

"Can I help you?" he asked. He looked at me like he looked at the rest of them. With tired eyes, not registering that he knew me. He was ashamed and I was ashamed and we pretended he didn't spend his days doing this.

"*¿Qué? ¿Hablas inglés?*" Mike asked. "*No español.*"

"Can I help you?" my dad repeated. "I don't speak Spanish."

"*Sí, sí, yo quiero tacos.*"

"*¡Viva México!*" Gina Lynn shouted. She had her phone up, recording it. I clenched Caleb's hand, but I said nothing.

We weren't Mexican. My dad's great-great-great something or other had come from Peru and my mom was Puerto Rican. We'd lived in Hollow Oaks my whole life. My dad had never left

New York. It wasn't even the good New York. Not the city, with its sparkling sidewalks and energy, or Long Island, with its celebrity summers and palaces. We lived in a part of New York as forgotten as the houses that filled it.

My dad tried to play along. He helped Kyle find hemorrhoid cream, because it was his job. He didn't know that they'd add sound effects to his walk and label the video "Stay in School." When they found the cream, and he picked it up to give it to Kyle, he didn't know someone would add a comic book splash over his back saying, "Too Many Tacos. Ass Is El Fuego."

"Smile for ICE," Gina Lynn said.

He looked at me, and I stared at the floor. I don't know if he recognized Caleb. Or if he just saw me holding a boy's hand and that was enough of an explanation.

Later, I sat at Gina Lynn's house with the rest of them, watching them upload it, seeing the comments people posted, laughing when I was supposed to.

I don't expect to be forgiven for it. I can't forgive myself, but this is what happened.

When we left Gina Lynn's that night, I told Caleb I needed to stop by the store for something and had him leave me there. I waited until my dad got out of work, sitting on the trunk of his car.

"You should know better, Ellie," he said when he came out.

"I'm sorry," I told him. I was, too. It hurt to watch him cross the parking lot in his wrinkled vest and old, ragged clothes. He couldn't replace them because he'd spent all he had buying mine. The ones that let me belong to a group of people who made a name for themselves through his humiliation.

He said nothing on the ride home and went right upstairs to bed. I took Fred for a walk and cried in the comfort of night.

When my dad left for work the next morning, he didn't say good-bye. We never talked about it again. The only thing he ever said was that I should have known better.

Maybe it's better I'm gone.

chapter sixteen

Gretchen turned me into a hashtag. I like that.

They don't.

"Who gave this to you?" he asks.

"Nobody. They were on every single car when I got out of school."

The wall pays for this news.

"Fuck. Fuuucckk." He drags the second one out, as if it's the only way to summarize what they've done, how eventually even the perfect plan fails.

I stare at him. He's wearing shorts, standing in the doorway of the room, holding one of the papers.

Shorts. That means it's spring.

I disappeared in November.

How many months has it been? Five, at least. Is anyone still looking?

I wonder if a body can survive the winter.

"What were you thinking?" he asks.

He shouldn't have asked. His brother moves from the wall and it's them, together, in the same dance. But it's different now.

They're not as soft. They don't cry. Neither one of them begs as their drumbeat violence fills the room.

The paper floats to the carpet. From the floor, I look up at myself. It's an old photograph. A school photo from last year. Taken out of the yearbook. It was before my hair faded. Before Kate chopped off the moldy remainder. The blue streaks look terrible. I look like I was trying too hard.

I *was* trying too hard.

#WheresEllieFrias screams in white from the black bar under my picture.

The guys land on the floor, fists and hands and anger collapsing with them.

"You shouldn't have brought her here," he says.

"I didn't see you complaining."

"Fix it. You have to fix it."

He takes out his phone, dials, waits. There's a pause, and his expression changes. He's charming. Sweet. The person she trusted when she ended up here with him.

"Hey, Gretchen. Yeah, it's Noah. How are you? Listen, about these flyers . . ."

I watch his brother instead. Those eyes. The steel sees right through me. It always did. He never saw me. All the pretty promises were just words.

"You don't know what you're talking about," Noah argues on the phone. "Will you fucking listen?"

It's weird to hear him beg. To believe there's any power in it. He should know better than anyone how little pleading does. He tries to speak over her, tries to change her mind. He's not listening to what she says in reply. At least not processing. All he hears is no. He doesn't know how to hear no.

"Fucking bitch," he says, smashing the phone against the

wall. "Come on. Let's go. We're going to fix this place. She won't remember where it was."

"Do you think we should move her?" Caleb asks. "What if—"

Noah punches another hole in the wall.

"No, not yet. The weather. And with this. No. Fuck. We are so fucked."

I should feel relieved. Happy. Something. But they leave, forgetting again about me, letting me wait while they find ways to hide what they've done.

Maybe I'm too angry to feel anything else. And I am angry. Just not about the right things. The things I would've expected to be angry about. I'm not angry about being here. I'm not even angry it happened. Mostly, I'm just angry that it could. That it keeps happening.

I'm angry that it's spring.

They'll come back. They'll paint over the holes. Maybe clean the carpet. They'll clear the closet where they store the little treasures they've kept. And then they'll go somewhere else.

I lie back and wonder. Wonder what I'm waiting for. What I'm even holding on to anymore.

chapter seventeen

I should've been angry with Caleb. I was, at first. After that night, with his friends and the video and my dad, I tried to pull away from him. I took longer to respond when he texted, or I found reasons to stay home and curl up with Fred and a bowl of macaroni and cheese rather than be with him. I told myself he wasn't them or the videos, but still he was part of them, and I hated how it spread to me when I was around him.

But there's only so long you can lie to yourself. I'd learned to fit Caleb into my life, in the places I needed him, and I felt him missing in those days that followed. I missed how it felt when he'd call me pretty.

Eventually I gave in and we sat by the lake, in the back of his car, and I made him two people. I separated that night from the others, because we do these things to protect ourselves.

"You seem upset," he said.

"I'm fine."

"Is it what happened? The other night? You've been . . . quiet. Tell me, Ellie."

Over time, it had grown softer to be with him. I don't even know what I mean by that, but that was how it felt. At first, being around him, kissing him, his hands on me, all the physical space between us was like forcing yourself to sit on one of those cold, metal folding chairs for hours. It wasn't right, but we did it anyway. In the months since, though, it grew to be comfortable. I sat, resting my head against his chest, his hand on my hip, and we seemed to finally fit.

"It's not right. What they do."

I had to say it. It was between us, and I wanted there to be nothing between us. I wanted him to be the guy I imagined him to be.

"Gina Lynn and Noah and them?" he asked.

"They're people, Caleb. They hurt. It hurts to watch them hurt. It's not funny."

He leaned his head down on top of mine. "That's why I like you. You're not like them. You're so different from them."

"They're your friends, though."

"Are they?" he asked.

The sky turned from orange to pink to purple while we sat there. I thought about it. I didn't know how to define a friend. I didn't even know what made me *me*.

"You're right, Ellie. I'm sorry."

I'd been trying to convince myself that what I felt for Caleb was special. And then, he validated how I felt. He heard me that night, and he agreed it wasn't okay what they did. That's how it happened for me.

It was a word that I'd reserved for coffee when fishing and relish on hot dogs and my father and Fred and various shades of blue.

"Caleb, I . . ."

When you fall in love with someone, it's better when it's in summer. Summer is a stolen season. It's time out of time, and everything that happens in summer feels so much more infinite. I'm glad I fell in love in summer. I'm glad that night existed. Despite all the nights that came after, despite everything that happened, I'm glad I knew what it was like to be heard.

"I love you, Ellie," he said.

Who can say what makes something true? Sometimes a thing is true, and then maybe it's not true anymore. But it doesn't mean it never was. Caleb did love me. I believed it then and I still want to believe it. I have to, even if everything else says he didn't. But I wish I could understand. I wish I knew how something can be true and reverberate the way it did that night—and then be so carelessly false. I wish I understood how a person can hold such contradictions.

I wish I understood how easy it is to lie.

Later, I tried to tell Kate about it. She was packing for school, and I said the words I hadn't said to Caleb.

"I think I'm in love with him," I said. He'd said it and we'd spent the night in his car, and I didn't say it but he knew. There was no way he didn't know.

"Which of these do you like?" She held up two shirts. One was a plain green T-shirt and the other one was a Beatles shirt. She didn't listen to the Beatles, and I wasn't sure what she was even asking.

"I don't know. They're fine?"

"I don't know which one to bring," she said.

"Can't you bring them both? I'm sure you can bring two shirts."

She threw them both to the side of the bed and picked up another one instead.

I wish I had known more about Kate, had known why she wanted to get away. Even now, all I know is that she needed to get rid of who she was here. I don't even know that because she told me. I only know because now I understand how time can weigh on you and how a place can turn you into someone you don't want to remember being.

But on that day, I didn't understand and I wanted to ask her about Caleb.

"Kate, did you hear me?" I asked.

"Yeah. Caleb." She didn't say anything else.

"It's a big deal," I told her. "I love him. I've never felt like this before. I kind of need to talk to you about it."

She stood with her back to me. "What do you want me to say? Do you want my permission to let him break your heart?"

I was surprised, because she'd never mentioned anything about him. Nothing except to say once that she knew of him and she knew Noah. All she'd said was that she never understood what girls saw in them.

"He's sweet," I said. "He tells me all the time how pretty I am."

She nodded, still not turning around. "You *are* pretty, Ellie. You don't need Caleb Breward to say it to make it true."

I sat in the chair by her desk and played with her cup of pens. She went back to packing and I sat in the hot oppressive silence.

After she closed her suitcase, she sat down on the edge of her bed and tossed me the Beatles shirt.

"The Brewards are assholes," Kate said. "You can do better."

"You don't even know him."

My dad explained the Bechdel test to me once when I was younger. I forget what movie we were watching, but it was one he stayed awake for and he tried to make the whole idea of female relationships in film make sense to me. It was something he'd picked up in film school. I listened because I loved hearing him remember the person he'd been, but I didn't really get it. I didn't have friends, and I didn't think much about boys, so I couldn't understand the nuances of what he was saying.

Looking back, I realize Kate and I failed the Bechdel test. We failed at every test. Worse, we failed at opportunity. She hated Hollow Oaks. Hated everything it stood for, and she hated Noah Breward. It was something in the way she'd mentioned him before, but I didn't ask. I didn't ask why she stayed in a town she hated for an extra year, doing nothing but helping me dye my hair and borrow her clothes. I didn't know anything because I never asked her to explain. I used Kate, even if I didn't know it yet.

Wisdom is a privilege of the dying and the dead alone.

"You know what comes next," she said. "How long have you been together? A few months? That's not very long. If you tell him you love him, you must know what comes next. You have to know what he's going to think you're saying."

"I know. He's gonna be a senior in a few months. I know relationships move faster for him. He's been sweet, though. I already told him I need time, but that's just it. I've been thinking about it. I know what's next, and that's what I want to talk to you about."

Kate walked around her room, cleaning up signs that she'd ever lived there. It was nineteen years of her life and she was trying to erase it entirely. I watched her walk around and I waited for her advice. I waited to be told it was okay that I felt this way about Caleb. Or for her to tell me that it wasn't. I wanted someone to tell me what I should feel, because I didn't know if I could trust myself.

"I love him, Kate," I said.

She only nodded and kept cleaning. It was hot—a midsummer day—the humidity almost as heavy as what we weren't saying. She walked through her room, still wearing her hoodie. She always wore it, like it was some kind of armor.

Maybe it was. Maybe Kate always felt like there was something she needed protection from. I wish I'd asked her. I wish I had asked about Hollow Oaks and Noah Breward and what kinds of things there are to hide from in a small town.

chapter eighteen

Their father looks like them. I'd seen him on TV and around town, but never close up. I recognize both of them in him. He has Noah's anger, his entitlement. It sits on him, waiting to be called upon; the lines in his face show the places where it's weaved itself into him wholly. And in his walk and his confidence I see Caleb.

"How stupid do you have to be?" he asks. It's directed at them both, sitting on the edge of the bed like obedient children. It's amazing to watch them cower. To see that they have weaknesses, too.

Mr. Breward, or Wayne to his friends, as he says during his campaigns—insinuating that we are all, sincerely, his friends— moves with military precision. I don't think he ever served, since it would've been mentioned at some point during all the years he held this town in his hands, but he could command an army.

"I called Adrien," he tells them. "I'm not sure I'm ready to get him involved, though. I think we can make this go away, but I need you to hold it together. Keep a low profile for a while."

"No one's going to listen to her," Noah says. "She's like this. She's always starting stuff. Nobody listens anymore."

Mr. Breward pauses and looks at his sons. "There's another one, too. I don't know her name. Adrien's trying to find out. But I did dig up what I could on this Gretchen girl. You're right; she's got a habit of causing trouble, and that works well for you."

"What about the . . ." Caleb starts to ask, but he can't say it. None of them can say it aloud.

"Just clean up. Get this room fixed." They've already repaired the wall and cleaned some of it, but it's not done. And time isn't kind when you have secrets.

"Adrien wants us to stop by there tomorrow," Wayne Breward continues. "He'll probably have something." He takes in the room, brushing his hands along the walls, the table, the bed. I can hear his footsteps on the carpet. It's a weak carpet. A weak carpet in a room for weak girls.

"This one's almost ready to turn over," he says, "and then it won't be our problem anymore. I just would've preferred that you'd had more self-control. Especially after . . . It's too soon. I don't know what you were thinking. They couldn't have been worth it. One night isn't worth losing everything. What was it? An hour? An hour's worth throwing your lives away?"

They don't respond, looking at the carpet. Their dad sighs. "Just keep yourselves out of trouble. And don't tell your mother I was here."

When he's gone, they wait. Processing. Maybe they're trying to figure out who the other girl is, but how could they tell? There are too many. It's hard to keep track. We all become names. Things. Colors and the clothes we wore. We aren't human. Of all the things that make a girl, a soul doesn't seem to be one of them. Not here.

"Let's get this place cleaned up," Caleb finally says.

The closet is never open. But now it is, and they go through the pieces they found from each of us. They save something from every girl. A collection of the hurt, a trophy case of their victories.

I know each item so well. Perhaps the lip balm, if they'd found it first, would've been added to the closet.

Hair ties, a sock, a bracelet, and earrings. Just things that each girl carried. Things they kept as some kind of reminder. I watch them go through each item. There were more girls than I remember.

Noah lifts a bracelet, a stringy thing that was ready to fall off but hung on. Faded yellows and blues and greens. The girl who wore it was the prettiest one of all. A porcelain doll, so fragile.

I wonder if she's the same girl. The one who came forward. I wonder if Noah knows it when he touches the bracelet, if he remembers her at all, or if he simply yearns for whatever he's missing when he sees it. I wonder what he finds in the little pieces he's saved.

I wait for me. I want to see them take me out and throw me away like the rest.

But they didn't keep me here, because they want to pretend I never happened.

Caleb holds the trash bag while Noah makes these girls disappear for good.

"It's just this garbage and we're done." He grabs another handful of girls.

You'd think by now, it wouldn't hurt. The casualness, the way they are with each item. Caleb pushes the trash down into the bag and waits for his brother to finish.

People say you can't fall in love in high school. That relationships you have when you're young are meant to be stepping-stones to what real life brings, they say. But I feel the hurt of it.

I thought I loved Caleb. And while he erases these girls from their history, like he erased me from everything, I feel the shards of it in my blood.

Every last word and memory broken apart. Rushing through what's left of me.

It wasn't a fantasy with him. Like the way he smiled and moved, the growing thing between us was awkward. Still, I remember the love as much as the hate. It's a gnawing pain that I can't forgive. I cared for him deeply. And I believed in him.

Perhaps the worst dangers in our lives are the ones we invite in.

Noah dumps the rest of the items into the bag before doing another sweep of the closet. It's just a closet now. Empty except for the dresser the people before left behind. He pulls it away from the wall, checks underneath, making sure the remnants of what they've done are all removed.

He nods and Caleb closes the bag, tying it shut, holding it over his shoulder. The same way he'd slung my bag over his shoulder on that first day by the river. A sadistic Santa Claus.

I don't know where I'll go when they're gone. The walls are freshly painted, the room just another room in another house. The last record of what happened here sits in the bag Caleb's holding.

Neither of them moves. Noah keeps looking into the dark closet, seeing something that's not there. I wonder if he's mourning this place. Mourning that it's over.

"Are you worried?" Caleb asks.

"Not really. They're not going to believe her."

"But what about . . . the flyers. If she tells the right person. We didn't move her. All they have to do is walk out back and—"

"Don't say it. Don't say her name," Noah says. "She doesn't

exist. We've been over this. This is about Gretchen and the other one, whoever it is. They're trying to distract us, trying to get us to say the wrong thing. They've already asked about her. We've been through it. We're clear, so stop bringing it up."

Looking at them now, they don't look like monsters. Noah's perfectly trimmed nails and hands, when they're not pulsing with the violence he has within him, make him look gentle. Soft in places. His hair, his clothes, everything about his posture is on target with whatever makes him seem safe.

And Caleb, with his awkward confidence and constant smile. Charming. Sweet.

They look like a sitcom.

"Say it," I whisper.

Noah shuts the closet and they're done here.

They turn out the light. Caleb pulls the door closed, the trash bag hitting the frame as he leaves me alone with the bed and the closet and the carpet and the always-and-forever brown walls.

"Say my fucking name!" I scream after them.

Being dead is agonizing. But at least when everyone ignores you, it doesn't sting the same way it did while you were alive.

chapter nineteen

D ad and I were never religious. I went to Sunday school and Saint Elizabeth's, but it was mostly for show. We both had too much else happening in our lives. We were too busy to worry about what God was up to all the time.

Besides, it was hard to get answers about God that made sense. I asked the priests and nuns at school, and when we went to Mass on Sundays, I would try to piece together the stories. There was the Gospel and the Old Testament and the way the priests tried to make it relevant to what was happening in the world.

But the stories were told out of order. Just bits and pieces of someone's life, and we were told He was the only one who really knew. How could I understand these disjointed parts when I didn't understand my own scattered stories?

I didn't know my mom's parents. She was part of my dad's life, then I came, and she was only a story, too. The grandparents I knew died when I was eight. She went first—cancer—and my grandfather followed close behind. I always hoped someday someone would love me that much. That someone would follow me into death, because living wasn't worth it without me.

It seems silly. I was so afraid of being alone in death. As if the real pain isn't on the people left behind.

Now I know it wasn't a romantic gesture on my grandfather's part. He wasn't desperate to keep my grandmother company; he just couldn't bear how quickly her space in the world closed up and left nothing in its place. They're not the same thing. Not at all.

"Where do we go when we die?" I asked Father O'Connell one Sunday. I used to fall asleep dreaming that my mom had meant to come back, that she'd turned around after leaving but she'd died trying to return to me. It didn't explain the cards, but I was young and I could still live in two realities. The one that was and the one I wanted it to be.

"If we're good, we go to Heaven and get to be with Jesus," he told me.

"Why Jesus? I don't know Him."

"Because Jesus loves you and wants you with Him," he explained.

I liked Jesus just fine. I felt sad when I looked at him during Mass, hanging on his cross. They told us we should be happy about it, that He died for us, but it didn't look like something I wanted to be happy about. I thought it was selfish to find joy in His pain just because it made things better for me. I didn't know Jesus well enough, and I certainly wasn't open to dying for Him.

He used to watch us during lunch at Saint Elizabeth's. I'd peer over to the side and He'd be there. I felt ashamed, sitting at the lunch table and being upset they'd run out of french fries when poor Jesus was suffering next to me. But when the kids would make fun of me or knock my tray onto the floor, I'd look at Jesus. I'd ask Him for help. No matter how much I asked, though, no matter how much I hurt for His suffering, He never seemed to be there when I needed Him.

"I don't want to be with Jesus. I want to be with my dad," I told Father O'Connell. They put a lot of stake in Jesus and what He wanted, but I just wanted my dad. I could count on my father. Jesus's track record was a bit spotty for me.

"God is all of our father."

"No, my *father* is my father," I argued. "What happens to him if I'm in Heaven with Jesus?"

I didn't want to die and be separated from my dad. I didn't want God to think I was bad, and I didn't know how to be good. I tried to be good. But I failed, and I don't know the rules anymore. I don't know where we go when we die. I don't know if Heaven still waits for the good people, or if Hell exists, or if there's a lot of nothing. I only know what happened to me and I know what follows a series of mistakes. There was nothing in the Bible or in sermons that prepared me. There was never a list of what made good girls. And when you discover you're not a good girl, I don't know what you're supposed to do. There's no kind of reconciliation for that.

chapter twenty

I don't have to stay here. Maybe I'm weak, but I don't think that's it. I think I stay because it feels apropos. This room ended up being the most important part of my life. I guess it only makes sense that it'd be the most important part of my death.

Sometimes I do leave. I never go far, though. I walk out to where the trees are, where I can be among the quiet things I didn't notice enough when I was alive. They remind me how there's still so much good. I go there when it's too much. When I can't see the good anymore. When I can't feel it or I can't remember, I go to the trees and I listen. I hear the birds sing and I wait for the sunlight to play games in between the branches. I remember how my feet always made the same sounds when I'd walk down a path covered in dry leaves. That crunching sound that announces to the world it's fall.

I can go other places. I just don't.

Right after it happened, there was one time I did. I was scared and my first thought, once I understood what was happening, was to go home. I thought maybe I could go to sleep and wake up and it would all be a mistake. There's no sleep in death, though. It's just time passing along the endless loop of itself.

On that one night, I went home and found my father crying.

He sat at the kitchen table, our laptop on, and my picture—the same one from the yearbook that Gretchen used on the flyers—filled the screen. I was memorialized by that one school photo, a thing I had to do, and I'll forever be that girl now.

The kitchen was dark. The only light came from the computer, and my father was washed in it, in the tints of my picture glowing on the screen.

I watched him cry. It took a while, me sitting there with my dad's pain surrounding me and helpless to do anything about it. He stared and clicked on the laptop and then stared some more. Eventually, when it seemed like he was out of tears, he got up and went to bed.

My dad had so many dreams. Ideas of how the world should be. How it could be. When he was able to stay awake, he talked about them. He told me about the films he'd wanted to make, the ideas he had of what he could still make. But agents and film producers weren't rushing to Hollow Oaks for stories about people like us. He told me the ideas he'd had, and then they died between us.

I want to believe he still held on to those dreams. Even though they were on pause. Sometimes I thought I saw them in the back of his smile. But that night, after he saw the things people had written about me online, I watched as something in him snapped.

I couldn't go home again after that. I didn't want to watch him unravel. I didn't want to believe that there was nothing left for him, either.

I'm sure it was hard for him when I disappeared. I'm sure he worried nobody really cared. These things happen and they're in the news and they're part of everyone's lives, but not really. They're someone else's problem. You still try to care when you remember to, but eventually, something else comes along.

However, there's not caring, there's being human and forgetting, and then there was . . .

I can't decide what to call it. I can't call it apathy. Apathy doesn't bite into your soul.

My father had always been strong. But strength is a tourniquet. It isn't a well. We can't tap into it endlessly as the hurt spreads and takes out all that's good. Strength dies because it can only hold off so much pain. When my dad saw what they'd written, he couldn't fight anymore.

I'd been missing for less than a week.

After he left the kitchen and went to bed, I sat at the table and looked at the screen. He'd left it open, because he couldn't bear to close it, but he couldn't keep seeing those words, either. There was my picture, and then there were his pleas for information. The police were requesting anything anyone might have known about me. Pleading on my father's behalf.

Below my picture, below my father's attempt at connecting with the people left in Hollow Oaks and our surrounding area, were the comments . . .

Sure, I'll help, but only if she's my reward. I'd like to find her and give her a good spanking.

That was the first one. The first thing anyone on Earth— after my father—had to say about what happened to me.

My dad was taken down by twenty words. Twenty callous combinations of letters that were put out into the universe without thought.

It got worse from there.

She looks retarded.

Typical. Welfare family and welfare kid. Glad she's gone.
Who cares? Probably trying to get attention. Teenagers today.
Idiot parent. Nobody cares about your dumb kid.

I was a slut, a loser, a freak, mentally ill, pathetic, privileged, disposable, spoiled, worthless, and a lot of other things. But after 136 comments, still nobody cared. It took until number 137, and even then, he didn't care. He just wanted to call the others out.

So my dad gave up, I went back to the room with the brown walls, and the world continued to fall apart.

Now that Caleb and Noah are done with me, with all the girls, with what happened in that place, I go home. It's time. I don't know if anything's changed, but as soon as I see my dad and Fred, I realize how much I've missed them. How much I've missed home.

This place is full of me, even though for my dad, it probably feels empty. Hopelessly so.

I miss it all so much. Even my room with its remnants of the people I wanted to be, with all those pieces scattered, trying to make the right kind of girl.

Dad's on the couch when I get there, watching the news. The living room is dustier than it was when I was alive. A coating of dust covers everything. There's a glass and a dish on a tray table beside the couch, but he's not eating. They're both empty and I get the feeling they've been there awhile.

One of the bulbs in the overhead light is burned out. I remember how I had to constantly replace them. Funny how many lightbulbs have burned out in my short life. How we accept the creeping darkness into our lives. We run to the store and replace them. As if light is that easy to hold on to.

Fred is curled up next to my dad. I squeeze in beside him

the way I used to and his ear twitches. I imagine petting him and even reach out my hand. There's no connection, though; it's only the memory of what his fur felt like on my fingers. Still, he wags his tail like he knows.

My dad coughs.

It's nearly twilight. The room is dim and the half-burned-out light does nothing. The news drones on about stocks and politics and sports. My dad isn't listening. Not really, but the sound is comfortable.

I settle into the recollection of it all. The normalcy. The mundane. If I was still here, I'd probably be making dinner or doing homework.

"Oh, Ellie, why didn't you listen?" my dad asks.

I wonder if he knows, if he can feel me here beside him. I try to reach out to him, across whatever there is between us. He doesn't see me. Doesn't know. He's watching TV and talking to the news. Fred falls asleep and starts snoring.

I'm gone.

The permanence of it still doesn't make sense. I'm not really gone. Not exactly. My body isn't here, but I feel the same things. I want my dad to hug me. I want to curl up against Fred, to feel his whole body across the length of mine, to listen to the rumbles he makes when I pet him. I want to fall asleep on the throw rug and hope there's a snow day tomorrow, because I'm too tired even to walk to my room.

I still need to be someone, to be remembered. Isn't that the same as being alive?

"The case of Ellie Frias, the girl who disappeared in early November." The newswoman says my name the same way she delivered the information about the recent public works cuts to the snow-removal budget. She's going home after this, having a drink, wondering what landed her in a market like this. A dirty place, a relic.

My face appears on screen. The perpetual yearbook picture. Of course.

The bored anchor continues.

"When Frias went missing, a full investigation was launched, but the police were unable to find anything. They determined at the time that she likely ran away. Law enforcement officers and child psychologists across the state agreed that it's not uncommon to find a teenager desperate for an escape from her life. While the case remains open, at this time we are told no new information has been presented to the police. We aren't sure what brought on this renewed interest. All we've been told is that they are reviewing a possible link between Ellie Frias and two girls who've come forward with some shocking allegations. Cassie Haddom is live in Hollow Oaks with more."

A woman, barely older than me, appears. She's not accustomed to spring here. She's wearing a jacket and scarf. Locals are in shorts.

"Thanks, Maria. That's correct. Two young women have come forward with accusations against boys in town who they believe may have a connection to Frias. We are told one, in fact, was previously questioned about a relationship he had with the girl."

The screen is cut in two to allow Maria and Cassie to discuss my life, my relationships, and the investigation.

I don't know why Cassie is in Hollow Oaks. She's standing on a street with no houses, and she has no information. She could have reported from her office, and she could have avoided looking out of place with her cold and her shivering.

"Have you been given any names, Cassie?" Maria asks.

"Not at this time. Names and details are not being released yet. We believe some of the parties may be minors and we're told there are other pressing privacy concerns."

I don't own privacy anymore. It's another function of the living, I suppose. My name is spread across the television, with a terrible picture of me on the bottom right, below Cassie's face. A study in contrasts. The successful and beautiful woman, and the unwanted mess of a girl.

Dad turns the television off. It's weird to be on the other end of a news story. I'm sure he's relieved they're looking again, but it's hard to hope. It's been at least five months. Even if they find me, he must know there's not much chance I'm found alive. All that's left now is closure, but that's not a guarantee. Some people get closure; others just go on living because it's the only option.

If there was one thing I would wish for . . . one more thing on my massive pile of wishes, it would be the ability to tell him. To tell him that I didn't run away, that I didn't leave him willingly, that I wanted to live. I'd tell him that I love him. Tell him all the things I should have said and didn't. Because we don't.

"Ready for a walk, Fred?" Fred looks up and whines, stretching himself out across the sofa. "I miss her, too. All the time."

He goes to get Fred's leash, leaving the dirty plates and ignoring the burned-out lightbulb. When he comes back for Fred, I see the tears before he wipes them away. He edges past me as he takes Fred and they head out.

I don't follow them. I don't want to be aware of how I can't feel the breeze as we run. How I can't differentiate between temperatures or watch my breath remind me that spring takes a bit longer here. I can't hug either of them or tell them I'm sorry. I can't and so I stay, not crying the tears that don't come.

Instead, I go up to my room when they leave.

I haven't seen it in months, but everything's been moved around. Dad, the police, who knows who else . . .

My diary sits on the dresser, opened and inspected. I imagine what it must have been like, a team of people reading my secrets, trying to decipher me, trying to find connections between the little pieces I left them.

I want to get away from this place.

Those were the last words I wrote in my diary. A week before. They taunt me from the dresser. They told the police what they wanted to hear.

The thing about my diary is that I lied in it. I obscured the truth. I never told even the empty space around me the whole story. I was afraid someone would find it, read it, know me. I wanted them to know a different girl. A better one. I didn't want someone to tell my dad about the parts of me he would have been ashamed of.

I try to picture it, having a stranger in here, looking through the objects and creating an image of a girl. I try to imagine the Ellie they found. Who did they ask about me, and what did they say?

Next to my diary is the box of mementos I'd saved. The things we all hold on to while we grow up. Our soul in a shoe box. That's what a girl becomes. She becomes a shoe box of fishing line, concert ticket stubs, hastily written notes from study hall, a dog collar, a pair of parrot earrings, the diamond heart from a boy she thought she loved. She becomes the things she can't bear to throw away. Things she holds on to but that aren't part of the girl she's become. Or the girl she wants to be.

Am I these things? What would someone know of me from this room? It's all pieces of other people. Of the lives I thought were more than mine.

Nothing makes sense. Nothing in this room makes me a girl. I have no secret music collection, no life passions, no real interests. Just cutouts of the lives I wanted instead. Looking around my bedroom, it's so clear now. I never *was*.

Seeing it makes me angry. I missed it, but being here hurts.

I never wanted much. I only wanted to be a girl.

I know I wasn't very good at it. At being a girl. At being human. I hurt my dad. I didn't say the things I should have said. I wasn't Kate's friend. I was selfish and naïve. I wanted so badly to be a girl that I fell for a boy I thought loved me. I fell for the first boy who called me beautiful. I fell in love with those words and I believed them and I let him make me think I was special. I chased those words until I fell for the wrong boy. Until I fell in love with the boy who killed me.

I don't want to think of these things. Not here. Not in my room. A place I wanted to come home to and have it feel warm again when I arrived. But I can't feel warm here, because my room is like the houses Caleb and I visited. It's like the house and the room where I died. A place that belongs to a ghost.

It suits me better dead. My room is like a tomb. Which is fine, because it's the only one I'll get. Since nobody knows where to find me.

chapter twenty-one

B y the lake, there's this hidden spot. You'd never notice it. There's the road and the trees. It's something people pass all the time, seeing just the road and the trees. But if you look closely, if you stop and pause, there's a break in it. And in that break is a path that's dusted over with years of leaves and branches—dusted over with all the parts of life we don't notice because we're too wrapped up in the human parts. Who said what about whom. What someone did. What they meant by something. But in the quiet between all the worry and all the things we fill our minds with, the world goes on.

Kate and I found this place once. Right before she left. She'd finished packing and we walked along the road toward the lake. She was leaving in the morning. I wondered which shirts she'd ended up packing. I hadn't really been paying attention. Of course, I didn't realize there was something else in what she was doing. That she didn't care that much about shirts. That she was trying to decide what parts of herself to keep when she moved on from Hollow Oaks.

"Hey, come here," she said. Cars didn't come out this way

much. One had passed twenty minutes earlier, but it was just us on the road now.

I followed her as she dragged me into the trees. "Check it out. There's something back here."

Two of the trees rested, broken in half, one hugging the other. They made an archway over the path. I ducked under the trees, one of the branches scraping the back of my neck as I shimmied underneath, and we crossed into what was left of a picnic spot. There was a table, splintered wood with one bench. The sign that used to say something about the place was rusted over and coated with what happens when we forget places. I don't know what you call that kind of rot.

"This is awesome," Kate said. "It's this entire secret world."

It wasn't a world. It was a small circle on the edge of a cliff overlooking the lake, where people had sat once, eating sandwiches. It was another memory in a town full of nothing else.

I sat on the bench seat, looking out over the water. People were boating. It was still summer and there was still that quiet comfort of knowing the day would take forever to die.

"You don't seem very excited," Kate said, sitting next to and above me, on the picnic table itself. She peeled loose pieces of wood from the top, splinters becoming dandelion seeds. Her nail polish was already chipped.

"I can't believe you're leaving."

She lay down across the table, her long legs kicking off the back, and she squeezed my face. "Ellie, baby."

"Don't do that," I said. "Forget it. Forget I said anything."

I didn't know how to have friends. I knew we weren't actually friends. Somewhere in the back of my mind, I knew I was probably nothing more to her than someone to fill the space in her boredom. I certainly wasn't a good friend to her. I didn't know her. I didn't ask questions. But having a sort of friend was still better than being alone. Mostly, I wanted to believe we were friends. Or that we could be. I liked Kate. I just didn't know how to find Kate through all my thoughts about me that waited between us.

"Don't be sad. Come visit me," she said. "Come discover the exciting world of Ohio."

"You picked it," I reminded her.

She started to play with my hair. The chopped mess from where the blue had faded was growing out. "You should let me redo this before I go."

"Why are you going to Ohio?"

She smiled. "It's the only place that would have me."

"Seriously," I said.

Kate wouldn't look at me. "I don't know. There's just . . . I needed space. This town suffocates you."

My father had said it before, too. I never felt it, though. Not then. I liked the town. Except for how sad it was. The way things got left behind. I didn't like that, but I blamed people, not a town. I didn't have big goals, so I never felt like the town was stopping me from reaching them. All I really wanted was to be someone.

"I think I'm going to sleep with Caleb." Kate kept playing with my hair, kept looking past me, at the trees. "I mean, I want to. Not because he's asked or anything. Really."

"He hasn't asked?"

Asking implies communication. We hadn't talked about it. Not exactly. He'd pushed further each time, finding new parts of me to explore, but we hadn't said anything about it. His hands went further, and things moved forward. He'd hinted at it. He talked about how good we'd be together, but we never actually said the words. He never asked me if I wanted to and I never brought it up. He simply tested the line and pushed just past it. Far enough to move us closer, but not far enough that I stopped him.

"No. I mean, he wants to. I can tell. He hasn't really asked or anything. But he definitely wants it to happen," I said. "I do, too."

"Are you sure? You really think you're ready to have sex?" Kate asked.

"I am." I paused. "Yeah. I think so. I think I want to."

She sat up and returned to pulling the wood of the table apart. "It's a big deal, Ellie."

"Is it?"

"You're kidding, right?"

"Well, I mean, it's a big deal for my church. And my dad might be mad. But it's not like people don't do it all the time. You have, haven't you?"

She sighed. Parts of the bench had been white once, and now the paint was peeling, crackling off in strips and flakes. She slid to the edge, where the white was trying to hold on, and slipped a painted fingernail underneath a piece of it, watching it flutter on her hand before the wind took it over the cliff.

"Ohio was the farthest my parents would let me go that wasn't here."

"Kate? Have you? Why won't you answer me?" I asked.

She was pretty. Older. All the things I wished I was. She knew things that she never said, but they rested on her. She walked like she understood the subtle places of the world, and her eyes always felt full of stories. Yet she didn't explain. She never said anything and I didn't ask. She held herself apart from it, and now I realize that sometimes, we do whatever it takes to survive. I wish so much that I'd asked her what had hurt her.

"No. I haven't. It's not really . . . We don't have the same kind of friends."

"I have you. You're my friend."

"We don't have similar experiences, Ellie. My high school years were . . . well, I wasn't where you are. I didn't really get involved with guys."

"So you don't think I should?" I asked.

"I think you should do what you want, but I also think you need to consider what someone like Caleb will expect. You're not going to be his first, you know."

I hadn't asked him. I thought there was a chance he'd been with other girls, but I didn't want to know. I hated the thought of it, because it made what we did feel less special. It made it feel like something people do. Not something *we* did.

"I think I'm okay with that," I lied. "I just . . ." But I couldn't finish, because I didn't have anything to say. I wanted her to tell me what it would be like, but she didn't know and I felt like I was losing the only person I had to ask about these things.

Kate picked another piece of the white free and blew it out to the lake. "Can I just ask you why?"

I should have asked what she was asking *why* about. Why were we friends? Why did I care about Caleb? Why was it summer? Why is a big question with a hell of a lot of answers. But I had a hard time seeing beyond myself. I talked about Caleb, because that was what I wanted Kate for.

"He listens to me. I like how he listens," I said. "I like the way he makes me feel like I'm important. When I talk, he does this thing with his head. He leans to the side and it's like he's got this way of listening. Like he wants to make sure he doesn't miss anything. That's what I mean. I literally like the way he listens."

"I listen," Kate said.

"It's not the same," I told her.

It wasn't, because it wasn't just about how Caleb listened. There was more, too. More I couldn't say. Saying it aloud made me feel weird. Wrong or something. I didn't want to tell her that when I went home most nights, after he dropped me off somewhere, that I could still smell him on my clothes. I would walk from wherever I was, thankful for the night as I pulled my lips together and tried to remember what he tasted like. I would think about what we'd done. The things he'd tried and how they felt. With Caleb, there was a recognition of something I'd never experienced before. He called me beautiful, but it was more than just feeling pretty. It was the realization of this sexual part of me. This thing I was and the way we affected each other. I wanted to know what it was about me that stirred that in him.

It's not a big jump from the boy who bites your bottom lip to the one who makes you wonder what happens when someone is a part of all of you. And time, especially when you're fifteen, fills itself with the steps along that path. I called it love. I told Kate I loved Caleb, and to some degree, I think I did. I loved him because he'd sat with me one night in the summer and he'd listened. He'd validated how I felt. But more, he guided me into something new that was waking up inside myself and I didn't know this was something very different than love. Maybe they're often linked, but at the time, I thought they were the same.

"I still don't get it," Kate said. "All you're telling me is that he pays attention to you. Why does it matter anyway? You said you were sick of everyone calling you names, of noticing all the ways you were different. Why is Caleb so important to you? What's so special about him? Or is it just because he notices you in the right way?"

"I don't know."

She turned around to look at me, but I felt like shutting down. I couldn't answer her. I didn't want to tell her that, for me, being loved equated existing. I needed Caleb to love me, because it meant I was someone. It meant I *was*. But I didn't know why Caleb. And because I couldn't say what made him special, it just made me feel worse about all the things I felt when I was with him. He was fine, but maybe Kate was right. Maybe he was in the right place and he'd said the right things and I liked feeling noticed. But if she was right, then why did I want to let him touch me so badly? Why did I let him do the things he did if I didn't think he was special?

"It's fine, Ellie. I'm sorry," Kate said, and she sat next to me on the bench. "Look, you don't have to know. You don't need to have all these answers. I just worry about you. I've been lonely, too, and I know how it can mix things up in your head." She smiled and started playing with my hair, braiding it into small sections. "I don't know. I don't know a lot of things. I know you think I do or whatever, but I don't have a clue. I'm nothing special myself. I don't know much about guys or relationships or even what you're going through. I'm . . ."

I looked at the lake. Clouds were rolling in, like they do in summer storms. It's warm and comfortable and everything makes sense. And then you're running home, trying to keep the cold from getting into your skin, watching the lightning crack the sky apart.

I never knew what she was. She left the next morning.

And then . . . well, then I died.

chapter twenty-two

This place always calls me back. Nobody's coming here anymore. No one is looking, but I go back. I hope. I hope maybe they'll see me here. And that they'll find me.

I wonder if I stay here because someone should. Because somebody should watch over where I am. Someone should remember me.

It's a strange place when it's empty. It never truly feels empty to me, of course, because it holds so much inside it. The brownness spreads off the walls to the floor. The carpet is still stained. They aren't removing the stains. They were here before. Dark stains too faded to make out for sure. They could be blood. They could be anything. Any stains that may have come later blend in. One person's pain added to another's.

Kneeling on the carpet, I can't feel the burns now. The burning that tore up my knees belongs to my body, and my body doesn't belong to me. When I stare at my knees, they're only the idea of knees.

Somewhere in the deep and buried stains are more pieces of me. Tears, blood, and all the other things I was that they took. It's hard, when you're not a whole girl to begin with, to lose even more of yourself. It's not right that they get to have those things, and nobody even sees.

So many things make a girl. So many things that you can't hang on to.

At first, I tried to be good. I heard those voices in my mind.

Ellie, be agreeable. Good girls don't argue.

I let the carpet tear into my knees, let the blood spill in places while they found parts of me to devour. I was silent, always silent, like a good girl.

I remember how close the bed was. I could see it, but I didn't earn that. I didn't get that kind of luxury. I was a hands-and-knees kind of prize.

It was just motion. Hands. Arms and mouths. Places on my body that I thought of when it was quiet. Sometimes accidental brushes in the shower, and sometimes at night, especially after Caleb. But they were secret places. And now they weren't. All these places were opened and discovered and colonized.

They were an army of monsters, giant claws and teeth. There was no kindness in their touch or their words or their lips on mine.

I made it a story. Something from Lovecraft, a descent into the otherworld. I told myself it was only a nightmare. I promised myself that if I was good, it would be over.

His hands were so dirty. I could see the dirt under the fingernails in the hand on my jaw, the fingers pushing my lips apart. The monster, with a multitude of arms, kept me captive. Later, Noah's hands were soft. But they didn't feel it when he hit me.

I knew I'd die remembering the contrast in their fingernails and how my knees burned.

Agreeable. Good. Don't cause trouble.

All the voices.

I tried. I was good for so much of it.

And maybe it was all true. Maybe it was because I wasn't good. Because I couldn't be agreeable. Because when I couldn't be good anymore, when I finally screamed and begged and fought, it got so much worse.

Brutality. That's what it was. A control that extended beyond me, beyond us, beyond this place. It filled the room that night, and I could have cried or begged or fought, but nothing could dispel it. It was something in us, something in the way we were, the way we all are. I was a sacrifice, a testament to it, but I could have been anyone.

That hurts most of all.

I could have been anyone.

It wasn't my eyes, or my hair, or my pleas that drove them. I wasn't pretty after all. It wasn't something I'd said, some way I'd looked. I wasn't special.

In my head, I tried to place blame. I thought about the clothes, the $18 jeans, the things I'd said to Kate. I remembered the unsaid promises I knew I'd made to Caleb that summer. I found blame in me, because I had to make sense of it all. I had to have a reason, because a reason was the closest thing there was to being special. A reason, even if it was blame, was something I owned, and ownership was better than just being.

Being anyone. Being a girl was all that landed me here. Having all the parts they wanted, but being nothing more than that.

Maybe we are a cookie recipe. Maybe nothing makes a girl.

I claw uselessly at the carpet now. My hands are smoke. A memory of hands and there's nothing there but the carpet. I thought I knew what it was like to be invisible. I thought I could disappear, but now, I fight to touch anything real and I vanish.

Whether or not anyone likes me—whether or not I like me—I don't want to blame myself anymore. I only wanted to belong. I wanted so badly to be taken in—by someone, some-place. Anyone. Anyplace. I wanted it enough to screw up and lose myself, but I am still not to blame.

I did exist. I *do* exist. I'm phantom knees and hands and the memory of what makes a girl, but I'm still real. I was real then, too. Even when nobody noticed.

No matter how bad we are, no matter the mistakes we make, we exist because we make them. We exist because we screw up and we're wrong and we're broken, but those are all the things that make us real. Those are all the things we are.

I didn't deserve this. Even the most confused and lost girl, even the most screwed up of us all, doesn't deserve this. Death isn't the consequence for making a mistake; it's the punishment we force on girls because they couldn't be good.

Only girls have to die for wanting.

chapter twenty-three

The attorney's office is stuffy. Well, I can't actually feel that it's stuffy, but I can sense it. I can glean it from the way they all sit, uncomfortable, not looking at one another. The attorney speaks with a drawl, a man out of place.

"What's this your father's told me about some nonsense with the ladies?" Ladies is supposed to mean gentility. He says it as an insult.

I came here because I could. Because they don't know I'm still here, and it feels like revenge. The meaningless revenge of the dead girl.

Noah responds first, clearing his throat, still looking to the side as he speaks. "It started with this girl, Gretchen, from school. She's one of those girls. She's always making a problem out of everything, always going on about misogyny or male privilege or some ridiculous issue she has. She's so annoying."

The attorney—his nameplate says Adrien Deschaine—leans back in his leather recliner. He would be better matched to a pipe than the black pen he clicks throughout the conversation. Slow, methodical, timekeeping clicks.

"I looked into her background," Adrien says. Click and pause.

"She's quite the instigator, but I don't think you'll have much trouble with that one."

Noah nods. "It was . . . I just . . . yeah."

Adrien clicks his pen again. "It's the other one, though. She concerns me. I'm wondering if she could possibly be an issue. There's not a lot to dig up on her." Click.

The guys shift in their chairs, eyes trained on anything but a living person, waiting. For a name or an explanation. There are too many and they can't tell which one.

I like watching them as they squirm, seeing how they run through the mental list of the things they've done, unable to differentiate between us. Unable to identify what happened when. Suddenly aware that there are so many of us who could take them down. So many they assumed were weak.

"Who is it?" Noah asks.

"Right now, you understand there are no charges, correct?" Adrien replies. "You're aware the police have merely begun to gather information, and I only have limited access thanks to a few friends I have in the department?" They wait for the click, but he keeps his finger poised on the pen, pausing. He waits for them to nod, to confirm and acknowledge. "So you are also aware that it would be bad form to consider any kind of response to these claims?" Click.

"We won't say anything."

"It's important you don't, because if this does become a case, we make sure the burden of proof falls on the girls. Make them prove it wasn't consensual, which is very difficult to do. It's easy to walk away from these things, as long as you know what to say."

"Thank God for that," Noah says.

I want to hit him. I want to punch Adrien with his careless

words. I want to ask where the case is for me. Ask if the burden of proof falls on the dead girl, too.

"This other girl," Adrien continues as he looks down at the file he's prepared, "Kailey Howe. She says she doesn't remember how she ended up with you in the first place. What's the story on that one?"

"She was one of Caleb's," Noah says. "The redhead, right?"

Caleb nods, and I imagine feeling nauseous. I imagine my stomach turning over. I remember sickness.

The way he said it—*one of Caleb's*—like she was part of a set. Like I was.

"You remember her?" They both nod. "So what's the story?" Adrien asks again.

"There isn't one. She came over, we hooked up, end of discussion," Caleb says, but his eyes stay focused on the papers on the desk in front of him.

"Was she drunk? High? Anything she can use to say she wasn't able to consent? This is important, too."

"No." Caleb looks up. "She's lying. Just like Gretchen. They're all liars. Are you gonna fix this?"

Click. Adrien puts the pen down and shuffles his notes and files back into a folder. "These cases are really tough to prosecute. Charges like this are hard to prove. You're lucky, too, because this Gretchen one has a bit of a past. She did say she saw a doctor after, which could possibly be a challenge. Realistically, though, given her background, I think we can say it was consensual. We can argue that she's feeling rejected. That's assuming anything comes of this."

"She wanted it," Noah insists. "I don't think we have to argue that. She was into it."

Adrien smiles. "Your dad said you're both pretty well-liked.

I'm sure it's hard on these girls when they realize you're not interested in anything long-term."

Caleb holds his hands out in front of him, spreading the fingers apart. "I have a girlfriend."

"How will she handle this?" Adrien asks.

"I don't know. She's gonna be pissed. I'll figure it out, though."

"Please do. Especially with this Kailey one. There's very little I can find on her. The only thing is, given the timing, we may have the advantage. It's been what—ten months?"

"Nine," Caleb replies. "And I hooked up with her before I started seeing Gina Lynn seriously, so hopefully it won't be a problem."

Nine months.

Summer. This happened in summer.

This happened while I thought we were falling in love.

I've never heard of Kailey Howe.

This whole time, even after what happened, I still held on to hope. This belief that somehow Caleb was two people. That I'd loved him and something in him had gone wrong between that first time we'd met and the last time we were together. I wanted to believe that the person he was at the end wasn't the same person I'd known and spent those moments with. All that is gone now.

While I fell asleep on those nights last summer, thinking of the way he'd learned to kiss me . . . When I'd started to feel the things I'd expected, the things I'd wanted to feel . . . While I was lying there, wondering if it was too soon to go further.

All those things I was thinking, was imagining, was wanting . . .

He was there. In that room. In that house. He was there with other girls. Doing those things to other girls. This was a part of him the whole time.

"Okay, so with Kailey," Adrien says, "it'll be a question of why she waited. It sounds like they're pulling all kinds of things out of the air, hoping something will stick, and that actually works out for us."

"What about . . . Gretchen made these flyers," Noah says. He takes me out of his pocket, folded into pieces, and passes me across the desk to Adrien. "And the news said the police are reviewing the case."

Adrien unfolds me. Looks at me. Remembers. And then he smiles.

"The police already questioned you on this. We have a lot in place and it's going to be hard to find a connection now out of nowhere. Just because two girls said something happened. *Allegedly* happened."

I don't hear the rest of the conversation. I leave before I can. Before they can continue to erase me completely.

I pass their father in the lobby, flirting with the receptionist. He didn't even go in, trusting his attorney to guide his sons through these kinds of accusations.

Outside, I try to find somewhere else to go. Maybe I should return to my body. Wait by it. Wait for the rain to come, to reveal what they've hidden. Wait so I can show everyone exactly what they've touched. Maybe I can remember flesh and bone and blood and the things that used to be mine. Before they were theirs, too.

chapter twenty-four

was wearing the $18 jeans and a black sweater. Sneakers. I
had my hair in a ponytail because I didn't know how else to
wear it.

If you try finding a missing girl who was wearing a sweater
and jeans and wore her hair in a ponytail, I imagine you'll
realize what she already knew: Some people blend in so well
that, when they're gone, it doesn't seem like they ever were.

I think the elastic came out before I made it to the carpet.
It's meant to hold your hair away from your face, not to save
you. I remember swallowing my hair as I fell. It caught in my
throat, quieting me while I cried.

You get to relive these moments on a loop. I know there are
probably details that contradict each other. Ones that maybe
came from another part of the night or from pieces of things I
acquired in my life. I've moved them in where they don't fit to
fill out the story. But I know what happened. I know it because
it plays in my mind for every second I don't focus on something
else.

The jeans were first. The sweater was merely annoying; the
jeans were prevention.

"Someone's been waiting for this," he said.

I'd spent more on the underwear than I had on the jeans, but if the jeans weren't going to protect me, the purple silk had no chance.

Caleb touched me the same way he had before. I couldn't stop myself, letting his fingers in because he'd been there already. I was angry at my body for not understanding. It never listened to my mind.

"I like that. I knew you'd be good, Ellie."

Good. Always about being good. I don't know what that even means anymore.

"Why can't I turn around?" I asked. "Let me look at you." I still didn't know. Didn't understand. I thought something was wrong, but I also thought this must be normal. This must be what happens, must be how it is. I knew the first time would be strange, and I figured this was what it was like. Still, I couldn't escape that he didn't want to see my face.

He kept one hand on my back, pushing me down into the carpet. When I began to cry, the hair spilling from my throat, he whispered, "Shhh," and put his other hand over my mouth. I could taste myself on him.

I'd imagined having sex with him. We'd gotten closer and closer. That night, I'd planned on it. It had been more than a year since the day we'd met and almost eight months since Gina Lynn's first party. I spent lots of nights, staying up into the early hours of the morning, wondering. Even practicing, hoping. I'd hear my dad leave for work and feel ashamed, because I was still awake with these thoughts inside me. Picturing Caleb, watching his face in the moment it happened. I wanted to see his eyes in that instant, when he was forever a part of me. Instead, I had to stare at stains on a ruined carpet.

How do I reconcile that I wanted it? It was my darkest secret until I didn't want it anymore. Not the way it was. But even then, while I spoke unheard pleas against his hand, I felt my body rise to meet him, felt myself welcome him in. I told myself I would get used to it. I thought it would be like our first kiss and that, eventually, we'd find a place where we were both comfortable.

I keep blaming myself, because I don't know what else to do. I still feel the phantom weight of him bearing down on me. Can remember his fingers pushing against my lips, gagging me while he did this thing to me.

That's it, though. This was done to me. I blame myself, but it wasn't something I did. It was nothing I controlled. That wasn't what I wanted. I wanted to be there with him, to be a part of it. I wanted to give something in return for something, a reciprocal moment. That was how I'd pictured it. I didn't want this, and even while my body tried to make sense of what my mind already knew, I realized this would never be what I had hoped for or imagined.

At first, I was sad and disappointed, but I tried to think it was normal. However, as he grew more violent, as the carpet tore into my skin, as I cried and shook and tried to fight back and he pushed me farther down, I knew that this was nothing like I'd planned.

And then there was what happened after. When the door opened for Noah, it became something so cruel, so unimaginable, so outside the realm of possibility. That's when I realized it wasn't a mistake. That Caleb *enjoyed* this. That he'd always wanted it to be this way. That he liked it more the harder I cried.

When I think of those things, I sometimes think I'm glad I'm dead.

I don't want to be dead, though, because there are so many

things I miss. I miss that chill when winter comes without warning and you don't have a coat when you walk outside, only to be reminded that the cold isn't beholden to you to give notice. I miss sitting in the living room and eating cookies that are more sugar than food, worrying about who gets kicked off a pointless reality show competition that's probably rigged anyhow.

These are the things that make life. This is what a girl is. This is what they took from me.

Where they put me, there's nothing but dirt. They didn't even give me a rock or a stick as a remembrance. It's just me and some dirt.

I watched them do it. Watched them stand out in the night, the moon swimming under clouds, Caleb holding the flashlight and complaining it was too cold.

He was cold. I was dead, but he was cold.

I can see it. Now that the house is cleaned up, the bank will sell it for nothing. The couple who buys it, maybe they're young. Maybe they think it's a great deal because they don't know what kind of place it was. They don't know the things that happened here. Their kid will play in the backyard. He'll bring his friends home and they'll play soccer over where I am. They'll live and exist and never know that I'm still waiting for someone to see me, right under their feet. When the grass grows in, it'll be like I never existed at all.

That night, I died slowly.

All the clichés, they lie. I didn't see my life flash before my eyes. There wasn't a warm comforting light. It was me, trying to breathe, seeing Caleb over me, remembering his smile in those first days. It was the feeling of my windpipe giving in, the desperate realization that this was it and there was no way out.

I died seeing beige. Beige and the boy I thought I loved.

Dying was my art. It was my achievement. I was a pointless girl in a pointless town with a pointless life. Dying was the point; it made me someone.

They were careless when they got rid of me. They left me with nothing but a tarp, a few ropes, and my clothes, torn, then hastily and poorly replaced. My sweater was inside out and backward when they threw me into the ground. They didn't bury me. Burying implies care. I was thrown into the dirt, an inconvenience.

They waited only a few days to bring another girl to the room. There was no panic or fear in them. What they did to me didn't matter. They barely even remembered.

I stopped paying attention to time after that.

How do you kill someone and leave her to rot in the ground, then shower, eat a sandwich, watch TV, brush your teeth, do all the things that are part of life? All the things you took from her? Why do you feel entitled to continue? Because you don't think she was entitled to these things, too?

That night, I sat and kept guard. I hoped they'd come back. I hoped someone would drive by, would see the dirt, would find me. I waited until they did come back three days later, until they did it again and again.

I watched the snow come, covering where I was, letting the world forget me, too.

Going back there now, I only remember where I am because I spent a lot of time memorizing small details. The way the light hits the branches by the tree on the edge of the property, cutting across the yard like a scythe. I remember the angle of the spot from the back door, a slider into the kitchen, through which they'd dragged me out into the yard. I recognize the shadows that the shed throws across the ground, landing right where my head is, darkening the patched bruising on my face and neck that's gone now, along with other pieces of my flesh.

After I stopped breathing, I had a hard time making sense of it. There are no guidebooks to being dead but not going anywhere.

Noah left to buy ropes and a tarp. Probably from my dad. I still wonder if he sold them to him, if my father gave Noah the tools to get rid of his own daughter.

By the time Noah returned, Caleb had forced my body back into my clothes. The torn jeans hung on my limp body. My hair was matted and covered my face.

After their dad came and helped them, Caleb walked away, toward the house.

"I'm taking a shower." The four words my boyfriend said after he and his brother raped and killed me.

I hate that word. I hate it being a part of what I was.

Rape.

It brings with it connotations, assumptions, a whole steamer trunk full of other people's ideas of it, because other people only know it as a word. A concept that's discussed, argued, demonized. If you actually know what it is, if you live it and experience it and know what it is beyond a word, you have to carry that word with you. You're now "rape victim," "rape survivor." Your identity is attached permanently to a word you hate.

I'm also a murder victim, but murder carries with it what it is. People don't debate what defines murder. Politicians don't argue the body's ability to fight off being killed. There's no talk of a "murder culture." No one says that you asked for murder. What you wear doesn't excuse being killed.

Yes, I wanted Caleb. But I also wanted to go home that night and have my dad knock on my door five times in the morning until I woke up, because I stayed up too late playing on my phone. I wanted to go to school and complain about homework, just like I wanted to have sex and wake up the next day happy I did. I didn't want to be held facedown against dirty carpet. Didn't want to be passed between them, to have them in the places they went.

I didn't want anything more than what plenty of girls want. To be loved. To fall in love. To lose my virginity and be happy about it or regret it, but to have been given a choice.

The futility of rage in a dead girl is almost funny. But as I stand over where my body is and wonder if I can slip back inside of it, the way they did with such ease, I don't want to laugh. I just want someone to find me.

chapter twenty-five

The problem with summer is that it doesn't last.

Caleb and I sat in the park, two people among the masses. I wasn't used to sitting with him anywhere in the sun. Our relationship seemed mainly to exist in the hours between twilight and darkness. Borrowed from time in a dying season.

"It's weird to be the only one going back to school this year," he said.

"Only one of what?" I asked. "I'm going to school."

The last day of summer, the day before school starts, always feels both endless and like living on fast-forward. Under me, the metal of the bleachers seared my legs, but I didn't want to move. Didn't want to let the day end. Kids played sports on the fields around us and moms worried over grass stains and heatstroke.

"Sorry. I meant in my family. It's always been Noah first, then me. It's weird to be in school and have it be all mine. I can't remember anything that was only mine."

"It must suck having siblings. I'm too selfish to share with anyone," I admitted.

Caleb laughed, turning on the bleacher. Sun continued to

settle into the sharp ridges on the metal bench, burning the backs of my thighs.

"I don't think you're selfish, Ellie."

"You don't know me that well."

He considered it. And in truth, what did we really know? I knew him in the ways he wanted me to know him. I knew the things he shared, and he knew what I did. We knew each other as extensions of ourselves, as ideas of another person. But we only knew what we wanted the other to know. He didn't even know where I lived.

Caleb and I knew each other as you do when you start to discover love. We knew that this other human being, this *other*, found the things in ourselves we wanted someone to find. I knew I liked being part of Caleb and Ellie. I liked following an *and*. I called it love and I believed it, because it made me feel like I belonged somewhere. At the end of *Caleb and*.

I suppose Caleb could have been anyone, too. Except he wasn't.

"I know you're not like anyone else I know," he said finally. "And I know mostly selfish people."

It's hard to remember him. It's hard to isolate those feelings, to recall him in those days. Caleb before. All my memories of him come through the screen of something else. I know I felt things about him then. I believed the things he said, but now, I don't know how I did. I think of what Adrien said. About the girl named Kailey. And I don't know how to remember that day anymore.

I can't explain him. It aches to think of that afternoon on the bleachers, because I know what came after. I can't remember loving him without knowing what he did, and that makes me hate myself. Because somehow, I still do love him. Or, at the very least, I love this memory of him. Even when I know what he was. What he was all that time. Even with all the anger, I can't remove this part of him from my life. I can't change the way I felt.

"I don't want to go back to school tomorrow," I told him. "I like this too much."

"Me, too. You're the best part of my summer."

"Really?"

"Of course." He leaned forward to kiss me, but I didn't let him, sliding backward on the bleacher. I wanted him to tell me more. To explain what it was he saw in me that I didn't. To let me know what was special. Maybe even then I knew it didn't make sense. That real love feels different. It doesn't make you ask someone why. They don't have to tell you, because they show you instead.

"Tell me about Noah. Or about college or about something you haven't told me," I said. "Tell me about you, and then you can kiss me."

He shrugged. "I don't know. I don't know what to tell you. It's always been me after my brother. He does everything first. It's just the way it is with us. Sometimes I feel like the extra kid. The one my parents had in case Noah fails."

"So make something yours. Make something that he doesn't have," I said.

"What?"

"I don't know, but there's more to life than following Noah into everything. There's more to life than being a backup."

His hand, which rested on my knee, tensed. "Is there?"

"There's college. If you can't find it now, I'm sure you can find something there." Something somewhere else, but I didn't say it. The idea of this coming to an end in a year scared me.

"I don't even know if I'm going," he said.

His family had money. Caleb and I never talked about grades, but I knew that he would get wherever he needed—or wanted—to go, because he could pay for it. Noah was no scholar from what I'd heard, but he'd managed to get into the local college just fine.

I was naïve, but not that naïve. I knew what power was.

"I'm sure you'll go to college," I told him. "Whatever it is you feel like you're missing, maybe you'll figure it out there."

"You realize, by next summer, we might not be in the same place?" he asked. He had never spoken a more honest statement.

"I'm not going anywhere," I said. "But you'll probably be sick of me anyway." He leaned over to kiss me again. "Will you be?"

I wanted him to argue, to promise he wouldn't grow tired of me. I wanted him to say something, but all he did was slide closer.

"This is depressing. Let's talk about something nicer," he said, and he moved his hand upward, teasing the edges of my shorts with his fingers.

"That's not talking," I pointed out.

"Shhh," he said, and his fingers pushed into the flesh of my thighs as he kissed me. I knew what he was asking, what he was testing.

I stood up. "Not here."

We walked back to his car, his arm around my waist, his fingers on my skin below my tank top, while the two of us stayed silent.

That night, I almost let it happen. We left the park and let the day die from the back of his car, going further than we had before. I didn't stop him; I didn't slow it down. Time did, running out until there wasn't enough of it, and when he dropped me off on the other side of town, I walked home thinking about what came next for us. Trying to feel the word *yes* on my lips. Trying to imagine what it would be like.

The next afternoon, I sat at lunch, alone. I didn't have lunch with anyone I knew, and it was the first day of school. Every year is a new year. Trying to find your place again. The few people you'd held on to the year before have changed. Summer sweeps in and shapes us all, and then September comes and we have to start over.

I was hanging on to the way Caleb had kissed me the night before. The way that he'd undressed me and we'd stopped because we'd run out of time, but how I knew that the next time, all I needed to do was say one word. I thought of all that, but I shouldn't have believed any of it. Because all of that was part of summer, too.

"Are you Ellie Frias?" She stood over the table, her hair shining and perfect, like everything else about her.

"Yeah. I went to your party," I said. "Parties."

Caleb had invited me to a few more of Gina Lynn's parties over the spring and summer. She and I had talked. Not about anything important, but he'd introduced us. Several times. Plus, I'd been there with her that night. When they'd filmed my dad.

"I thought you looked familiar," she said. "So, listen, this may sound random, but are you with Caleb Breward?"

"I am," I said. She knew this. Or she should have, but she didn't remember me and I'd seen her several times that summer.

"Like for real?" she asked.

I pushed my yogurt to the side and looked up to respond. "I think so. I guess. I mean, what do you mean?"

She smiled and lifted her hand, waving one of her friends

125

over. The other girl was equally golden, although it was false. She was spray-tan pretty, while Gina Lynn just made the sun chase her. I never caught her friend's name.

"Did you know Caleb's got a girlfriend?" Gina Lynn asked her friend.

"Seriously? I thought you guys were—" She stopped with a look. The secret language of girls who can speak secret languages and still make people listen.

"See, the thing is, Ellie . . . It's Ellie, right?" Gina Lynn sat down and put her hand on mine.

"Yeah, Ellie." Even I was caught in her spell. My brain wanted me to remind her that she'd asked me literally seconds earlier. That I'd told her before. But I nodded and said it again, hoping she'd learn it and I'd become a word in her vocabulary.

"Caleb and I go way back, you know? You just moved here, right?"

"No. I mean, I've always lived here. I think we talked about this before."

"Really?" She looked at her friend, who'd sat beside her and was texting. "Didn't you say she was new?"

"I don't know. I've never seen her before."

Being dead suits me well. Sometimes, I feel like I came into my own after dying. That this was who I was supposed to be all along. It's not much different than being in high school. Things continue, life happens, people have conversations, and I'm still on the edge of it all.

Gina Lynn grabbed the girl's phone. "God, who are you even texting?"

"What the hell?"

I went to stand, picking up my yogurt, thinking that somehow the conversation, or whatever it was, was over. But Gina

Lynn turned back to me and gestured for me to sit. Obedient, I did, and I waited while they argued about someone named Ben.

The cafeteria was subterranean. All the windows were small portholes in the upper third of the walls, hinting at natural light. Strips of fluorescent hung above us, and I listened to the buzzing, a subtle sizzle that went unnoticed in the din of lunch. Underneath all the conversation, the music, the sound of the maintenance guy mowing the lawn from the ground overhead, there was a barely distinguishable hum. I liked the way it kept humming, music for the attentive few.

" 'Kay, back to you, Ellie. Sorry." The spray-tan girl sat chagrined, while Gina Lynn held her phone. "What I was trying to say was that, well, Caleb and I have always kind of had an understanding, you know?"

"I don't."

"We're kind of a thing. But it's like a whenever thing, you know?"

"Wait, what are you saying?" I thought about the night before. How he'd touched me. How we'd been so close. How I almost told him I didn't need to go home yet when we realized what time it was. I remembered the way I'd tried to say yes, tried to see what would happen. I remembered how he'd told me he loved me.

"I just broke up with Trevor. You know him?" Gina Lynn asked.

I didn't. Why would I know him? She couldn't even remember my name and we'd met multiple times. Throughout the summer, I'd seen her with guys, but she was never with any one more than others. Except Caleb.

"I don't think so," I said.

"Yeah, well, anyway. He's whatever. But you gotta understand. Being single sucks, right?"

"I guess."

"So, yeah, the thing with Caleb is that he's kind of my boyfriend when I don't have one. And that's gonna be an issue, right, I mean, if you're in the picture?"

"Are you asking me to break up with him?" I asked.

She laughed, her hair spilling around her like she was in a damn shampoo ad. "You're cute, Ellie." It was the exact same way Caleb had said it when we'd first met. "Good talk, hon."

She left, handing her friend back her phone, and the other girl shuffled after Gina Lynn. I stared into my cup of yogurt, blueberry swirls clinging to the interior edges of the plastic. I had no idea what had just happened.

By the end of the day, I couldn't stop thinking about it. Couldn't make sense of the night before. I wondered how things could change so fast. I stood at my locker, trying to gather my books. Telling myself that it wasn't real. That Gina Lynn was confused.

"Ellie." Caleb stood behind me, his hand on my back.

I didn't want to turn around. Didn't want to see his face, in case he told me she wasn't wrong.

"Ellie," he said again. It was the fifth time he'd said my name, but nothing had followed. I waited for him to say something else.

I'd told myself school would be different this year. Some people knew who I was now, although they still didn't know me. But I was attached to someone else and they acknowledged me because they had to. Sure, it was ephemeral recognition. It was the way you recognize the guy who works at the pizza place when you randomly run into him at your doctor's office. Nothing but the way we deal with an illness, or a flat tire, or something that just has to be and we have to let it. But it was something.

I knew what Caleb was going to say, and I knew what I'd lose if he said it.

"Turn around, Ellie," Caleb said.

I did. He was smiling. That awkward expression that he always wore.

"At lunch . . . I mean, today . . ." I couldn't say it. Couldn't make it true. "Do you want to go somewhere?" I asked.

It hadn't even been a full day. Things don't change that fast. Not in real life. I kept telling myself that I'd misunderstood. Even though I had known since lunch what was coming.

"Ellie," he said again.

"Just say it, Caleb. Stop saying my name."

"Fine. This isn't working," he said.

"Why?"

"Come on, you knew it wasn't going to last."

"You didn't answer my question," I said.

He pulled me close to him, holding my shoulders and leaning into me. His hair brushed my neck, and I wanted to kiss him. He could turn it off, but I couldn't. Nothing had changed for me.

"I'm sorry, Ellie."

"What happened? It was last night. Last night, you said you loved me."

He sighed. The warmth collected against my collarbone. His body was tense against mine. I tried to remember what else we'd said the night before. Tried to remember what happened in less than a day.

Caleb pulled away, shoving his hands into his pockets. He

stared at the locker beside me, not looking at me. I had stopped existing for him. "You're sweet, and it was fun, but it's just not a good time," he said.

"Why not?" I asked. I kept asking questions he wouldn't answer.

"It's my last year. I have college applications and I should get my GPA up and our dad has us working a lot on another place. There just isn't time."

I don't know why I didn't cry. Not until later that night, at home, in my bed. I took it in, and I tried to see him as someone else. Not Caleb. Not this part of me, this person who filled my life where I was lacking. The person who was going to leave that emptiness behind because he had to fill out a college application.

"I can wait," I told him. "We don't have to see each other every day. I can help you with school. My grades are okay."

"You're a sophomore." I was, but I was in advanced classes. He didn't know that, because we didn't talk about school. We didn't talk about anything, but I only realize that now. I only know now that we were entirely resting on the surface. At the time, I still thought it was okay that all we had were summer evenings in the back of his car. Borrowed nights in other people's houses. Conversations cut off by kisses. I thought that was the same thing as love.

"Caleb, please don't."

"I'm sorry. I really am. I promise, it's nothing you did. Maybe things will change. Maybe in a month or two, when everything settles."

He kissed my forehead and left me there with my textbooks poking me in the side from my bag. I stood with my fingers against my lips, trying to remember. Trying to hold on to where he'd kissed me.

The next day, he and Gina Lynn were together and everyone knew it. I didn't hate her; I couldn't. I saw how his arm fit around her waist, saw how they smiled together and how the whole school watched them, envious. I knew they made sense and we didn't.

When I went home that night, after seeing him with her in the hall, I threw away all the clothes Kate had picked out. Everything she'd given me. But in the morning, before dawn and while my dad was sleeping, I snuck back outside and dug through the trash can. I changed my mind because I believed I could exist in a way that wasn't touched by him.

I saved a few things. Two T-shirts, a black sweater, and an $18 pair of jeans.

chapter twenty-six

N ow that the room is sterilized, wiped clean of what happened here for good, I drift. There's nothing left in the house anymore. I don't know why I stayed except I didn't know where else to go, but now, I can't even justify that. So I walk through town. I accept that I'm here and that I'll probably always be here. I rediscover Hollow Oaks. The park. The school. Stores where I bought aspirin and pencils and hair dye. The one on the hill, where my dad was—is—but I don't go in there. I can't see the sameness of it, can't look at him continuing because I might come back. He'll never leave, at least not until there's a body to bury. And even then . . . I don't know. Maybe he'll hang on to it. Maybe he'll stay because while this town is what it is, it's also all that's left of me.

There's this entire freedom of not being seen, but I don't know how to use it. I move from place to place, trying to get a sense of what's happening, trying to piece together what they know and what they don't. They can't find me. Even though they know I'm gone, there's nothing they can do. This thing has been introduced into the world, but it just festers and the world goes on.

I don't want to go home again. Home is the worst place. It's all the things I need to feel, held away behind an invisible veil.

So I walk instead. I observe. Hollow Oaks. The oaks were taken down for the factories, and the factories sit empty in their space. The name became ironic.

One of the factories, right on the river, is a brick behemoth. The age on it shows. Spray-paint tags, broken windows, padlocks and chains designed never to be cut or opened. Where there used to be a sign, an announcement of what this was, of what creation came from the hollow vastness of it, is now a darker patch of brick. Just a hint.

Once upon a time, there *was*.

That's the theme of this town.

This was where my dad worked. I sit on the hill behind the factory, a small hill that drowns itself in the river a few feet farther from where I sit. The silence of it isn't disturbed by my presence. There are no crunching branches when I settle. An owl continues its melancholy keening. The river knows where it's going and it takes no notice of me.

When Kate left, I had nobody to talk to anymore. I guess I could've gone to my dad, but I'd crossed that chasm and I didn't know how to get back.

I hadn't known loneliness before. Not really. I'd known the idea of it, but since I'd never had anyone, I had only imagined loneliness. I had to imagine love and so the absence of it was just something I guessed at. But now, I knew what it felt like to miss someone. To have someone fit into your life and take parts of you for themselves, only to abandon you and those pieces without care. To leave you with pieces missing and somehow changed, while they tore away the parts they'd loaned you for a time, too.

When Gina Lynn burst into my life, into my quiet, I learned. I'd thrown myself into whatever I had with Caleb so fully that I couldn't figure out what was left without him.

It's a dangerous companion, loneliness, and it scares me now, as it takes my side by the river. I can't last an eternity with no other friend.

The owl agrees.

I sent Kate an e-mail that night, trying to put it into words. I sat alone, needing him, and I hated that need. Kate replied with a sad face emoji and a promise that she'd call soon. She never did, but I never reminded her, either.

Death is a mirror. It's a reflection of the things that happened and the shimmering edges of what could've happened instead. There are all these pieces. Each memory, each moment. I sift through them, trying to put them together. Trying to understand why I can't move on. I cling to the idea that I'm still here because of something unfinished. Believing in those ghost stories I read as a kid. Because otherwise it means this is it. This constant reminder, the regret and what-ifs just spreading into forever.

Maybe Father O'Connell was wrong about Heaven, or maybe I just wasn't a good girl.

Maybe this is Hell. An endless flood of all the things you should have said, could have done, and the constant knowledge that you put yourself here.

There aren't other dead people in this place. It's a small town, but not small enough that I'm the only one ever to die. If I had been, I'm sure they'd be looking a lot harder. So why is it, even in death, I'm all alone? It doesn't feel fair that this is my punishment.

I listen to the owl. Over the trees, beyond the river, a white burst of light drenches the night. Pollution from the store on the hill, constantly invading even the quiet places.

Time passes through the night. In death, time is forever. Night becomes day and time means nothing anymore. I stay on the hill by the water, by the factory, until the owl goes to sleep and cars begin to pass.

The thing about Hollow Oaks is that it's not a place that creates people. The whole world is made up of places like this, I think. Places that churn out lives, but those lives fill space without shaping it. We don't make it onto the news. Even during the weather report. Billowbrook and St. Agatha do, our neighbors hinting at what we can expect, but Hollow Oaks only exists to the people who live here.

So when the news vans arrive, one, two, and then a parking lot full of them, it's something people notice.

Cassie Haddom, the reporter I saw that night while I watched TV beside my dad, stands in front of the police station. She's figured out the weather now, and she's trying to blend in, but the way she shivers when she thinks nobody's watching still identifies her as an outsider. She sips her coffee, waiting for something. A crowd of reporters builds around her.

When a police officer steps out of the station, the reporters become a mass of cameras and microphones. I don't recognize the officer, but then again, I never had much cause for knowing the town's law enforcement.

"Good morning," the officer says. "On behalf of the Hollow Oaks Police Department, I'm Officer Shannon Thompson."

She's young. She looks like she's barely out of high school. She tries to cover for it. Posturing as confident, authoritative

"We are confirming that, effective immediately, the department will be launching a full-scale investigation into two claims of alleged sexual misconduct against Noah and Caleb Breward, sons of Wayne Breward. Wayne Breward is well-known in Hollow Oaks and in the surrounding area, serving not only as the town's tax assessor, but also recognized for his work in real estate."

This is why the reporters are here. They're here for a name. A headline: Sons of Local Politician and Real Estate Mogul Accused of Sexual Misconduct.

Misconduct. I wish they'd call it what it is. Misconduct sounds like something you do to earn yourself a time-out as a toddler.

"Two young women have recently come forward with similar accusations. We will be determining the validity and strength of these claims, as well as cooperating with the district attorney's office regarding what we find. As of now, no formal charges have been brought. In addition, while there have been media reports that this may be linked to the case of Ellie Frias, who has been missing for approximately six months, we do not have reason yet to connect the cases. Of course, should that change, we will investigate as expected. At this time, we do want to ask the media to respect the privacy and rights of both the Breward and Frias families. We will not be taking questions, but we welcome any information you may have about this situation. Thank you for your attention."

The storm of questions echoes through the parking lot. Officer Thompson takes her prewritten statement and rushes back into the station, as reporters follow. I wonder what happens when she goes inside. Does she want to be the voice of this? Does she want to be the one reporters link to the questions that go unanswered?

I watch Cassie, who doesn't move, readying herself for a

quick report where she is. I don't know why Cassie feels like the one I should follow. Maybe because she was first. Maybe because she was here before any of them. Maybe it's the way she said my name.

"This is Cassie Haddom for WLKV News, coming to you from the town of Hollow Oaks. As you just heard, the local police department is now revealing that the accusations we previously reported on, claims of sexual assault, involve the sons of Wayne Breward. Breward, as many know, has built an empire in the region as a real estate professional, capitalizing on the economic downturn by assisting mortgage lenders and banks with maintaining abandoned, or zombie, properties. He is also the tax assessor for Hollow Oaks, and the Breward family is well respected here and beyond for their work during and after the economic crisis."

She pauses, reaching for the scarf she's not wearing.

"We will be following this investigation and reporting to you with anything we learn. Again, this is Cassie Haddom reporting for WLKV News from Hollow Oaks. Back to you."

She and her cameraman pack up their equipment, while the other reporters, having gotten nothing else from Officer Thompson, begin their own stories.

I head past them and enter the police station. I wish I could tell them how close they are.

The lead detective is old. Older than my dad, and he doesn't want to work on this case. He sighs every time Officer Thompson speaks. I figure he's in charge, though, because everything gravitates toward him as they discuss.

"We have to get the girls' stories again and confirm them before we give anything to the Brewards," Officer Thompson argues.

The conversation happens around a table—one of those sort of plastic-over-wood ones that show up in church recreation halls and schools. The few items in the room are a coffee-maker that was burning coffee before I was born and a vending machine. Only two of the beverages are available—water and root beer. The little lights that warn you not to feed your money into the machine, that tell you someone beat you to the last Sprite, form a vertical row behind the lead detective's left shoulder.

"Shannon, those boys have every right to know what's being said, what we have. It's human decency," he replies.

"I hate to say it but Gomes is right," the other officer says.

"This is bullshit and you know it," Officer Thompson says. "We give them that information, we may as well throw the case out. Do you think Adrien Deschaine is just going to sit on it, is going to leave even one detail for us to turn over to a prosecutor?"

"I don't like it, either," the other young officer replies. "But either way, we're stuck. If we don't tell them what we have, they'll turn that on us and we won't get anywhere anyway."

"What if they weren't Wayne Breward's sons? Would that make a difference?" she asks the detective. Gomes.

"It doesn't matter, because they are. This town isn't going to let us forget that," Gomes says. "Tariq can go talk to the boys. We'll call Gretchen in at the same time. Shannon, I want you here with me. She'll probably feel better talking to a woman."

"What's the point?" she says. "We can't help her."

Gomes says nothing, leaving her alone with Tariq. Their roles have been assigned and that's that. As the door shuts behind him, Officer Thompson turns to her partner.

"You could have backed me up, Tariq. You know there's something here."

"I do, but what good does it do if we get the whole thing thrown out before we even start?" he asks.

"He's going to make it impossible on them. How am I supposed to get a girl to open up? I know he's just . . . Gomes. But if I'm a teenage girl, he's a nightmare. He doesn't get it, and he doesn't know how to talk to them. How to listen to what they don't say instead of worrying about what they do."

She stands and moves to the vending machine, debating between the two options. There's a quiet pause and she leans against the machine, pushing her hands hard against it. "Do you think they know where that girl is?" she asks.

"Who?"

"I don't know. These girls. Those kids. Anyone. How can a girl disappear?"

"She can't. People don't just disappear."

"Tell that to Alex Frias. She was fifteen. We should've found her," she says.

"We will. We'll find her," he replies. "I promise."

chapter twenty-seven

The cops bring Gretchen in first. I already know her story. At least most of it. I saw it happen. I watched his hands, saw the bruises he'd left in places only I could see. I could have breathed in the plaster from the walls if I still had lungs.

She looks different, but not in the way she's walking or how she's dressed. Her hair is shorter, but that's not what it is, either. It's that she holds herself with the fear still clinging to her. She hasn't forgotten; the memory is in the way her shoulders hunch, protecting herself from the outside, and in how she sits at an angle, keeping her eyes on the door. She's in control of herself, but it's in spite of the fear. I don't know how much time has passed since it happened to her, but the fear has made her work harder to breathe.

Gomes sits across from her, Officer Thompson beside her. She leans in and offers to take Gretchen's bag, but Gretchen clutches it closer to herself.

"I'm fine," she says.

"Okay, Miss Van Elkland," Gomes says. "I'm the detective leading this case. I understand you made the first claims of assault against Noah and Caleb Breward. I also understand you played an integral role in getting Kailey Howe to come forward with her accusation, and that you've been building a social media campaign to generate renewed interest in finding Ellie Frias as well?"

"Why do you make it sound like a bad thing?" Gretchen asks.

"Miss Van Elkland—" Gomes starts.

"Gretchen. Please call me Gretchen."

"Gretchen, these are very serious accusations, as I'm sure you are aware. You claim that on the night of April 4, Caleb and Noah Breward raped you repeatedly, as well as physically assaulted you. Is that accurate?"

"Yes."

"I also understand that you saw a doctor after the incident."

Gretchen nods. "I did. But he said . . . they said it doesn't prove anything."

"Who is 'they'?" Gomes asks.

"The doctor. The people at the hospital. They had someone from the hotline there, but they said the results . . . they weren't enough."

Gomes reviews his report and writes something down. "We want to help you, but you can understand that we have some challenges ahead of us. Without any kind of proof . . ."

He doesn't want the case, but he doesn't want this damaged girl in front of him, either. He just wants to work somewhere where these things don't happen. He still wants to hope that there's a place like that.

"I have proof," Gretchen says. She puts her bag down and takes out the lip balm, placing it in front of her. It sits on the table between her and Gomes. "I found this. In the house where they took me. Kailey and I weren't the only ones."

Gomes stares at it. "I'm positive you don't think I can arrest someone because of ChapStick."

Gretchen sighs and looks to Officer Thompson, continuing to tell her story. But she speaks to Thompson now, not Gomes.

"I met him in class," she says. "It was that required writing class the college makes us all take as freshmen. He thought it was pointless. Honestly, he was a bit of a tool. He complained a lot. But he was also . . . I don't know. Funny? It was distracting during class. The class was boring. There was something about him. I found him both repugnant and kind of cute in a weird way." She ties the cords of her bag around her finger, pulling them tight until the blood collects and turns the finger purple. She loosens the cords with a sigh.

"Was there a previous relationship?" Gomes asks. Gretchen still won't look at him, but she continues.

"No. He stopped me one afternoon after class. Asked me if I had notes from the last lecture. He said he'd missed class because his brother was sick and he could use some help. I pictured a little kid. I didn't realize his brother was fully capable of taking care of himself."

She shakes her head, running her fingers over the knuckles on her opposite hand. Her breathing catches and she shakes her head again to avoid crying. "I told him I did. I said I had the notes, but I needed them to study so he needed to copy them. He invited me over, said he'd copy them in his dad's office."

"So you went to the house?" Gomes writes it all down.

"No. Well, yes, but not his house. It was empty. Not completely, but it was . . . I don't know. It was like a house, but not really. There were only a few pieces of furniture and it was dark. He brought me to a room with a light in it. And a bed. It was him first, but then his brother . . . Caleb. He came in and they both . . ."

Officer Thompson gets up and grabs a box of tissues from a small shelf in the corner. She hands them to Gretchen, who pushes them away. She can't say it. She doesn't want to have the word grow inside of who she is.

"What can you tell us about the house? Do you know where it was in town?" Gomes asks.

"I don't. I wasn't paying attention on the way there. It wasn't near much, but I don't know. I'm not from here. I live at school and I was talking with him on the ride. I thought . . . I just didn't think . . ."

"It's okay," Thompson says.

Gretchen nods. "When it was over . . . when we left . . . it was dark. There were boxes and stuff by the room. It was in the basement, but I don't know. It was a house. A random house that felt like any other house. Except it was somehow . . . it just felt forgotten."

Gomes sighs, but writes it down. He knows how hard it is to find a place that's been forgotten in Hollow Oaks. That's every place.

"From what we've seen, you have a tendency to get behind these . . . what do you call them? Women's issues?" he asks.

"What he means," Officer Thompson says, and she turns to glare at her colleague, "is that most people who know you would say you identify strongly as a feminist, right?"

Gretchen nods. "But I didn't want this. I don't feel redeemed because it happened to me personally. I'm not basking in the revelation that the things I believed, that the things I value on a big scale, that they're going on here. I would give anything for it not to be true."

Gomes closes his folder and puts his pen down. "Talk to me, Gretchen. What are you hoping to accomplish?"

"I don't know what you mean. What's there to accomplish? I just need someone to know. I need you to stop them."

"I mean, what's your motivation? Is it money? The Brewards are extremely wealthy."

"That's not appropriate," Officer Thompson says.

Gretchen laughs. "My parents do fine. We're fine. I don't need money."

"What is it then? This is a big accusation, and you're not giving us much to work with. Is there something else behind it? I hear it's helping you achieve a big online following. Are you enjoying being the leader of a revolution?" Gomes asks.

I get it. I do. I know he needs to say it, because someone will. I know he needs her to be ready, but I also know that she's just a girl sitting in a chair with nothing but her bag and a box of tissues. I know she's no revolutionary.

"Do I have to continue? Should I get a lawyer?" Gretchen asks Officer Thompson. She turns to the side so she and Gomes can't see each other.

"Can we have a minute?" Officer Thompson requests, and Gomes takes his file.

"I have what I need," he says, and leaves the two of them in the room.

"I apologize," Thompson says. "We don't get many cases like this, and we're all under a lot of pressure. He does believe you. We all do. It's just that . . . it's going to get worse."

"I know. It's not like plenty of people haven't said it already. It's not like I don't know how these things go. That's the one thing my supposed online following has taught me. I know all about the kinds of things people say."

"I want to help you. We all do."

"I shouldn't have even stayed. I thought about moving back home. Leaving school."

"Why didn't you?"

"It's . . . someone needs to say it. Why aren't you looking harder? Why didn't you find Ellie Frias? How hard can it be to find a girl?" Gretchen asks.

"Like I said, we're under a great deal of pressure—"

"You should be. I don't know where she is, but I told you what happened to me. That should be something. The rest is on you now."

I go and sit beside Officer Thompson after Gretchen leaves, resting my intangible hand on her knee. She's crying. I'm grateful for her, even if she feels like a failure. At least she's asking.

It's impossible in a town like this. It's impossible in any town. Girls disappear. Girls are brought to secret places to be used and nothing is done, because it's how things are. Because they're only girls.

"Fuck me," Thompson says, and she leaves, turning off the light in the room.

I sit alone in the dark.

_____

chapter twenty-eight

While I wait for the cops to talk to Kailey Howe, I go to school. I don't know why, but I guess it's because it's something that was part of me. Leaving the house, getting back into the town, it fills me with the things I was, and I walk into school, remembering how I felt every day when I got here. How when I started, it was scary. New. But by the time I was a sophomore, it was just a place I had to go. Routine. Part of the normal.

School has always been an odd place for me. It was comfortable at times. At Saint Elizabeth's, I liked school itself. I liked when I was in classes. Unless the teacher got a call or needed to go into the hall with a student or there was a sub. When the teacher was there and I planned my day so I could avoid being in the room too early, I liked it. I loved the things they knew and how they were excited to tell me about them. I didn't care what I learned. I loved hearing about the American Revolution and learning how to count in French. I loved reading short stories and watching videos about the planets. Information thrilled me.

But then there was lunch. There were the minutes between classes. The bus rides. There were the comments. The things girls wrote about me on the walls in the bathrooms. There was Greg McCarthy, the boy I'd thought was cute in sixth grade, who passed me a note and asked me to wait for him after lunch. There was the group of kids who waited with him. Who laughed, took pictures, as he threw tomato sauce all over my shorts because he'd heard Anabelle Henry say I had my period. There was the time Nate Lambert tripped me walking down the hall during a fire drill. For no reason but because it was funny.

Those things all disappeared in high school. When I did. Kate helped me escape them. And then Caleb made me count.

The halls of the school are empty now. Except for one kid, running somewhere. His sneakers squeak on the linoleum. Under the row of lockers to my right, there are pens and a tin of breath mints and pieces of paper and someone's watch. The daily detritus of teenagers. Tonight, they'll be swept away and replaced tomorrow with more pens and paper and maybe a ring and an empty water bottle instead.

There's a sign on the wall. The tape on the top left is loose, so I have to bend down to read it. It's for drama club auditions. For a play that already came and went, but the sign's still there.

I walk past the auditorium. I wonder if they had an assembly when I went missing, if the police came or if the principal stood on the stage asking for information. We always had assemblies about the most random things, and I know in the movies, they have them when something dramatic happens. But that probably doesn't happen in real life. I wasn't as important as yearbook photos and class ring orders.

When I see Caleb, he's sleeping. In the back of a classroom, his hoodie up, the teacher talking and ignoring him. There's nothing on his desk. He couldn't even be bothered to bring a notebook to school.

The police are questioning girls he's hurt, and he sleeps. He hasn't been arrested. He just continues and has the opportunity to do it again, like he did when he threw me away.

If I could tell him, if I could communicate somehow, I don't know what I'd say. That I thought I loved him? That I believed he loved me? Would I tell him how agonizing it is being dead? Would I ask him why? Why he lied? Why he hurt me? Why I didn't deserve to be alive? Or would I leave him in silence, the way he left me?

I don't think it would accomplish anything, but I wish, for just a moment, that I could tell him. That I could let him know how I still see it all. How I remember. I wish I could show him how much better I know him than anyone.

After the bell rings, I wait in the hall during passing. Kids come and go by me, through me. This is what life is. We breathe, we go on, and we don't remember.

The boy at the water fountain won't know tonight that it was between his third and fourth classes that he was thirsty. He won't know that the girl he's liked for a year walked behind him while he was drinking, that she slowed to give him a chance to stop her. She won't remember that her pen came loose when she accidentally took the corner and crashed into another girl, that it joined the others under the lockers. It won't matter to her that the pen she got later from the boy who sits next to her in chemistry was the pen that he got from the girl who sits behind him in history. He won't know that the girl who sits behind him still has the same gum on her shoe, but the pink's lost now.

Caleb stands by Gina Lynn's locker like he stood by mine. He has his arm around her, one hand resting on her hip, and he whispers something into her ear. She laughs.

"Hey, Caleb. Out on parole?" The guy who yells it is familiar, but I can't remember his name. Brett maybe. Or John. Or Ezekiel. It could be anything. He could be anyone. Just like I was.

Caleb smiles, turning away from Gina Lynn. "Some girls just can't stand that I'm taken."

"You shouldn't joke about it," Gina Lynn says as the guy in the hall continues by them.

"Why? It's a joke. Like I'd waste my time on trash like that. I have you."

"I know, but people might think you're not taking it seriously."

He kisses her. I haven't seen him like this in months. I've seen what he really is. What really happens, but with Gina Lynn, it's still the game. It's still the softness I wanted to believe he had in him. He doesn't hurt her; he kisses her and he means it with her. It's like the way he was on those summer evenings. The boy I let into my life. The boy I called my first love. But now, I can see the rot behind the smile. I can see what he is and I wonder why I never noticed it before. It's so clear to me now.

"You need to stop worrying," he says. "Besides, you've got my back, right?"

She nods, but for a moment, she hesitates. He closes her locker and puts his arm out, waiting for her to fill the space. She looks down the hallway instead. She looks through me, looks past where I stand, by what used to be my locker. She opens her mouth, almost says something, but then blinks. Forgetting whatever it was she was thinking, she slides into the place he made for her.

They pass me. His arm around her, her smiling, and I remember why I haven't come back here. There are no places left in this town where they aren't.

chapter twenty-nine

've never seen Kailey Howe before. She's small and thin. Red hair. Young. They usually are. Except for Gretchen, they're always young. I think they figure we're the weakest. Kailey might not even be in high school, but I can't be sure. She's so tiny that she could be older than I'd expect, but she looks like a child.

Thompson lectured Gomes earlier on trying to listen better. He's the lead on the case, but he knows he's not cut out for dealing with these girls. He doesn't want to be here, but I admire that at least he asked questions. At least he's trying to make sense of how we think.

Now, he shifts in his seat. Even he knows it would be hard for anyone to look at this girl and assume she has a motive. Like I said, pretty and sweet. Good girls. That's how you get people to listen.

"I was running," Kailey says. She looks at Gomes. She stares directly at him while she speaks. Waiting for him to tell her she's wrong. That it didn't happen. That he can make it disappear. "I always used to run. Every morning and every evening. All summer. Even in the winter, although not there. But I don't really run anymore."

"And you were running that morning?" Gomes confirms.

"I was. I usually took the route by the lake."

"Your parents have a cottage there?"

Kailey nods. "It's a little place, but we go there in the summers. Except. Well, they're selling it now."

"How did you meet Caleb Breward?" Gomes asks.

"Like I said, I was running. I liked to do at least six miles, but it was warm. I was on mile four and the sun was really bad that day. Even that early. I'd paused to catch my breath, and he was in his car. I didn't see him at first. I was so focused on how hot it was."

Caleb and I spent a lot of time at the lake. I wonder if it was a morning before he came to get me. Before we'd spent the evening in his car, kissing and whatever else we were doing. I wonder if he'd cleared the taste of Kailey Howe from his lips with me.

"I'm sorry. Can I have some water?" she asks, and both Thompson and Gomes stand to get it. He nods and Thompson heads out, before Kailey continues. "I'm not from around here, so I didn't know him. He stopped and he started asking me where I was from, my name, you know, typical stuff. He asked if I needed a ride. If I was okay."

"Did you get in the car with him?"

She shakes her head. "That's just it. I didn't. I talked to him for maybe . . . ten minutes. Then he left and I continued my run. But there's this hole. In my memory, you know? Like we talked, I shook off the heat, and I went back to running. But then I don't remember how I got from the side of the lake to that house. I remember the house, though. Or at least I remember the room where they had me."

Officer Thompson returns with the water and Kailey drinks it, giving Gomes a chance to review his notes. Where Gretchen was angry, Kailey is sweet. She's easy to root for. Vulnerable. She has none of Gretchen's bad attitude. No inherent expectation that nobody will believe her.

They're both telling the truth; it's just easier for Gomes to hear it from Kailey.

"Thanks," Kailey says, handing the plastic cup back to Thompson, who takes it and sits, holding the cup, waiting. "It was . . . I don't know how to explain it. It wasn't a real house. Does that make sense?"

"Not really," Gomes admits, and Thompson sighs.

"He means he doesn't understand how it wasn't," she says. "Could you describe it?"

Kailey nods and looks down at her shoes. They're new running shoes, top-of-the-line quality, but they look too new. Too unused. It's well past Christmas, but I get the impression she got them from her parents, that they tried to encourage her to keep at it, to start running again. That's what makes a girl. She builds an escape for herself and someone comes along and turns it into the one thing she dreads.

"I don't think anyone lived there," she explains. "It wasn't a model home, though. It was . . . It felt dead."

"And you woke up there?" Gomes asks.

"I'm not sure. I don't know if that happened or if I just can't remember. I remember running. I remember being on the side of the road, talking to him in his car. And then I remember him on top of me on the bed. I remember that house, and I remember them coming into the room. Both of them. There were two of them. After he . . . he brought someone else in. And then they both . . . at the same time."

Officer Thompson stands, putting the cup on the table. She heads toward the tissue box and Kailey shakes her head.

"I don't need those. I don't cry about it anymore. I can't. It happened. There's nothing I can do about it, and I'm trying to move on."

"What made you decide to come forward only now?" Gomes asks. "It's been almost a year."

I remind myself it's his job. That he needs to prepare the girls for what's to come, if this gets to trial. It makes sense, but I hate how he pushes them, how he passively accuses them, how he makes it their fault. I hate that he has to do these things, because it's more important that Kailey is ready for it than that anyone looks at her. Hears her. Helps her. She has to be ready to convince people, because they can't simply believe her.

"I didn't know them," Kailey says. "I didn't know how it happened, and I knew nobody would believe me. So I tried to pretend. I tried to be okay. I wasn't okay, though. My parents asked why I was different, but I just told them I was fine. I quit running. I was afraid to go outside. I went back to school and I did my work, but I stopped spending a lot of time with people. I just didn't want to be alive anymore."

Gomes clears his throat and reaches across the table to grab the cup, but Kailey flinches. He sees it and pulls back, making a note in the file.

"I spent a lot of time online," she continues. "Looking for them. For anything from this town, anything that could validate what happened to me. I heard about Ellie when she went missing. I thought maybe . . . but then she disappeared again, even from the Internet. People forgot. And then, a few weeks ago, I saw the posts. I saw what Gretchen wrote and I e-mailed her. I asked her to tell me about where it happened. That was what I needed to know. I had to know if it was the same place. She tried to tell me about them, but they weren't that different from so many other guys. It was the place that made me sure. They did it again after me. To her. And I'm positive they know where that girl is. Ellie. I think they did something to her."

"Unfortunately," Gomes says, "while we can try to find a connection with Ellie, this isn't about her. We're working on building a case against them for your assault."

"I'll never win," Kailey says. "There are too many things I can't remember. But there must be something. Something about that place. I know I'm not the only one. There isn't just me and Gretchen."

"We'll try," Thompson promises. "We'll fix it, Kailey."

I don't know what bothers me most. That Kailey Howe, a girl I don't even know, may be the catalyst for them to look harder into what happened to me. That last summer, as I thought I was falling in love with Caleb, he was doing this to her. Or that every time something like this happens, someone promises to fix it.

This whole town has been built on promises nobody remembers to keep.

chapter thirty

A town like ours, a town that lost before it even started, makes it easy for people like the Brewards. We see them as an example of what can be. Amid broken factories, a river so shallow it seems like it's close to giving up, the endless snow and winter, and entire streets of houses that just didn't work out, the Brewards keep holding it together. They succeed off the pain of others, but people have a strange way of admiring the strength of it.

Hollow Oaks was destined to fail. Our history is of failure. Before any of us, before we were a town or even a state, the area was passed from one group to the next. It was native land, and then British, and then American. But it was a place that wasn't fought for, wasn't worth keeping.

After the factories came and went, the town went on. What else is a town supposed to do? But in the last ten years or so, when people realized that the loans they had were impossible to maintain, especially with no jobs and the weather what it was, Hollow Oaks slowly turned into a ghost town. There are still people here, but when I was growing up, the high school had more than a thousand students; when I disappeared, we were down to 349. I was 350.

Now, the media has nearly doubled our population.

Cassie stands in front of the hardware store, the dim evening light making her a shadow. She's shivering, of course, but she's learning to fake it better. Her cameraman waits beside her.

"Ms. Haddom?" The man behind her isn't from here. The people in this town look aged. They look years older than they are, but he doesn't. This man is old, but not aged. He's distinguished; that's the word I was taught means you have money.

"Charles?" He nods. "Great, we're about ready, so I'll do a quick intro and then we can get started."

The cameraman points the camera at Cassie and, apparently, Charles. She smiles and waits for him to gesture it's time to start.

"Good evening. This is Cassie Haddom reporting for WLKV, again from the town of Hollow Oaks. We've been following the investigation into claims of sexual misconduct against Noah and Caleb Breward, sons of Wayne Breward, real estate developer and local politician. Although the police have not indicated what kind of progress has been made in this case, we have been told that the Brewards already retained the services of Attorney Adrien Deschaine and that they are confident, if charges are brought forward against the boys, that the case will be settled swiftly and without further disruption to the family. With me now is Charles Schaffer, a local businessman who has recently started a group to assist the Brewards. Charles, I understand you're friendly with Wayne and his sons?"

"That's right, miss. Wayne and I have known each other a long time. I'm the VP of business development over at J&M Holdings, a mortgage and financial firm. We're in St. Agatha, so I've done business with Wayne multiple times over the years. I know what kind of man he is, and that extends to his sons."

"I see." Cassie swallows. "I understand you've begun a fund-raising campaign to generate support for the Brewards?"

"These boys have their entire futures ahead of them. It's concerning that they're being forced to take from their college savings to defend themselves against baseless accusations. We would like to help by showing them we all know what kind of people the Brewards are, and that everyone in Hollow Oaks, St. Agatha, and our neighboring communities is standing behind them."

"From what we've been told, the Brewards are among the wealthiest families in Hollow Oaks. Isn't that right?"

"I don't understand your point," Charles says.

"It seems perhaps fund-raising would be unnecessary, that they have the funds to hire an attorney and that—"

Charles cuts her off, his distinguished expression growing feral. "You're not from around here. I'll excuse your assumption that this is about money. This is about the fact that these boys, models of integrity and perseverance, are being denigrated by a corrupt press, the biased media, and an inept local police force. They are watching their futures be dismantled slowly. Their potential careers. Families. Their entire lifestyle is being destroyed. All because some young women have a hard time being responsible for their own actions."

"Oh?" Cassie asks. "You know these young women as well?"

"I don't need to know them, miss. I know their type."

"What type would that be?"

"The girls who desperately want to catch the eye of boys like Noah and Caleb Breward. They're well-liked. As you noted, they have money. They represent some kind of conquest for these girls. And they're boys, after all. Boys like that kind of attention. But this . . . this circus . . . it's too high a price for a little fun."

"From what we've been told, these boys have a strange idea of fun, Mr. Schaffer. What about these girls and their futures? Are you saying they're not entitled to those?"

"I don't like your tone, sweetheart."

Cassie pauses, and I watch her balance her career and her reputation with the desire to hit him. Her shoulders square and she tenses, but she stands tall. She breathes in and smiles.

"I apologize. I appreciate your time, Charles. There's a reason you're here, I believe. You have a website you'd like to share, where people watching can donate to your . . . fund-raiser?" It's in the word *fund-raiser* she says everything she can't actually say. The way the word curls up at the beginning and she mumbles its close.

"Yes, we are at www.brewardsupportfund.org, and we've had a wealth of success already. I assure you that this town and the towns around here know the truth."

"Thank you again. As I said, we do appreciate your time. Our viewers will reach out with further questions."

Cassie wraps up the interview and Charles leaves, less distinguished and less respectable now. When she's done and he's gone, she turns to her cameraman, her hands shaking.

"I'm going to get fired for this, Gus," she tells him. "This case is going to ruin me. This town is a mess."

He nods, and she stares out into the evening, shaking and shivering.

The ringing comes in a matter of minutes. Cassie rolls her eyes and picks up her phone.

"Hello?"

There's a pause. Someone on the other side is yelling. Cassie nods at Gus and he unwraps a pack of cigarettes. It's a brand-new package. He hands one to her and she takes it, listening to the yelling on the other side of the phone, waiting for Gus to light her cigarette. She coughs when she inhales.

"No," she says to the person on the other end of the phone. "I'm not sitting here and defending that. I'm not listening to it. These girls . . . they're in college. High school. Where are they going to come up with money to hire an attorney?" The person on the other end speaks again, and Cassie sighs. "I don't care. It doesn't matter if the state will prosecute. If they even do. It's bad enough that, if this goes to court, those girls could end up on all our TVs. It'll be impossible to keep their names secret in a town like this. I'm not being a part of demonizing them before we get started. He wants to claim the girls are just heartbroken? That the boys' futures are being ruined by some kind of drama? Well, I'm not doing it, Gwen. I'm not feeding into it and I'm not giving them more to work with."

Gus watches her, flicking his cigarette.

"I can't, Gwen. I just can't," Cassie says. She hangs up and crushes the cigarette she smoked once under her foot. "This shit is disgusting. How do you do it?"

Gus shrugs. "Bad habit."

"That was Gwen."

"I figured."

Cassie paces, but she doesn't go anywhere. She looks around, although it's only them on the street right now. "She's pissed," she tells Gus. "I'm being too confrontational with the locals."

"She'll get over it. She hired you for being confrontational."

"I want to do something. I'm sick of waiting for updates and interviewing assholes. I want to actually help."

Gus finishes his cigarette and picks up his camera. "So let's help. You lead. Let's go talk to someone who knows something."

"Who?" Cassie asks.

"Alex Frias? He's got to be wondering what's going on, right?"

"No. That poor man . . . No, he's been through enough. He's keeping his distance right now. Let's let him have that. If this turns out like it might . . . like it looks like it's going to, he'll have plenty of time to talk to us."

"I don't know then. But eventually we've got to find someone. We can just start asking. Someone will have something to say."

"People aren't going to want us intruding."

"Well, maybe this town needs some intruding. It's been almost half a year since a fifteen-year-old girl went missing, Cassie. And now two other girls are saying there's something else going on here. It sounds to me like this town has a hell of a lot to dig up. Go grab yourself a shovel."

chapter thirty-one

They're so smug. Both of them. All of them. Adrien sits with Noah and Caleb around a large conference table. Officer Thompson and Detective Gomes wait. There's a tape recorder, but it's recording nothing but pens scratching down questions and notes and the sound of the ceiling fan spinning.

They won't say anything. Every question must go through Adrien first. It's an exercise in futility, but the police should get something official on record. Should try to do their jobs right.

I hate how I feel captive, that they can do this, that they control me even in death. How do we let another person have this kind of power over us?

"I'm not sure there's much more we can tell you," Adrien says. It's been a circus of vaguery. Lies and excuses.

"We still need to clarify a few things," Gomes explains.

"As we've said, these young women are confused."

"There are several things that are unclear," Thompson adds. "How did Kailey Howe get to the house? What house are both girls referring to? Their descriptions are consistent, but they don't match the Brewards' home. Is there an existing relationship with Noah and Gretchen? Because he says there is, but she says they were barely acquaintances. That she was only with him to loan him her class notes. And while we have alibis from the boys for the time Ellie Frias disappeared, we aren't clear why these two girls, who don't know each other and are not connected to Ellie, are insisting that there's more to that story. So where would you like to begin?"

I like how she will walk out of here, exhausted, maybe head home and cry, stressing about how little she can do. But in here, in front of them, she refuses to let them get away with it. She makes them answer the questions nobody else pushes them to answer.

"You have a lot of questions, and I'm not sure we need to go through this again," Adrien says. "However, I will allow the boys to answer if they like."

Allowance. It's the way they live. The world allows.

"Gretchen has wanted me since day one of class," Noah says. "I don't know the answers to the rest of it, but there's nothing in her accusations."

Gomes nods. "Caleb? Anything to add?"

"About what?"

"Officer Thompson just pointed out where the inconsistencies are in your stories versus the accusations from these girls. Were you listening?"

Gomes may not be a good man. He doesn't really understand about the girls, but he's also not all bad. He doesn't believe the Brewards, and he likes truth too much to let his doubts about the whole thing interfere.

"Not really," Caleb says.

"Tell us about Kailey Howe," Gomes pushes.

"What about her?"

"How did she end up with you? She can't remember."

Caleb shrugs. "I don't know. I don't really remember, either. But she's probably just upset because I didn't call her after."

"How did you meet?" Thompson asks, and I admire her for not reaching across the table and throttling him.

"She was out running."

"So you just interrupted a girl while she was running?"

Adrien puts his hand up. "I don't think—"

Caleb smiles and leans back in his chair. "It's fine. I didn't interrupt her. She stopped. I was driving and she heard the car. I could tell, because she slowed down as I pulled alongside her. When she saw me, she stopped and walked over to the window."

"What made you decide to stop?"

"She was hot. I'm a guy. She was wearing those yoga pants, and I was alone. I saw her, she looked at me, and I invited her in. Obviously."

"Obviously," Officer Thompson says. "You're saying she got in the car then?"

He nods. "She jumped right into the passenger seat. Hell, I don't know. Maybe that's stupid. Getting in the car with a stranger, but girls can all be pretty stupid at times." He looks at Officer Thompson as he says it.

"Where'd you bring her?" Gomes asks.

"I can't remember," he says. And they're done with the conversation, because Adrien intervenes.

"I think we've been more than forthcoming. From now on, I'd prefer you coordinate with my office if you need more information. These boys have responsibilities and they can't drop everything for every girl who comes along. It's unfortunate that some girls don't understand that every relationship isn't forever, but these boys have lives to live now."

When they leave, Gomes and Thompson sit in silence for a moment. The fan whirs. Thompson leans over to shut off the tape recorder and slams her fist against the table once it's off.

"It's bullshit," she says. "Get a warrant. Get a list of every house they've fixed or worked on for the last year. Call in their alibis. This is all bullshit."

Gomes watches her and she tries not to break down, but soon she's crying and he puts a hand on her shoulder, awkward and uncomfortable at the display of emotion.

"Shannon."

"Just don't."

"I can't get a warrant. Right now, we have nothing. They're humoring us because they want to look good for the press. They want it to appear that we're investigating these sorts of things, but with what we've got, there's no way they're letting us take this to court. You know that. You must know that. We don't really have a case. We have weak evidence that will be torn apart if we tried to go to trial like this."

"It's not right," she says.

"No. It isn't. But it's the way things are."

"And we do nothing?"

Gomes shakes his head. "I didn't say that. You're right. We'll find a way to get that list of houses. See if anything matches the description the girls gave. Filter through the crap we've gathered by asking the town for information. Review the statements we have on file from November. Talk to Alex Frias. I don't think the case is over. I just think it's going to be nearly impossible to get it to stick unless we find something we can use."

"But we'll try?"

"I don't believe a word those boys just said. They're arrogant and they know something. This case has bugged me from the

164

beginning, and their names keep coming up. I know it's an up-hill battle in this town, but there are coincidences and then there's this."

Thompson gets the tape recorder and the files. "I want to find that girl. It's been too long, Gomes."

He nods.

I follow them out. They head to different offices and process everything they have privately. I hover and wait, but it's the middle of the afternoon and time works differently when you're dead. You'd think eternity would slow things down, but it's only when we're living that we assume time is endless. When it actually is . . .

I don't know. I notice so many things now.

chapter thirty-two

loved my dad. I know I've said it, and I know I didn't act like it at times, but I did.

I don't know what happens, what line gets crossed that transitions a girl from seeing her dad as the entirety of her world to viewing him as an embarrassment. For years, we were best friends. Fishing, the movies he slept through, cooking on the grill outside when he was home in the summers. I was his little girl, and he was everything. And then, he wasn't. I woke one day to realize that to be liked, I had to give up the one person who loved me. That's a pretty shitty way to introduce a girl to growing up.

There was one night. One night amid so many others. I was thirteen. Everyone else was going to the school dance, but I didn't want to go. Didn't want to stand alone and wish someone would talk to me.

My dad was scheduled to work and I had big plans. Macaroni and cheese with maybe a movie. Or an episode of TV if I was too tired to commit to two hours.

"Ellie," my dad said while I stood in the kitchen debating if

I preferred shells or elbow noodles. These were priorities at thirteen.

"Have fun at work."

I'd had shells three times that week, but I liked the cheese better than the weird powder that came with the elbows. It was thick and creamy, not fluorescent orange salt with some fake cheese flavoring.

"Put down the mac and cheese," my dad said. "Turn around."

I closed the cabinet, putting the shells on the counter. I wasn't much for change.

My dad was standing in the doorway, but he wasn't wearing his work vest. And he had a battered old suitcase in his hand. I hadn't even known we owned a suitcase.

"Where are you going?" I asked.

"*We're* going. I called out for the weekend. Go pack some things."

"For what?" In all my thirteen years, we'd been two places— my grandparents' house each summer for a week, until they passed away, and, once, we went to Lake George. Everyone went to Lake George.

"Grab some things," he told me. "And bring something dressy. It's a surprise."

"We can't . . ." I looked at the pile of bills. At the ragged jacket he'd left on the kitchen chair, the sleeves starting to come apart at the seams. "I mean, I don't want you to spend the money."

"It's fine, Ellie. I've been planning this. Go get ready, okay?

I didn't want to push him about whether we could afford it. I don't know what he gave up. But he was excited, and I didn't want to lose this chance, so I packed a bag and followed him to the car.

During the ride, he kept talking, but he wasn't saying anything. I could tell he was excited about the surprise, although I had no idea what it was. We drove into the sunlight and I tried to guess. I tried to run through possibilities.

As we pulled up to the train station, I felt his excitement seep into me. The station was an ugly place, but it brought you to places that weren't. I pictured other places. I stared at the posters, faded and out-of-date. Images of cities and landmarks and skylines, all changed in the years since the posters had been made. The station was a memory of the things other people had done and the world that was. Like everything else in Hollow Oaks, it clung to a memory and forgot how to keep living.

"Two for New York," my dad said to the person behind the glass window.

"New York?" I asked from beside him. The poster on the wall of the city was from years ago. Before 2001. A skyline with buildings that were no longer there. A reminder of what we'd all lost.

The bored ticket person took my dad's credit card and printed the tickets, checking the clock. "You have twenty minutes. Platform two."

There were three platforms. In a town that never went anywhere. We were the only ones waiting.

"What's in New York?" I asked. I knew there were millions of things in New York. Theoretical things. Things I'd always wanted to see. There were the images I had of skyscrapers and taxicabs and Times Square and all the things on TV. In movies. I'd felt all the things my dad probably missed about living when he said those two little words. It was a city with the same name as the place we lived, but not the same place at all. I suddenly felt all the things he'd put on hold when I was born.

I knew why New York. I knew what was there. What I didn't know was why today.

"We'll visit my old dorm," my dad said, not answering the question I didn't ask. "And then we can see Central Park and you can pick whatever show you want to see on Broadway. Or, really, we can do anything you want."

"I don't even know what there is," I said.

"It'll take a bit to get there. We'll check your phone. See what's playing."

I looked at the battered suitcase beside him on the gray platform. Felt my own bag over my shoulder, where I'd shoved some clothes and an Easter dress. I felt like a runaway.

"What's happening?" my dad asked, watching me try to make sense of a world that had always existed just fine without me. "Don't you want to go?"

"What about Fred?" I asked.

My dad laughed. "Tom's watching him." Tom was our neighbor. He didn't go out much, and I knew nothing about him except that he was old. And he brought me candy on Halloween because nobody went to his house. It was as old as he was, and all the kids had stories about Tom. It didn't help that half our neighborhood had been forgotten. That Tom's house looked like the others, except he didn't have boards over his windows. It was easy to make him something he wasn't, but in the end, Tom was just an old guy who was too tired to cut his lawn.

"Thanks, Dad. Really," I said.

I was excited, but it was a lot of pressure. I didn't know how to be alive. I realized it as the train took off from the station. As my dad showed me where the suitcases went and I was surprised there was a bathroom and a café on the train. Everything amazed me, because I only knew Hollow Oaks.

We scrolled through list after list on my phone during the train ride. Broadway shows. Restaurants. Tourist sites. My dad didn't say anything, except to reiterate that it was up to me. So I tried. I tried to pick the right thing. The one that would be special. The one he might be happy I picked, would be happy that he'd given up so much for.

Entering New York on a train is depressing. The train rides along all the hidden parts of places. The houses people forgot. The businesses that are trying to be remembered. And then as the city gets closer, it's crowded and kids play outside on basketball courts with no nets, and buildings cut the sky open. But the pretty ones—the ones that shine and fill the scars of the sky with light—they're still in the distance. The ones by the train are ugly. We're not supposed to look at those. We're supposed to think about the ones in the background.

We all want to be part of something, but not the parts of it that make it true.

"So, what do you want, Ellie? What do you want to do?" my dad asked while the train slipped into the darkness of the tunnel, delivering us into the city without having to continue looking at its edges. Trying to make us forget what we'd seen. So that when we walked outside later, we would believe that this was all the city was.

"I don't know," I said.

I didn't. In a place like Hollow Oaks, in a town that never moves, you don't let yourself want. You don't think about all the people living lives that might have been yours. Living in places that breathe. You try not to think about the way every day, on the ride to school or work, more and more families and people disappear. More yards grow so high you can't see the front steps to the houses anymore. More lives are consumed by a place, while somewhere else, other people just go on.

I can't really fault them. What kind of life is it to live waiting for it to end?

"We have the entire weekend," he said. "Anything you want."

"It doesn't matter. Why don't you pick?"

I didn't know what I wanted, except that I wanted him to remember, too. He'd lived before and I wanted him to feel that again. I didn't know anything but Hollow Oaks, but for my dad, life had been stopped. Paused. I wanted him to walk through New York and find that again. To remember.

That's what we did that weekend. We visited his dorm and saw musicals and ate lunch that cost more than my dad made in a week and I stood in the center of the world. I watched the lights and felt the city breathe, and I was a part of it all. I was so happy to be a part of it. The world was a mass of people and sound and light. Of noise and hope and potential. And for a few moments, for three days, I felt like a girl who *was*. I wore my Easter dress to the shows. A waiter called me miss and called my father sir. We were special. My dad and I forgot who we were there. We lived for three days as other people.

Then we took the train home.

If riding into New York is depressing, riding home is like dying.

chapter thirty-three

Officer Thompson and her partner, Officer Tariq Malik, sit in Detective Gomes's office reading through pages of something. None of them look hopeful.

"Not sure which is more concerning. The number of these properties the Brewards have worked on, or the number of them that exist," Gomes says.

"If we narrow it down to the area by the lake, given the little Gretchen remembered and where Kailey was, there are fourteen." Officer Thompson circles something on one of the papers. "Fifteen."

"Somebody is lying. Someone has to be, because none of this makes sense. If they have this kind of access to these places, and both these girls are describing the same location, how have there only been two accusations? This feels systemic," Malik says.

He puts his notes down and goes to the whiteboard on the wall. There are scattered words and ideas on it, but nothing linking Kailey and Gretchen, and nothing linking me to either of them. But he looks at it anyway, hoping he'll see something new.

I always wondered about magic. About coincidence. I

wondered if there were forces that controlled how life unfolds, or if it was just chaotic spinning. I wanted to believe that time revealed life, that it held on to the most important moments until they were right, and then it dazzled us with its power. But after Caleb, after that night, after everything that happened, I believed a lot less in magical forces and the power of time. I started to see it all as a hopeless and out-of-control disaster.

When she comes into the station, though, when she breaks the silence, I don't know what else to call it. It's the closest thing to magic there is in real life.

She looks nervous when she enters. She picks at her nail polish, flakes drifting in a silvery pink snowfall onto the station floor.

"I need to speak with Detective Gomes," she says.

The person at the desk nods and disappears down the hall. Gomes comes out, leaving Malik and Thompson in his office with their papers and notes.

"Gina Lynn?" he asks.

She looks up from the plastic blue chair by the window. Her eyes are bloodshot.

"Can we talk?"

"Sure," he says. "Come on back."

She follows him, her boots dragging on the floor as she forces herself to walk forward, to take the steps toward his office. All of what she is, what she was, has been fading in small drips since she entered the station. She looks behind her as she goes. The way she probably did as she drove here and walked inside. Afraid someone will see her.

"Officers Thompson and Malik you've met before," he says as they stand in the doorway of his office, while he grabs a notepad and the tape recorder. "We're working together on a case."

"We'll stay out of your way," Malik replies.

"Can you come with us?" Gina Lynn asks. She turns to Gomes. "They're working on the Brewards, right? It's the same case?" He nods. "They should come with us."

"Is this . . . Are you sure?" Gomes pauses, but Gina Lynn doesn't say anything else. "Okay."

By the time they all settle in the room, she's shaking. Her thumbnail is back to its natural pink, the flakes she picked off leaving a trail of bread crumbs through the police station.

"I lied to you," she says once they're all sitting. "I lied to you, and you have to know, because it could be . . . I'm afraid I killed her."

"I'll get some water," Thompson says.

Gina Lynn looks around the room, taking in its drabness. Sometimes the whole world seems this bland. But maybe it's only my world. I was never a colorful girl.

"Why don't you start from the beginning?" Gomes suggests. "That will probably be easiest."

She nods. "I lied. It's not the beginning, I guess, but I lied because I didn't think it would matter. Nobody knew her. When you were asking about her, when people were looking, they couldn't find anything because she wasn't someone anyone noticed."

"Who is this? Who's this *her* you're talking about?" Gomes asks. He knows. Or at least he thinks he does. But he wants her to say it. He wants to hear it from her.

"Ellie. Ellie Frias."

He looks up, his eyes registering surprise, but he tries to cover it by nodding and turning his notebook page.

"When she disappeared," Gina Lynn continues, "I didn't think it was important. It wasn't the first time, and then, when you asked if I was with Caleb, I said I was. Like I was, you know? But not the whole time, and now . . . Look, I didn't think it was related, but do you think . . . Is there any chance he's really involved?"

Thompson comes back in and puts the water down in front of Gina Lynn. She waits for someone to explain what's going on, but nobody does. They all just watch Gina Lynn. For a girl so used to being stared at, she's nervous as she shifts in her seat and refuses to make eye contact.

"Are you saying you weren't with Caleb Breward the weekend Ellie Frias went missing?" Gomes asks. Thompson goes to speak, but Malik shakes his head and she closes her mouth. "The weekend you and your mother insisted to us, six months ago, that Caleb Breward was in your house?"

"He was, but not totally. It was only a few hours. But. Look, the thing is . . . Okay, so you need to know a little bit about Ellie and Caleb. You know they had a thing, right?" she asks.

"They dated," Gomes confirms.

"Kind of. He says it was nothing. It wasn't very long. I saw them together like twice maybe over the summer. We hooked up early in the year. And then again once school started. Maybe the first weekend? So, she wasn't really in the picture, you know? And she had her own issues."

"So then why would you think he was involved now?" Thompson asks.

"Right before she left. It was Halloween weekend. There was a party at Caleb's house. Everyone went. But she wasn't invited."

"Why?"

"Nobody knew her," Gina Lynn says again. "You had to see that when you looked, okay? When you were trying to find her, you couldn't. Because nobody knew anything. She wasn't online. She didn't talk to anyone. No one knew anything about her. She wasn't someone we cared about." She pauses. "I don't mean it like that, all right? We weren't glad she was gone. It's just that when she disappeared, it wasn't even a thing. Her desk was empty, but that was basically it. She was a desk."

It's callous, but she's right. I was furniture and she didn't care, because why should she? I'm not angry at her. It's not her fault she didn't know me. I could have tried harder, could have pushed myself to be something better, but I was happy to be furniture, too.

"That's harsh," Malik says.

Gina Lynn nods. "It is. But you tried to find her. You looked for her every day for like a month or whatever, and you didn't find her. Why?"

"There was no sign of her," Thompson says. "And we had reason to believe she chose to leave."

"Exactly. There was no sign of her missing. No indication something bad had happened. But be honest. There was no sign she ever even existed, was there?"

After deleting my Facebook account, I didn't go online much. My search history was boring. Schoolwork. E-mails. After Caleb broke up with me, there was the one e-mail to Kate but she hadn't replied again, and my phone was empty, too. Nobody texted me before him and nobody texted me after. Even my diary was filtered and embellished. Trying to be more interesting than me. Giving the police reason not to suspect anyone else.

"Look, I'm sorry. I'm not trying to be harsh. I really do want to help," Gina Lynn concedes.

"Go on," Gomes tells her. "Where was Caleb that weekend?"

"You asked me about that night after she went missing. That whole weekend. I told you I was with him. My mom said he was at our house all weekend, and he was. Sort of. But he went out that Saturday. For most of the day. My mom was on a date or whatever. Caleb took off that afternoon. He came back after midnight. Later, he asked me to say he was there the whole time, and I couldn't believe he had anything to do with Ellie. Not after what happened on Halloween."

"What happened on Halloween?" Thompson asks.

"Nobody told you? Ellie was there. She wasn't invited, but she came anyway. She went to Caleb's house, to the party. She was wasted and she was all over him. It was embarrassing. They'd broken up at the end of the summer, but she wasn't over it. She begged him to take her back and he . . ." She pauses and the officers wait. They've stopped writing, letting the tape recorder get it all. They're hanging on to what she's saying. The small details and how they tear everything apart for them.

"After they broke up, there was one time. Early. She stopped him in the hall. Asked him to talk to her. He was really mean. I thought it was funny, okay? I laughed at her. He was my boyfriend and she was in the way and I didn't care if she was hurt. She didn't come to school for a while after that. She was in my French class, and I noticed she was missing. And then she tried to talk to him right before the party. It ended up the same and she missed school again, and it was just sort of what happened with them. So, when she showed up that night, it was annoying."

"What happened?" Thompson asks.

"He humiliated her. He told her he was sorry and that he wanted to be with her. He kissed her in front of everyone, but then, he just laughed at her. He made me record it. We had these videos and we thought it was funny. I deleted it, though, because she ran outside crying. I'm not that much of a bitch."

177

"What you've got is that he pretended he liked her and then said he didn't?" Gomes asks.

"Not exactly. He got up from the couch. We were sitting together and she was in the doorway. He kissed her and she held on to him, but then he moved away from her. He dragged her into the room and he asked what she wanted him to do. He told us she tasted like dog food. That she had to eat dog food because she was poor and her dad was an illegal."

"You guys sound like a really great group of people," Thompson says. Malik and Gomes look at her, Gomes scowling, but she shrugs. "What? Should I be impressed? I'd like to know what this has to do with Ellie going missing. I'd really like to find her and if this helps, great. But otherwise, we're just remembering the things people did to that poor girl. Who does something like that to another person?"

Gina Lynn starts to cry. "It was all so pointless. She left, and Caleb went after her, but when he came back a while later, he ridiculed her all night in front of everyone. She didn't go to school for, like, a week after that. It was the kind of thing she did. She'd skip days, sometimes weeks, at a time. So, when she disappeared, well . . . it wasn't really new or anything."

The cops look at one another and Gina Lynn sips her water.

"Your boyfriend disappeared for most of the day when a girl went missing, asked you to lie for him, and you chose to do so? Because he'd already made fun of her and because she missed a lot of school?" Gomes is having a hard time understanding.

"He spent the night at my house Friday. That was normal. Then, that Saturday, sometime around three or whatever, he went home to change and shower and do whatever he did. This was what we did basically every weekend. It was only weird because he was later that Saturday. I'd already gone to sleep, but he had a key and he woke me up when he came back. It was after midnight, because I usually don't fall asleep until around then."

"Did you ask where he'd been?" Thompson asks.

"I did. Not right away, but yeah, later. The next day, I guess."

"Because you were sleeping?" Gomes asks.

"Well, no. I mean, I was, but when he showed up . . . no. I wasn't sleeping. Look, he was my boyfriend. He still is. I don't know if he's involved. But it's just . . . what if he is and I lied?"

"Did you and Caleb Breward have sex that night?" Gomes asks. "The night your classmate went missing?"

Gina Lynn nods. "Is that important?"

"I don't know. I'm trying to make sense of all this."

"I'm not the one who did this," she says. "I don't want to be the bad guy here. I should've told you, but it was all normal, okay? He usually took off for a while, you know? And she was . . . He'd been pretty clear a few weeks earlier that he thought she was pathetic. Why would he—? Why would he even be with her that weekend?"

Thompson has a hard time not raising her voice. "Let's say that your boyfriend, who had a prior relationship with a missing girl, did have something to do with it. He was gone for several hours right in the middle of the time frame when she disappeared. Knowing this, you not only agreed to lie for him, to give him an alibi, but you also lied directly to us when we asked you about it. We came to the school. We talked to everybody. Multiple times. Nobody had seen him that weekend, but then you and your mom insisted he was in your house for three days. That there was no way he was involved."

"I know. But I'm telling you now," Gina Lynn says.

"After six months. You've known this. You've had this information. You've seen us looking. You met with each of us in the days that followed, but only now, you've decided to tell us that the last six months were wasted? That you lied to us? Why would you do it?" Thompson asks.

"I'm sorry. I really thought . . . Look. I don't know how he could do this. He couldn't. I couldn't believe that. I can't. But now, I don't know. There are those other girls. And he's been so weird lately."

"Weird how?" Malik asks.

"Like, when I heard about these other girls, I said something, right? I mentioned it, and I said it was weird that his name keeps coming up when something bad happens to girls in this town. And he . . . He lost it. I've never seen him like that."

"What do you mean he lost it?"

"Caleb has always been sweet. Not that smart. But he was pliable. I'm not a very easygoing girlfriend." She laughs, but stops when they all stare at her. "Sorry. I just don't let him get away with much. I'm pretty jealous, and I didn't think there was any way he'd have this whole thing with her behind my back. Or these other girls. But when I said it that time, he was angry. He called me a stupid bitch."

"He's never hit you or anything like that?" Thompson asks.

"Hell no. I'd kill him." She flinches. "Oh my God. I'm so sorry. I can't believe I said that."

"It's okay. We know what you meant. Is that why you think he might have been involved? Because he seemed angry?"

"I don't know. I really don't. Not really, I guess. It was only that one time. After I said that. Since then, he's been joking about it. He thinks it's ridiculous. But I feel like something's wrong. I didn't believe it then. And I don't even believe these other girls. But I've been thinking about it so much. What if I'm wrong? He asked me to lie about that weekend, you know? That's not normal, right? He always left, but he never needed me to lie. I guess I figured it was just coincidence, but I don't know. Now, I just can't stop worrying about it. Wondering if I'm wrong. What if I could have saved her? What if she died? What if it was because of me? Maybe he knows where she went and she was sick or something and she never came back, and if I'd just told you . . ."

Gomes puts his pen down and looks at Gina Lynn like a father would. "It's done now. All we can do is try to fix it from here. Can I ask you some more questions, though? Maybe you'll be able to help us fill in some missing pieces?"

"Please," she says. "I want to help."

She doesn't know about the house, about anything Caleb's done. She doesn't know about us, about how we started or how we ended. She doesn't know about after. About Halloween and the things he promised me after we left the party. And Gina Lynn definitely doesn't know about that last night. About where he was and what he was doing. About what I did. Nobody knows. I wanted it to stay that way, but I guess even when you die, you aren't safe from your own secrets.

chapter thirty-four

At first, I was relieved. In the few days that followed Caleb's ending our relationship, it felt like things were back in place. I knew I didn't belong. I'd spent the months we were together with that always in my mind. Always reminding myself that this was pretend. I never forgot he'd used that word on our first day together, and I knew it would happen eventually. Seeing him kissing Gina Lynn in the halls, seeing them together, being alone, it all made sense. And at first, it felt like it should have been that way all along.

But that ease didn't last, and I started having a harder time sleeping.

Caleb didn't know me. I understand it more now, but he did want me. Even with all the other things that happened. And there was something about that desire. Something about how we talked less and less each week during the summer. How we spent more of our time together with his hands on me, exploring me. I liked going home after, liked how I could still feel it. I liked feeling attractive. He didn't see that my body was imperfect, that my hair was too dark, that I didn't look right. He couldn't stop touching me, and it was the closest thing I knew to love.

But then, I was alone, and suddenly nobody wanted me.

So I went to school, watched him walk through the halls, the two of them showcasing how they meshed so simply, and I went home to my dog. Eventually, I skipped school and just stayed in bed.

There were several times I needed to see him. I'd text him, but he didn't respond. So I'd text him again. I felt the room, my house, closing in on me. I needed something. I needed to know he missed me, that he felt the same loss.

He replied once. It was early October and I'd tried to talk to him that day at school. He'd told me to leave, but then that night, he finally responded.

Hey, Ellie. What's up?

That was all he said, but we have this way of working things out in our heads to fit what we want to believe. He used my name, so I took it to mean he was wondering about me.

I miss you. Are you free?

It wasn't what I wanted to say, but it was true. I missed him and I needed to see him. I thought maybe he would change his mind if he would just talk to me. Would spend time with me. We could go to one of the houses. I'd let him do the same things again. We'd almost had sex that last time we were together. Maybe if we did now, maybe he'd remember. Maybe he'd want me again.

I waited for hours, but he didn't respond.

I never got another text from Caleb.

What followed, what enveloped October, was darkness. Shame and humiliation. I was angry. I felt like a child—naïve and clueless. I hadn't expected it to hurt so badly. I hadn't anticipated that he would have that kind of hold on me.

I'd enjoyed being with him because he made me feel special.

Pretty. He looked at me. Most people didn't. Or if they did, I was somehow wrong. But when Caleb looked at me, when he kissed me and held my face in his hands and whispered words like *beautiful*, I felt what it might be like to actually be those things. When we were in the back of his car and I needed to head home, he'd tell me how badly he wanted me. He'd tell me what I did to him. I liked thinking it was something about me that did that. That it wasn't just because I was a girl, but because I was me.

I don't know what I wanted. But when he was gone and I was alone, it felt like those words were a virus. A dark, snaking disease that had infected me and left me hollow. I needed to be good enough again, needed him to tell me why he'd thought I was beautiful and then he didn't. I couldn't sleep. Couldn't eat. Couldn't think about anything but why. Why I was so ugly. So unlovable. Why I'd been good enough and then, in a day, I wasn't anymore.

It's impossible to go to high school and not hear about a Halloween party someone like Caleb is throwing. Nobody invited me, and I want to say it's because it was for people like them, and I wasn't one of them, but it was for everyone. Everyone but me. Yes, they were wealthy, but I wasn't separated from them by money alone. There was something else. It wasn't popularity, either. Plenty of people were rich and popular and were friendly enough. Whatever it was hung over me. Something I still don't understand. An aura of forgetability. An aura of average.

If I'd shown up and I hadn't been me, if the things that happened hadn't happened, I could have gone to the party, and come home, and nobody would have cared. But when I heard about it, when I realized he was inviting everyone in school to his house, to the place I'd never been invited, to somewhere

I was deliberately excluded from, something inside of me broke.

Dad was working that night. He left after lunch, and as soon as I heard his car pull away, I broke the lock off the cabinet in the kitchen where he kept the alcohol. He never drank. In fifteen years, I'd never seen him drink once. I don't know why we even had a liquor cabinet. The layers of dust on the bottles said that it was older than me. Maybe it had belonged to my mom. Maybe when they'd first gotten married, they'd filled their cabinet with alcohol because that was what adults do and they wanted to revel in crossing that threshold. I don't know. I only knew it was there because he'd mentioned it once and said that I should stay out of the cabinet.

I grabbed a bottle but didn't drink it. Not yet. I was afraid I wouldn't be able to walk to the party if I was drunk, so I put it aside until I was ready. Cutting my black skirt short and throwing on a tank top and black hat, I transformed into a sexy witch. I was one of twelve sexy witches at Caleb's house that night.

It was cold outside. Too cold for Halloween, but I drank as I went and warmed myself with it. I told myself he would remember. That he would see me and realize he'd been wrong. I walked through my neighborhood, with the echoes of people who used to be. The houses that were gone. The ones Caleb's family had fixed years ago, before I'd met him. Our neighborhood had been first. And when the rest of the neighborhoods started to fall apart, we were left behind, because we'd been poor to begin with. There was very little worth saving on this side of town.

I walked through the woods, by the lake, through a town that didn't care anymore. Until I reached where Caleb was. Until I got to what was left of Hollow Oaks.

His house sat at the top of the hill. Lights were on in every room, but by the time I arrived, I'd drank too much and they became one. An orb of light and it was still too distant for me to be part of it. I threw the little that was left of the alcohol, including the bottle, in the gutter at the end of Caleb's street.

He was sitting in his living room when I walked in, people surrounding him, with Gina Lynn on his lap. His hand was on her thigh, just below her sexy nurse's outfit. We were a bundle of stereotypes.

"I want to talk to you." In the entirety of my life, I can remember maybe five times I spoke with confidence.

"Ellie? You're drunk." He didn't move and Gina Lynn laughed, whispering something in his ear. "Yeah, I know. It's hard to let go when you've been lucky enough to taste this."

"I said I want to talk to you." I was having a hard time standing, but I had walked the however many miles it took to get here and I needed to know why. I needed to know when I'd stopped being beautiful.

All the things Gina Lynn told the police happened did happen. Caleb kissed me and it was the way he'd kissed me before. He put his hand on my back the way he used to, the way I'd known that he was claiming me.

"Jesus, Ellie," he whispered in my ear. "She's never going to let me go with you."

I looked at him, at his eyes, at the way he was smiling even when he wasn't. "I love you," I whispered.

"Play along," he told me. I let him make me a joke. I let him humiliate me, because I thought it was a game. Something he had to do so Gina Lynn wouldn't know that he'd made a mistake. That he had to be with me instead. After I ran away crying, I waited on the lawn. By the side of the house. In the cold, dark night where I was invisible.

"All right, talk," he said when he came around the house.

"I miss you."

"We've been over this. It's not you. We just don't work. You can't just show up here. You can't keep doing this, Ellie. You have to move on."

I started to cry. Drunk tears over my costume. The wind came and knocked off my hat. Instead of being the confident and beautiful girl he shouldn't have broken up with, I was a sad, pathetic mess in clothes that didn't fit right, chasing her hat down a hill while everyone else laughed about how poor I was. I fell at the bottom of the hill, although I caught the hat and hugged it to myself.

"Ellie," Caleb said, and he came toward me, sitting beside me. "What are you doing?"

"I thought you liked me," I said.

"I did. But you didn't think this was forever, did you? It was fun, right? Isn't that enough?"

I turned and kissed him. I wanted him to put his arms around me again, wanted to feel him against me. "I love you, Caleb."

"You don't want this," he said.

"I do," I told him. "I'll do anything."

"Let me take you home."

"No. Let's go to the lake. To one of the houses. Somewhere. Please?"

He looked up at his house and paused. There were people standing out front and I could hear the music from the bottom of the hill. "Let me get my keys."

I don't know what he told Gina Lynn. I don't know how he got away, but it was a few minutes and then we were in his car. I felt nauseous from the alcohol, but happy to be with Caleb. I thought I'd won.

"I missed you," I told him again as we drove. I figured if I kept saying it, he would remember he felt the same way.

"You're something else, Ellie."

"Did you miss me? Do you still like me?" I asked.

"I'm here, aren't I?"

He brought me to the lake and we spent an hour in the back of his car. My costume ended up on the floor. I let him back into the places he'd been. His hands were on me . . . in me . . .

I wanted him to remember. I needed him to remember that he'd found me beautiful.

"I want to, Caleb," I said. "I'm ready." He was on top of me and I knew it would only take a word. "I want you to."

"It wouldn't be right," he said, but he kept touching me.

"Why not?"

He kissed me, and I let him touch me, remembering what it felt like to be wanted. To be special. I knew I wasn't being good, but good would have to come later. Once he remembered, too.

"I'm still with Gina Lynn," he said as I lifted his shirt. Unbuttoned his pants.

"Don't you think I'm pretty?" I asked when he kissed down my body. He was talking about another girl, saying it wasn't right, but he was still with me. He'd undressed me. He was kissing me.

He tugged his shirt off and I felt him naked against my skin. I reached for him, ready.

"You're beautiful," he said. "Now, come here. Want to do me a favor?"

It wasn't what I wanted. It wasn't what I'd expected, but it was something I could do and he would remember. I told myself the whole time that he had to remember. He said my name that night and he kissed me while I did what he wanted. His hands got tangled in my hair and he kept whispering my name.

After I was done, I asked him again. "I want to," I insisted. "I want you to be first."

"It's late, Ellie," he said. "I have to get back. Gina Lynn's going to wonder."

He kept touching me, kissing me. His words didn't make sense.

"Please?" I asked. "I want you, Caleb. Don't you want me?"

"So badly. What if I call you tomorrow? Are you around tomorrow?" he asked. "Can you wait?"

I nodded and he smiled, kissing me again and helping me get dressed. I could wait, because it would be different now.

"Damn, Ellie," he said when were back in the front seats. "You're killing me. I can't wait until tomorrow. I bet you'll be amazing." He leaned over and kissed me, his hands rough against my throat. Nearly choking me. "God, I want you."

"We can just . . . I don't have to go home," I said.

He pulled away from me. "No, not here," he said. "I've got plans for you. I'll call you tomorrow."

After I did his favor, after I let him touch me, after he told me how much he wanted me and that he would call me the next day, he drove me to the gas station near my house. He didn't even say good-bye. And then he didn't call all day Sunday. On Monday, at school, he looked right through me like it had never happened.

That was when I realized how easy pretty words can be.

I didn't go to school for another week after that. He didn't post any pictures on the Internet. There was no cliché high school humiliation. Gina Lynn deleted the video. But it wasn't about that. I didn't care if people remembered what he'd said at his party. I just couldn't bear to see him. To remember what we'd done. How I'd begged him to stay with me.

I told myself to get over it. I tried to get over it. I didn't e-mail Kate. I didn't talk to anyone about it, because I didn't know what to say. Not that there was anyone to tell.

I cried and felt stupid and ashamed. I hated myself, but none of that made it go away. None of that made it better. I skipped school, but that wasn't fixing it, so I got dressed one Tuesday, went to school, and just tried to stop looking backward.

I ate my lunch in the hallway when I went back. A granola bar or crackers or whatever I could dig up in the house and toss in my bag. I'd sit on the stairs and listen to music and write in my diary. I wrote about things that happened to other girls. To girls as I imagined them. I wrote about wanting to visit New York again, about how awesomely successful I imagined my mom was, about being a singer. I didn't sing. I was in chorus class, but mostly to fill my schedule. I didn't know my mom. I wrote these things because if someone found my diary, I'd be far more interesting than I was. Even I didn't want to read about a girl eating a sleeve of Ritz crackers in a dirty stairwell at her high school in a hopeless town.

"This is one thrilling stairway."

I kept writing. I didn't want to hear his voice. Didn't want to talk to him. I knew as soon as he smiled I'd do the wrong thing and I'd forget that I was trying to move on.

He sat beside me and put his hand over mine. I tried to move my pen, but he pushed down. Not hard. Just enough to stop the words.

"I missed you," he said. His other hand stroked my knee.

You'd think I would've learned. You'd think I would've stayed away. Wouldn't have gone there that night. You'd think, after the party, after how used I felt when he abandoned me at the gas station and didn't call, after avoiding him and school for a week, I would have known better.

It's easy now. It's easy to look at that moment, to see what he was doing. It's easy to yell at myself and tell myself I was better than that. But all of that came later. It came with knowing who he really was.

You have to understand: I just wanted him to care like I did. I just wanted someone to love me that much. To be enough for someone. I was so afraid of losing the little I had that I was willing to do whatever it took to hold on to it.

"You haven't called or texted or talked to me," I reminded him. "You were supposed to call."

"I was busy. But I've been thinking about you. Come on. Look at me, Ellie."

Do you know how much I wish I could say there was something he did that was special? That I could defend it or rationalize it because there was a side of him only I knew?

There wasn't. Of course there wasn't. He was a teenage boy. He had too coarse hair and gray eyes and he walked like the ceiling was too low for him and he smiled crooked. He wasn't even very nice. But he was the one who found me sitting in the stairwell, and I thought that meant something. He kept coming back, and I believed he was hurting, too.

"I wish you'd called," I said.

"I know. But hey, listen, I wanted to see what you were up to. Want to get together Saturday night?"

"What for?"

He moved his hand off mine and reached behind my head, his fingers curling against the back of my skull.

"I was thinking maybe we could finish what we started," he said. "After my party. I haven't been able to stop thinking about it." His other hand slid up my side from my knee, under my shirt, his fingertips on my rib cage. "I can't believe I had that kind of willpower. You're really sexy. Do you have any idea what you do to me? I was hoping we'd get a chance to see each other. You haven't been around."

"You never called," I reminded him again. "You were going to call. You were supposed to. Almost two weeks ago."

He kissed me and pressed his fingers into my neck. "My dad had me working a ton. But you know I've been thinking about you, right?" I didn't say anything. "Oh, Ellie, don't be like this." He moved a hand back down to my leg, up my thigh. "You want this, remember?"

"You have a girlfriend. Remember?"

"Gina Lynn? No, that's over. I just haven't told her yet. Meet me Saturday night. It'll be just us. Come on, Ellie. You said you were ready."

"Caleb, I—" I pushed his hand down my leg, away from me.

"Shhh," he said, holding me against him, kissing me into silence. I hated how my body responded to it. I hated that I wanted to say no, to tell him he should have called. But he was right. I'd told him I was ready. That I'd wanted this. That I wanted him. And the worst is that, despite being angry, despite how much he'd hurt me, I still did.

"Ellie, come on. What can it hurt? I love you. You're beautiful. Let me show you, all right?"

I went. Of course I did. I was barreling down a road of mistakes and I couldn't figure out how to get back. I thought it would be special. I thought it would change something.

And it did. It changed everything.

He met me at the park and drove me to the house. He told me that it was quiet there, that he knew a secret place for just us. I wanted to believe him. I went there with purple silk under my jeans, hoping he meant it when he called me beautiful.

It was the last place I ever went. The last choice I made. I can't hate myself more for it.

———

FIRST, THERE WAS Caleb. Just us, like he'd said. It wasn't romantic and it wasn't what I wanted, but it was still just us. That part was true.

It didn't happen like it had in his car. He hurt me. He held me down. His hands weren't soft but demanding. He didn't undress me; he tore the clothes off like an animal. I cried and he laughed, but it was just us, and I thought this was the worst it could get. I figured I would take my clothes and he'd tell everyone whatever he'd planned to tell them and I'd go to school and see him with Gina Lynn and they'd whisper when I walked by. Talk about how pathetic I was but how I knew my place now. Knew my worth.

I realized it had been a game. I didn't know when he'd changed his mind, but I realized as he did this to me that he didn't want me. Not like I'd hoped. He wanted to hurt me. To make me go away.

When he got up after the second time, when he left me crying on the carpet and walked out of the room, I thought he was getting a towel or something. That he'd be back and he'd bring me home. I crawled over to my clothes, to my jeans and underwear. Hands shaking, I laid them out and tried to stand. I just needed to get dressed.

"What are you doing?"

I'd never met him. I'd seen him, heard about him, but we'd never spoken. I didn't know that voice. Not yet.

Caleb closed the door behind him and sat on the bed as Noah pushed me back down. I could smell the alcohol on him.

"What's your name?" he asked.

I tried to say it, snot building in my throat and the gargle coming out in cracks. He hit me, smacking me hard across the face. They learned from me. Never go for the face. After, they stopped hitting where someone could see it. They learned to work harder to cover up what they were.

"I asked you your name," he said.

"Ellie."

I was a canvas, a blank slate, until Caleb had begun to write out his need on me. He'd claimed what was his, but it wasn't everything. He and Noah found all the hidden parts of me. Passed between them, my body was their playground, and they bent me to their wills. They each were there and then, they made me do it at the same time.

They took off my sweater, and I was on my hands and knees, on my back, against the wall, while they shared. They ignored all the things I asked. All the ways I begged.

After they had ruined me, after they'd made their mess, they left me sobbing on the floor.

And I still thought it was over.

Caleb had said he wanted something that was just his. He didn't want to be where they'd both already been. He wanted something only for him. Something else that he could take from me.

I screamed. That was my mistake, but I couldn't help it. I was torn apart and I couldn't stop. I screamed. And then he hit me.

Harder and harder while he continued, still laying claim to the last part of my body.

The anger made him more excited somehow, turned him into an animal, and he slammed my face down. Noah helped, holding me while Caleb kept going.

I don't remember when I stopped breathing. I remember the dying and I remember being dead, but nothing changed. I was on the floor, screaming, my head throbbing and the blood spilling from my nose. He was in me. Then he wasn't, and he flipped me over, his hands around my throat, the ecstasy of power in his face.

"Dude, you're going to kill her," Noah said, but he was laughing.

I tried to look at Caleb. Tried to reach the boy I'd fallen for as the air went out of me. I couldn't see him anymore. Couldn't see who he'd been or the monster he was. Couldn't find anything in the wavy room, the world spinning toward darkness. Nothing but the brown walls and the memory of a boy who'd told me he loved me in summer.

And then I was there, but his hands weren't on my throat. I saw how he stood over me. I could breathe, but I realized I was doing it out of habit.

"Shit. We need to get something. We need to hide her," Noah said.

Caleb tossed my sweater over my body. "Call Dad."

chapter thirty-five

Kate's parents' kitchen is too bright. Painted yellow. A border with chickens runs along the ceiling's edge. Everything is in shades of sunlight. But they don't have any of the same light on them. They droop where they sit, heavy under something.

Cassie sits across from them. Gus isn't with her. This is information gathering. I don't know what led her here. How she's connected me to Kate or to the other girls, but she's here to ask the questions others forgot to ask, or asked and never followed up on.

"Your daughter and Ellie Frias were friends?" she asks.

Kate's father is older than my dad. A lot older. She was an only child, too, but she was planned. Her parents welcomed her into their lives. They were ready and had a crib and a whole room picked out. I was an accident.

I'd only ever seen Kate's parents in passing. We'd never talked. Nothing more than a grunted greeting or a wave. When I was with her, we were alone. In her room. Her backyard. We never brought each other into the other parts of our lives. Our friendship was something we each kept apart from us. Something we were still trying to figure out.

Kate's father drums his fingers on the table and tries to find the words. "They knew each other. I don't know if they were really friends. They weren't that close."

Cassie writes, capturing the way they speak, how they're reluctant to talk about me.

"She was home right after Ellie went missing, right?" she asks.

Kate's mom shakes her head. "It was about a month later. During her break from school. She's in Ohio, you know?"

"Right, for school," Cassie confirms.

"She took the year off after she graduated. She had to, and we didn't want her going too far. It was that year, that summer. She and that girl spent a lot of time together. But they were never friends."

"You're insistent on that. Why?" Cassie asks.

"Our daughter had nothing to do with what happened," Kate's father says. "It isn't right. She just wanted to go to school, and she came home and . . . Last summer, Katie never mentioned that girl. We saw her a few times, but they weren't close. She didn't spend a lot of time here. We only found out they were anything more than friendly neighbors after she went missing. Katie was home for the holidays and she said she'd worried about that girl."

I notice they call her Katie. It's deliberate. Kate never referred to herself that way. She'd never said it bothered her, but I knew her as Kate. She signed things as Kate. Yet her parents know her as Katie. It's weird how our parents know us as separate and different people from who we actually are.

Kate's father looks outside, through the window, up the hill to my house. To my kitchen. "I don't know what kinds of things that girl was or wasn't involved in, but it wasn't something Katie needed to be a part of."

"You worry about your daughter?" Cassie asks.

"Of course. She's our daughter," he says. He doesn't continue. He feels that should explain everything.

Cassie nods. "I assume Kate spoke with the police. You all did, I imagine?"

Mr. Prince—Kate's father—shakes his head. "They asked a lot of people in town for tips, but we were never called in to speak to anyone. Not officially. Although Katie went once. After Christmas. She told us she was worried. She mentioned that girl had some trouble with boys. Katie said she was afraid something had happened. We suggested she go to see them, tell them what she knew, and leave it at that. I don't know what came of it. They never followed up, and we didn't ask about it again. It wasn't good for her to be thinking about all that. That girl wasn't Katie's responsibility. Whatever happened to her had nothing to do with our daughter. We didn't need her worrying about those sorts of things."

"Our daughter has enough to worry about," Kate's mom says. "It's hard for her. For us. She can't . . . It's just a lot, and she's not strong enough. These things they're saying in the news. Would you want your daughter thinking about things like that?"

Cassie shrugs. "I don't have a daughter. But if I did, I guess I'd want her to know what to look out for. I'd want her to know what happens to girls."

Mr. Prince slams his hand down on the table. I can tell he didn't mean for it to be so aggressive, because he lifts it and cradles it with his other hand under the table, looking sheepish. "I'm sorry. But like you said, you don't have a daughter. Katie is . . . she's not well. That girl ended up in whatever situation she did because she made bad choices. Katie said she had trouble with boys. Our daughter knew better than to get mixed up in that."

Cassie sighs. "Has Kate been in touch with anyone back here?" she asks. "Do you know what came of the meeting with the police?"

"We just told you we didn't," he says and he gets up from the table. He makes a show of starting dinner, a subtle warning that Cassie is intruding. That her time is up. But she continues anyway.

"I'd imagine this would be something you'd want to talk to your daughter about. If she was close to Ellie. Even if they weren't good friends, I can't imagine it would be good for her to wonder what happened."

"My daughter," Kate's mom says, "like my husband said, she's had a hard time. In high school, she was . . . well, she was sick. Not well. You don't need to know, but she was in the hospital a few times. It was never easy for her to adjust back into things when she'd be there. When she'd go back to school, the kids weren't very nice. She didn't have many friends because of it, and we always tried to look out for her. To make sure she didn't get in trouble. Didn't get caught up in things that might have made her illness worse. We really wanted her to stay closer to home for school because of it. She insisted she needed to go away, but that was a very difficult choice for our family."

She looks at her husband, who nods slightly, and she continues. "We're trying not to get her involved. Katie needs to be kept away from things that upset her. Things that might make it hard for her. She's all alone there at school, and we can't . . . we can't fix it if she gets upset. She gets sick, you know."

After a year, it was something I should've known. I didn't even realize Kate was ill. All those afternoons. The conversations we had. She said she was in the midst of reinvention, but she had this sickness and I didn't know. I hate myself for not knowing.

"I'm sorry. I understand this is hard," Cassie says. "What do you mean she was sick? What kind of illness exactly?"

"I don't think it's really any of your business," Kate's dad says. "Look, like we said, she wasn't friends with that girl. We don't know anything. We've told you everything we do. My wife and I . . . we want Katie to move on. She's been doing better away at school. There have been no incidents. We'd like to let her keep it that way."

"I can't imagine it doesn't get back to her. Now that they're digging things up again," Cassie says. "The Internet alone—"

"She won't find out, because Katie and that girl were not friends. We don't know anything. She doesn't know anything. Can you please just leave us alone?" her mom asks.

Cassie does, but not until she makes them take a business card.

There was always a wall between me and Kate. I didn't know she was sick. She didn't know what was happening with me. Especially toward the end. We were friends, but not really, and now the only person who maybe could have explained, who might have been able to speak for me, is in Ohio and her parents don't want her to remember me. They can't even say my name. They just call me "that girl."

Kate's parents aren't hiding anything. They're just reluctant to admit I existed. Reluctant to let me into their lives. To admit what this town is. What people do. The things that are out there for girls. They don't want to face these things, because it's easier to believe they only happen to other people.

It's hard to get information in Hollow Oaks. Nobody ever wants to talk. Nobody ever wants to be inconvenienced by all the things that happen to girls.

chapter thirty-six

He sits in the same blue chair Gina Lynn sat in. He came right from work and he struggles to keep his eyes open. Playing with the skin along his nails on his left hand, he looks outside. Sees how the light from the store followed him.

"Mr. Frias, thanks for coming," Officer Thompson says. She guides him back to the same drab room. I don't know why I imagined there'd be multiple rooms, that these conversations wouldn't be repetitive. It's always the same here, and it shows even in the way that Gomes scribbles in the lines of his notepad as he waits.

"Do you have anything?" my dad asks. "Has something new come up? I've been trying not to watch too much of the news. It just ends up devolving into arguments and speculation."

Gomes shakes his head and adjusts in his seat. The fan is still going. It spins during all of these conversations, capturing all the pieces of the story. Only the fan knows the truth.

"Not exactly. As you know, we had very limited information before," Gomes says. "It's hard, even when we want to keep looking, to tie up resources with no direction. We don't want you to get your hopes up that there's been a breakthrough. However, we think, maybe, there's something that could help. We think we may have a starting point. There are still a lot of questions, though, and we're hoping you might be able to fill in some of the blanks."

"Is she alive?" my dad asks.

"We don't know."

"Is there a chance?" He wants to hope, and they want to let him, because it hurts too much to say it's impossible.

"We hope so, Alex."

"What we're trying to do is piece together new information we've received," Malik says. "Can you remember Ellie saying anything about Caleb Breward? About a boyfriend in general? Did she go anywhere in particular?"

My dad looks down. "I don't know. I know you asked me before, about him. If she was dating. What kinds of boys she might have been involved with. But Ellie and I, we didn't talk much. After she started high school, she spent a lot of time in her room and I didn't know how to talk to her. I didn't even know she had a boyfriend until you told me. Until you went through her diary and talked to other kids at school. We never really talked about those kinds of things."

He pauses and looks at them, ashamed. "Except . . ." He shakes his head. "There was this one time, but it probably doesn't mean anything."

"Anything could mean something," Gomes says.

"Well, she came into the store, while I was working, with some kids. Caleb Breward was one of them. They were holding hands, but there was space between them. It wasn't the way you stand with someone you're dating," my dad says.

It hurts me hearing that. It hurts because he noticed and I didn't. He saw what wasn't there, even when I pretended it was.

I wish I'd asked him. I wish I'd talked to him about Caleb or tried to find out what love looked like. How you can tell if someone means it when they say they care or call you pretty.

"So she never gave you reason to think they were serious? There was nothing else? He never came to the house?" Thompson asks.

"Never. She knew . . ." I hear him remembering. In his voice, I can see that morning. The fish and the bottles. I can see his mind replaying that time in the store. I see him putting it all together. "Why him, Ellie? Of all the people in this town . . . ?"

"You don't like the Brewards?" Gomes makes a note in the folder.

"There are a lot of things I don't like, but what good does complaining about them do? She deserved better."

"How long have you lived here?" Malik asks.

"Before Ellie. My family lived out past Ithaca, and Sierra and I—that's Ellie's mom—after school, we fell in love with this place. It had so much potential. We wanted to capture it."

"What do you mean?" Thompson looks at the clock. It's late. My father is exhausted, but he's trying to remember the right thing to say. Trying to give them whatever thread they need to find me.

"She was a writer," he says, talking about my mom. "I used to want to make films. We thought this town was the kind of place where we could do that. That there were stories here that deserved to be told. And then Ellie was born. Sierra couldn't stand it. It didn't take very long for the potential to start to feel like decay."

"That's when she left?" Gomes asks.

"Around. It wasn't just the town anymore. Sierra wasn't good at being a mom. She felt like it was stifling her. That we'd be stuck here forever and suddenly, all the stories that she wanted to tell felt like stories no one needed anymore. Stories of people she didn't understand. So she decided to go somewhere else. To find the ones she cared about instead."

"And as for you?" Gomes asks.

"I was working for Goodman and Sons for a while. Trying to do my best for Ellie. I knew there wasn't going to be a big career break for me anymore, but she was a perfect kid. She just lightened everything. I know it's cliché. A dad who thinks his daughter is the greatest thing ever, but Ellie was. I came home at night, especially after they started talking about layoffs, and I would feel like giving up, too. I thought maybe Sierra had had the right idea. But then Ellie would be sitting in the kitchen or playing in the yard. Just being Ellie." He pauses. "My daughter was my entire life. She *is* my entire life, and I have no idea what to do without her now."

"I'm sorry, Alex," Gomes says.

"I failed her. She had this whole life I didn't know about. I wasn't a part of it. I wasn't there for her and she was all I had. How could I miss so much? How could I let her down so badly?"

Thompson grabs the tissues. She's added that to her daily routine now. My dad takes one, but he doesn't use it. He just folds it over his hands.

"I need you to find her. I've been patient. She has to be somewhere," he says.

Thompson looks at him. "I know we've covered this, but there's absolutely no chance Ellie is with your wife?"

He laughs. "Sierra would've called right away. Like I said, she wasn't interested in being a mother. She would've been on the phone, making sure Ellie got back here as soon as possible."

"Sometimes, these things happen with kids and estranged parents. I'm sure, at Ellie's age, she wondered about her mom. Stranger things have been known to happen and at her age, she's going to surprise you. Maybe your wife thought—" Thompson says.

"Sierra and Ellie weren't estranged. Sierra was welcome here. I tried constantly. I never gave up on the idea of her coming back. She could have come back anytime." He pockets the tissue. "Look, the thing with Sierra . . . She chose not to be a part of her daughter's life. Ellie is fifteen. She won't be sixteen for a couple weeks. And you know what I got in the mail three days ago? A birthday card. She doesn't even remember her own daughter's birthday. She knows around when it is. And sometimes the cards come months early, when they're convenient for Sierra."

Thompson shakes her head. "I can't understand how—"

My dad cuts her off. "That's just who she is. Ellie and I know that. We've lived with it for years. We get it. But when you say maybe Ellie went to be with her . . . it's absurd. Maybe that happens with other kids. With different kinds of women. Not Sierra. Besides, if Ellie had wanted to, and if Sierra hadn't been the way she is, I would've been more than happy to send Ellie to spend time with her mom. She didn't need to run away."

"I know we've gone through it before," Gomes says, "but we need to cover all the possibilities. It's better to hope for something innocent like a girl trying to connect with her mom."

"I don't like the alternative," my dad admits, "but Ellie wasn't that kind of kid. We weren't close anymore, but she didn't run away. I told you then. Nobody believed me. I may not have known everything about her. We may have lost something along the way, but I know that. I know Ellie well enough to know she wouldn't have left. Not without saying good-bye. No matter what it was, Ellie would never have left me guessing."

The officers pause, looking at one another, knowing he's right. Six months is a long time. Maybe they hadn't had all the information. Maybe Gina Lynn had lied, but they could have tried harder.

"Right now," Gomes says, "we don't have enough to link Ellie's disappearance to anyone or anything with real proof. We still don't know where she is. What we do have, we believe, is hopefully enough to prosecute Caleb and Noah Breward on these new charges." He looks at the other officers and then back at my dad. "Alex, I shouldn't be telling you this. I'm *really* not supposed to tell you this, but I want you to know how hard we're trying. We are sincerely hoping that moving forward on this will bring out more information. There are a few things we're trying to tie up and they may bring us back to Ellie. I hate asking you to be patient, but I promise . . . we're still looking."

"If there's anything I can do, anything I can tell you, please let me help," my dad says.

Malik nods. "We will. You'll be the first person we tell as soon as we have anything useful. In the meantime, if you think of anything or hear anything, no matter how useless it may seem, please contact us."

Gomes reaches out to shake my dad's hand and squeezes. "We know we dropped the ball. But we'll make it right. I promise we'll find her."

My dad nods. "Please do," he says. "Even if it's bad news, I need you to find her. She needs to come home."

chapter thirty-seven

When you charge people like the Brewards with sexual assault, there's a media deluge. A town is put upside down. Local and regional coverage becomes national. People all over the country sit in their homes and imagine Hollow Oaks. They talk about the kind of place it is. The kind of people who live here. The kinds of secrets we must all have. Everyone has a theory and we're no longer just another town where people live and die and fade. We're a name that everyone knows. A name of a place where things happen to girls. As if it's unique to us.

Now that the media is here, there's no space left. The pizza place has to feed hundreds of members of the press. The school's courtyard is more film equipment than grass and trees. The front of the police station looks like a studio set. Everyone wants to know what comes next.

People discuss us online. They speculate as to what happened. As to who the Brewards are. Who the girls are. People everywhere talk about what did and didn't happen, and they prosecute and defend a group of people they've never met.

They condemn our town. Separate it from their own, where the same secrets pulse.

Gomes may have been disinterested in the case at first. Maybe he was tired. He's close to retirement and maybe he didn't want this. Maybe he was afraid of his reputation, of having this be how he's remembered. He didn't want to get involved in any of it, but when he's given the second stack of printouts, when he gets another pile of online comments that have come from all over, from people who couldn't find Hollow Oaks on a map, something changes in him.

He bellows at anyone who will listen. "This isn't a fucking witch hunt. Get these girls' names off the Internet. What's wrong with you?"

He's not yelling at anyone in particular. No one knows who gave up the names. Someone did, but they could be in this room or not. And it doesn't matter anyway. Gomes can yell. He can get angry. But no matter what he does now, the names are out there. Once a name is spoken, it doesn't get to be taken back. Sure, the media keeps saying the names have not been released, but what good does that do? Everyone knows and everyone has already decided if Gretchen and Kailey are telling the truth. The court of public opinion moves much faster than the law.

"There's something wrong with people," Malik says. Thompson nods. "Look at this one." He reads aloud. " 'Both these girls are lucky. Guys like the Brewards don't need to waste their time forcing anyone to do anything. I bet these girls are ugly. The Brewards probably did them a favor. If they were any good, maybe they'd have stuck around for more.' "

Gomes snaps at someone who brings in more pages for him to look at, and Malik puts down the stack. "I don't understand people," he says.

"There are plenty of calls to hang the Brewards, too. It's not all one-sided. Of course, the comments are just as vile," Thompson says.

"Yup. And plenty of calls to hang us, too," Malik adds.

Gomes pushes the papers away from himself. "Okay, let's just focus on what we can do. Let's make sure those two girls are safe. That's a starting point. From there, let's make sure that anyone else who wants to come forward can do so without being dragged through this. Let's find this house the girls described. Maybe, if we can do these things, we might have a chance here."

I know there are other girls. There were at least eight—well, seven since one is Gretchen—after me. But no one is coming forward, and I can't pretend I blame them. People all over the country know Gretchen's and Kailey's names. The cops tried to keep them safe. Tried to keep them anonymous, but Hollow Oaks wasn't ready for this case. Towns like this are never ready for these kinds of stories, no matter how many times they happen.

"I contacted the DA," Thompson says. "They're sending an advocate, setting up a meeting with the girls. She's going to help keep them from being out there too much. She'll do most of the speaking for them."

"Good. Liz started a website, too. She's trying to get more girls to come forward. There's no way there were only two," Gomes replies.

Malik nods. "I've been going through these lists," he says, holding out a folder with several printed sheets of paper. "Out of all the houses, there are four sites isolated enough. All four could fit the girls' descriptions."

"Well, let's get over there," Gomes says.

"Shannon and I can go, if you think you can manage everything else. Liz said info has been coming in, but . . . well, clearly it's going to involve some reading." He glances at the stack of papers.

"These people. It would be nice if they realized they're only making it harder on us. Do they even know they're just helping those boys?" Gomes asks.

Although he's not expecting a response, Thompson replies anyway. "I'm not sure some of them are opposed to making it harder. The Brewards have a lot of supporters."

Gomes picks up the papers. The station is quiet, despite the swarm of reporters outside. I wonder if he even wants to leave, given that he has to walk through them to get home. "Find the house. I'll be here filtering through the last dregs of humanity."

I want to help, although I can't. But being able to ride in the car with Thompson and Malik is nice. I like thinking progress is happening. I need to know they're getting closer.

"What happened here?" Thompson asks as they pull up to the first house. It's nearly fallen down. Weeds tug on the gutters and the roof has caved in. An animal scurries past the bay window on the inside.

"I don't think you could do much here," Malik says. "And I'm sure the girls would've remembered a hole in the roof."

"I think you're right. This is terrible, though."

In the backyard, there's a bike. One of the wheels came off and it's rusted, but once upon a time, someone rode it. Someone came home from school or work and there wasn't a hole in the roof. Once upon a time.

"This town is falling apart," Thompson says. "How are we ever going to clean all this up?"

"We count on people like the Brewards," Malik replies.

"They haven't done a thing here."

"They will. That's why people don't want to say anything. They don't want this house in their neighborhood."

"So we let the Brewards get away with murder as a thank-you," Thompson says. She doesn't mean it literally, but she's right.

As she backs out of the driveway, she looks through me while she scans the road.

When we pull up to the second house on their list, I feel the memory tugging at me. Caleb and I came here once, early on. The furniture had all been removed and the house just needed to be cleaned. We lay in the center of an empty kitchen, cool tiles on our backs, and I stared at where the refrigerator had been. I was happy for the people who'd lived here, happy they'd been able to take it with them. It was just a thing, but you miss things when you're forced to leave them behind.

"This isn't where it happened," Thompson says once they're inside. "Kailey mentioned a bed, and I can't imagine the boys dragging a bed here and then bringing it somewhere else. That's probably too much work, even for them."

They stand where Caleb and I fell asleep, their feet pressing down onto the memory of us. Malik flicks the light switch, which hasn't worked in who knows how long.

"It's sad, isn't it?" he asks.

Thompson nods, but the sadness is too much on top of everything else. They do a quick scan of the place, but it's just another house. Another ghost. Not the right one, though.

The road toward the lake is narrow. Clumps of leaves have rotted and lie discarded in piles along the shoulder. It's a pretty drive, except the potholes and ice heaves make it hard to focus on the way the birches and sunbeams play hide-and-seek outside the window. A chipmunk runs behind the car as we pass, diving inside a log on the other side of the road.

These are the places that people try to remember. We come out to the lake to breathe, to justify staying here.

I know they're in the right place. I've walked along these curves before. In the snow and in the rain. At night or under the bright sun at midday. I've stood and listened to the chipmunks and squirrels squawking over acorns.

Because I've had a lot of time to take it in now.

It's not far. These were my quiet escapes when it was too much in the room, but I wanted to be close enough to go back. When I was ready. When I let myself remember that it was my responsibility to be there. That I was the only one who heard them.

As we get closer, it all makes sense for the first time. I couldn't figure out what kept me here. Why I kept coming back. Why I'd walk in the woods but turn around and go back to that room, knowing what would happen. Knowing how much I'd have to remember.

I thought I stayed because I was scared, because I didn't know what else to do. But I didn't. I realize now that I stayed because I saw myself in the other girls' eyes. I heard myself in their cries and screams. I needed to listen. I had to experience it over and over again because I needed to give them that. I needed to make sure someone was there for them. I couldn't let them suffer alone like I had.

The car slows as we approach the house, and I feel all those nights coming back to me. Six months of it. I've watched so many girls be taken apart in there, and now, finally, someone else will know. Finally, I won't have to carry this by myself, alone, into forever.

There's nothing around the house. It's in the woods, far back from the road, the lake the only sign of people for miles.

Maybe it was a summerhouse. A place like Kailey's family had. Maybe the people who lived here and Kailey's family knew each other—the people who came into the town but weren't a part of it.

This is the same lake where Dad and I went fishing. A life that was shaped, on both ends, by this place. And by the boys who declared it theirs.

I'm not even sure if I mean the lake or my life.

It's a pretty house. On the outside. It still looks like someone could live here. They did a good job fixing the broken pieces. Someone even planted daffodils. I want to think they're beautiful, but I realize it had to have been one of them. Caleb or Noah. One of them had to go to the store, buy the flowers, and sit in the dirt, planting them. One of them had to believe that these yellow flowers deserved to live more than I did. Deserved more space in the ground than me.

Thompson and Malik walk through the rooms. Everything is in place. It's been transformed back into a home, and it waits for someone to love it again. Everything is as if someone will be back any day now, except for all the stuff in boxes in each room. I don't know what happens to the stuff when the banks finally come in and take over, now that it's all cleaned up. I wonder what happens to these parts of people.

"They left a TV," Malik says. "DVDs. A whole mess of their stuff."

"I guess they had other things to worry about," Thompson says.

The main floor of the house is clean, but it doesn't fit the description the girls gave. Malik looks through the sliding glass door into the backyard, and I want to lift him up, to put him over the spot where I am, to show him that I was here.

Thompson gets his attention instead when she opens the door to the basement.

"Wow, there's a lot more stuff down here."

Boxes fill the space in the basement. It was cold down here that night. I remember that. Concrete can't keep out the chill in the ground that stays here, even in the summer.

Thompson and Malik navigate the storage areas, check out the circuit breakers, press the buttons on the washer and dryer.

"Not here, either?" Malik asks.

Yes. Look closer. I could scream it but nobody would hear. I wish I could draw a picture, could show them the way the top box on one of the piles is crooked, because even the Brewards aren't perfect. *Look closer,* I plead in my head.

"I don't know. I guess not. But something's bugging me," Thompson says.

When Noah and Caleb started it, maybe here or wherever it was they started—since I don't know how long it went on before me—they were careful about everything. They had plenty of power and could get away with more than most people. They were smart, too. They chose us with a great deal of forethought. They planned the details and setup of the location perfectly. They made sure we wouldn't be believed.

Thompson walks past the piles, running her hand over the tops of the boxes. She gets to the back, to that pile, and I push the box, hoping it will fall. It works in movies. But in real life, the box doesn't do anything. My hands go through it.

Still, something happens. I know it wasn't me. After six months, I don't believe in luck. It wasn't a coincidence. She was just looking. Someone was finally looking.

"Come here," Thompson tells Malik. "Do you see this?"

Caleb and Noah, over time, grew careless. It's shown in the

top box on the stack, which has started to break free from the rest. If you look closely enough, there's a strange wooden surprise at the bottom corner. Dark wood amid cardboard and concrete.

"Let's move these," Malik says, and they drag the pile of boxes away from the door.

It was probably their son's or daughter's room. The people before. A hidden part of the basement. Where their kid wouldn't have to be part of the family except when they were hungry. Happy to be separate. Keeping company with a water heater and furnace.

When the pile is moved, the officers recognize it immediately. A small room. Hidden. A bed. Weak carpet. And they know. There's nothing left of all the girls who've passed through this room. Not anymore. But they know. Because places like this create energy that can't be washed away with new paint. All it needed was for them to come looking.

"Call Gomes. And get my camera," Thompson says.

While I wait with them for Gomes to show up, I remember it. I came here willingly. That afternoon, I stood in front of my mirror, trying to get my lipstick right. It was another of my dad's markdowns, but not orange like the others. I tried to make it work. Garish pink, but with just a little, I almost looked like the people in magazines. Like the girls I admired. As much as I could with my sepia-washed hair and skin. An old-fashioned photograph of a girl.

I don't want to die in a place like this. I don't want to be forgotten, to be left here. I don't want that kid, the one I imagined, to play soccer over my bones. I want someone to remember me. I want someone to care.

That's it, though. I want. I want. I want. Always. That's no good. Who cares what a girl wants?

chapter thirty-eight

When I went missing, they did look for my body. After they contacted my mom, who was out of the country, and they tried to get information from people in town, they looked for me in case I was dead.

They started searching for me by the river. It's like an unspoken assumption that girls who disappear end up in the river, I guess. Some kind of Ophelia complex. I didn't sing myself a lullaby and fall from a branch. It wasn't romantic. I was torn apart and thrown in the ground, wrapped in plastic. They don't paint pictures of girls in tarps, though, so maybe people can't shake that idea. A girl floating peacefully to her death in a wreath of flowers. Maybe we're all Victorian paintings or living poems.

Now, the team is in the backyard, digging. They all knew as soon as they saw the room. I watch them as they pull up the ground. By the shed, under a large gray rock, they find bones, but they're not mine.

"A dog," Malik says. "Probably the family who lived here, I would guess. They're pretty old."

It makes me feel a little better that I shared the ground with someone who'd been loved.

"Over here." A guy digging wipes his face and someone else joins him, marking the spot where the blue tarp juts through the earth.

That inch of plastic sends the whole team into work mode, digging and marking and photographing.

When one of them lifts the tarp, my foot falls loose. I'm still wearing my sneakers.

I don't want to see myself. I don't want to know what becomes of a girl.

I go to the front of the house and wait. The night settles overhead, but the lights from their lamps and cars don't let it through. The house is awash in white. It's quiet, except for the sound of digging. Except for the fear present when they take me out of the earth.

Thompson comes around the house, dialing a number on her phone. She's crying.

"Mom? Can I talk to Rana?" She sits on the front steps, her feet kicking at the daffodils. I don't think she knows she's doing it. It's a nervous habit to avoid thinking about what they found. She tries to keep her voice steady while the tears fall. "No, probably not," she says. "Do you mind keeping her there tonight? It's going to be late." She pauses while her mother responds. "Yeah, it's bad. Can you put Rana on? I don't have much time."

While she waits for the phone to be passed along to Rana, she looks up at the sky. Her hands are shaking and the phone slips, tumbling to the steps below her. She picks it up, her breath ragged.

But then suddenly, she's fine. The tears are quelled, her hands grow steady, and she focuses on the phone, holding it tight against her ear.

"Hi, honey," she says. "How's Grandma's? Are you doing anything fun?"

It shouldn't surprise me. She's young, but not that young. Plenty of people her age have kids. But I get it now. Why she's been so focused on me. On the other girls. It's the fear that's born with your child. The realization that you can't protect them, even if you make it your career.

Thompson smiles at hearing her daughter's voice. "I'm still at work, but I'll be home tomorrow night, okay?" Her daughter speaks and Thompson waits, running her free hand along the bush beside the stairs. Noise drifts over the roof from the backyard. "I'm sure Grandma would love to bake cookies," she says. "Well, you can ask her. I don't know if she has gummy bears, but why don't you see?"

The tears return and she bites her lip to avoid letting her voice shake. "Okay, Rana, I have to get back to work now, okay? But I'll see you tomorrow. . . . Yes, I'm very excited about your gummy princess cookies. . . . Give Grandma kisses for me, okay?"

She sits on the front steps of the house after she hangs up and gives in to the crying. Her tears soak the knees of her pants and she bends over, folding herself up. She tries wiping her knees dry, but the spots spread downward. Dark spots growing while she tries not to hurt.

On the other side of the bushes, a team of officers brings my body over to a van. The lights go down in the backyard, but Thompson doesn't move. She doesn't stop crying.

"How's Rana?" Malik asks as he comes around the house.

"She's alive," she says, tucking her phone into her pocket. "I can't imagine what Alex Frias is going to feel. I can't . . ."

"Are you okay?"

As the rest of the cops leave, there's no light anymore. This is one of the few places in town where the pollution from the store doesn't spread. I look up and the stars fill the darkness here. I wish I'd been able to see them when they put me in the ground.

"No," Thompson says. "I don't think I'll ever be okay, Tariq. I kept hoping, you know? I kept thinking maybe we'd find her. That maybe it was all just coincidence and we'd find her and she'd be fine. We took so long. I just can't forgive myself."

"It wasn't your fault. It wasn't anyone's fault. Anyone but those boys."

"What if we'd been able to save her?" she asks.

Shaking his head, he holds his hand out to help her up. They walk to the car in silence and I follow. I want to know where they're going. I want to know what comes next. I've waited so long to be found, but now, I don't know what this means for me.

Inside the car, Malik looks at Thompson. He changed spots with her and he's driving now. She sits with her face pressed against the window, shaking.

"Are you sure you're up for this?" he asks.

"It's my job," she says. "I have to be."

chapter thirty-nine

The Christmas lights are still tangled in the gutters. He never took them down, but I don't know if he lit them this year. I don't think he would've. He probably forgot they're even there.

"I'll do most of the talking," Gomes says, but it's not authoritative. He's not trying to lead the conversation; he's taking the brunt of it because Thompson and Malik are having a hard enough time walking to the front door. "He may be angry. He has every right to be angry. Hell, I'm angry."

My dad comes to the door wearing his panda bear pajama pants. I bought them for him a few years ago for Christmas. They were supposed to be funny. His T-shirt is wrinkled and there's a hole in the armpit. He looks like he was half-asleep.

"Come in," he says, and he opens the screen door to let them into the house. They follow him past the dark living room, down the hall, into the kitchen. The overhead light is on and there's one cupcake on the table, sitting in the middle of a plate that's too big for one cupcake.

"Do you want something to drink?" my dad asks. They

don't respond. He gets a glass out of the dishwasher and fills it with water.

"Alex, do you have a minute?" Gomes asks.

"I'm off today. It was . . . It *is* Ellie's birthday. She's sixteen."

The days after dying all feel like one long stretch of time. Not much different than the days when you're alive, but time doesn't work the same way. The sun goes up and down, but it's all one day. I didn't realize it was my birthday.

Thompson puts her hands on the back of one of the kitchen chairs. Her expression doesn't change. Her posture doesn't change. But her hands grip the wood of the chair, as she tries not to feel what she does. As she tries to hold it together because, like she told Malik, she has to.

She stands, quiet, her knuckles growing white, while my dad watches them. His eyes move between the three cops, and no one speaks for a while.

Thompson nods her head toward the cupcake. "Is that for her?"

My dad remains standing by the dishwasher, drinking his glass of water. "I couldn't ignore it. I mean, I don't think she's coming home, but what if she does? I can't have nothing ready, can I?"

Nobody speaks. The room fills with the silence. It's oppressive, especially to me, who doesn't have a way to break it.

"Did you need anything? Are you having any luck?" my dad finally asks.

"Alex," Gomes starts, but he can't say it. Not here. Not with the cupcake looking at him. Calling him out for missing it the first time. For letting six months pass. No one moves. Everyone just stares at the cupcake. Sitting there, on a plate too big for it, in the middle of the table. Remembering.

My dad knows before they say it. He watches as they look at one another, but not at him, each of them trying to find the words. He glances at Thompson clutching the back of the chair, at the way Malik tries to focus on the backyard through the window. At how Gomes stares down the cupcake and breathes in long, slow breaths.

My father realizes what they can't say and his knees buckle under him. He catches himself by hanging on to the counter. Several of the past-due notices fall to the tile. No one moves to pick them up.

"You're sure?" he asks.

Thompson swallows. A few tears escape, and she reaches up to wipe them away quickly, steadying herself with her other hand still on the back of the chair. She looks at my dad and nods. "We found her body," she says, but she can't continue.

"I'm sorry," Gomes says. "We'll still need you to come down to confirm it. Of course, if you can't right now, we understand. We don't have a lot of information yet as far as what happened, but the M.E. is coming out to do an autopsy, and we'll be running tests."

"How?" my dad asks.

"What do you mean, how?"

"How did it happen?"

"Like I said, we're working off limited information. We think . . . That is, this is all guesswork right now, but we found her in the backyard of the same home where the Brewards brought those other girls. They'd described the same house and we found it—her. In the backyard."

"They put her in the ground," my dad says, and he sinks to the floor, pulling on the panda pants and crying. He tightens his hands into fists and clings to the fabric. To one of the only things he has left of me.

My dad can't hug me good-bye. He can't hold me and tell me it'll be all right or comfort me after what they did. My father can't bring me to a doctor and tell me that we'll get through it. He can't even see me, not like I was. All he can do is clutch his panda bear pajama pants while he sobs on our kitchen floor, while he has to listen to words like *DNA testing*, *sexual assault*, and *decomposition*.

chapter forty

The police station feels cold. Although it's perception, not physical awareness, everything has a chill on it. Gomes brings my dad to his office first. He's not ready for the morgue. His daughter is in the morgue. That's not something you just walk into.

"I knew she wouldn't leave," my dad says. "I knew it."

"I'm sorry." Sorry is what Gomes has. Sorry doesn't fix six months, and it doesn't bring me home, but he can't say nothing.

"Why didn't you talk to them then? What if she'd been alive still?"

Gomes sits and opens the bottom drawer of his desk. It's so expected. The bottle. Tucked under an old manual. We find so much comfort in the ideas of us that we don't even notice when we become those ideas.

"They had alibis," he says. "We couldn't just start digging up backyards in town."

My dad won't sit. He walks to the board where the officers had written out the clues they'd had, where they'd tried for half a year to find something. The dry erase markers are faded now, but every part of our lives leaves an echo. In the new colored smears are the lines from previous notes. Possibilities that never came together.

"Who?" my dad asks.

"Who what?" Gomes fills a second glass.

"Who lied? Who walked in here, told you they were somewhere else, while my daughter rotted in the ground of an empty house?" I hate seeing him heartbroken, but his anger is new to me. I don't know which I prefer.

"Alex, it'll all come out. It's going to take a while. There are a lot of questions we all have."

"I want to know who. I need that. You owe me that."

Gomes puts the bottle back and closes the drawer. He unbuttons his collar. "I can't do that, and you know it. I wish I could. Believe me, if I could, I'd be right there with you."

When my dad sits, he does it like he's falling. A slow folding until he's smaller and the anger slips off him, sliding onto the floor and revealing the pain underneath. "Do you have kids?" he asks.

"I don't. Never got married. Never really had anything but this."

"You're lucky."

Gomes slides a glass across the desk, Post-its being caught up as it moves. Like a mini tornado of forgotten ideas.

"You don't mean that," Gomes says. "I know you're hurting, but you had something good with Ellie. I know you wouldn't give it up, even with this."

My dad stares at the glass. The liquid looks like oil. "It took me five years to stop resenting her."

"Your wife?"

He shakes his head. "My daughter. I resented my daughter

until she was almost seven years old. Can you imagine? Almost half her life. I spent half her life wishing her mom had taken her with her."

It doesn't hurt to hear him say it. In fact, it brings me some comfort. I resented myself for him. The guilt of my existence, when he tried so hard, always felt so heavy on me. When he admits that he felt the same way, it fades. Because the honesty doesn't mean he didn't love me; it means he had to work to love me and yet he did it anyway.

"She knew you loved her, Alex."

"Did she?" He starts to sob again. "Oh, damn it, Ellie."

Two grown men sitting in an old office, one of them crying and the other turning red from his own shame, should be the picture the media uses. People should see what goes on. What it really feels like. Because once the trial starts and everyone's watching, both men will stand resolved and stoic. But if they could see this, if they could see what this kind of darkness does to a person, maybe they'd feel it, too. Maybe they wouldn't make excuses anymore. Maybe they wouldn't shrug it off, because, you know, these things happen.

"I want to go there," my dad says, the words coming out as he swallows, nearly making him choke.

"Where's that?" Gomes makes himself professional again. Clears the desk. Rebuttons his collar.

"Where she was. Can I go there?"

"I can probably arrange that, but are you sure?"

"I need to see it. I need to say good-bye to her."

Gomes nods. "We'll set it up tomorrow. Do you want to wait until after . . . for . . . ?" He doesn't want to identify me as a body. I don't know why; it's all I was to Caleb. It's all any of us girls were.

"No," my dad says. "It's fine. It's probably best. Otherwise, I'll just stay up all night, telling myself there was a mistake. You know, for six months, I held on to it. I thought she might still come back. I told myself every night she would come home." He pauses. "She's not coming home. I need to know. For sure."

As they walk to the morgue, my father tries to be strong. He stares straight ahead, not speaking. Pretending it doesn't hurt. He moves his feet and he gets closer to where I am, preparing himself.

They haven't opened me up yet. They wanted to wait. My dad should see me as close to myself as I can be.

I'm on a table. The tarp is below me; nobody checks to see if it's become a part of me. If my body merged with it while I slept in the dirt.

It's gross. I'm me, but I'm not me. Gomes talked about winter while they were in the kitchen, talked about luck and the cold and how much the process slowed in the frozen earth. But I'm still a mass of rot. Festering on the table.

My dad stands back, in the doorway, holding on to the frame.

"I'm sorry," Gomes says again. "We just need you to confirm."

He nods, but he doesn't move. He stares at what I was and it sinks in. He sees it and even in the dream state he hung in as he walked down here, as he ran through impossible scenarios in his brain, telling himself it wasn't me, that it was just another missing dead girl, he didn't know it would be like this. He didn't know how quickly we all fade.

The houses don't decay like we do. A few weeds and some animals may invade, but we're far more fragile than wood. We're all just waiting to break into a million pieces.

"It's her," he says, and he turns and walks out. Nobody follows, because there's nothing to say.

I go home with him, and it hurts more than dying. He sits

in the dark in the kitchen, picking apart the cupcake. Pulling small pieces of it from its center, dropping them onto the table.

"I love you," I tell him, but he can't hear me. Fred sleeps at his feet, knowing something is wrong but unable to express it in any other way. It's the recognition of pain that even an animal feels.

The cupcake turns to crumbs. My dad sits in the chair, his fingernails thick with chocolate. Fred sleeps with his face on my father's toes. And I wait, across from them both, my hand reaching across the table, wanting.

Sometimes I'd sit like this. When he was at work. I liked how the world faded while I sat. But now it's just darkness and sadness and it has none of the ease of knowing you can turn on the light if it gets too uncomfortable.

He'd gotten used to listening, waiting for sudden sounds, lying half-awake every night just in case the door opened and I snuck back in. Now, the cars passing on the street outside aren't bringing me home. I didn't get bored on my great adventure and decide to come back to my life. The wind outside is howling and my body is being sliced open for evidence and nobody will ever eat my cupcake.

I hear him push the chair back. When he turns the light on, he scoops up the crumbs and throws them in the trash.

"Happy birthday, pumpkin," he says. "I know you hated it when I called you that, but . . ."

He shrugs and takes Fred for a walk. When he comes home, I'm already lying on the couch. He sits next to me and I imagine him covering me with the blanket, telling me to feel better. Kissing me good night before he whispers a warning not to stay up too late. Instead, he turns on the TV and listens to our lives as other people tell them.

"There is talk that new charges are being filed against Wayne Breward's sons, Noah and Caleb. Although the sexual assault cases will still be handled individually, we are told the investigation has led the police to a gruesome discovery. The body of Ellie Frias, who's been missing since November, was found behind a house where police believe she died. Limited information is available, but it's expected that, in the days to come, everyone in Hollow Oaks will be asked to remember the weekend of November 12. Cassie Haddom is live with what we know."

"Thanks, Maria." Cassie stands in front of the Brewards' house. The lights are all off, but their lawn has been commandeered by the media. They won't have any privacy tonight. "The police have recently arrested Caleb and Noah Breward on charges of sexual assault, but now, we're hearing talk that there will be additional charges due to the discovery of Ellie Frias's body in a backyard in Hollow Oaks. We don't know the details, but we do know that Caleb and Ellie had a prior relationship. When she went missing, he was cleared of any involvement. Right now, we are trying to find out what's changed."

"Do the police seem to feel there is a danger to the general public?" Maria asks.

"Not at this time. Sources say that while they can't go into detail, they are confident there is no credible risk to anyone else. We are also told that the Brewards, through their attorney, are cooperating."

"Thank you, Cassie," Maria says, and Cassie fades from the television. "In other news, the town of St. Agatha has recently undergone a restructuring in the permit process for new businesses."

My dad changes the channel. He settles on a Western. Something old with John Wayne I know he's seen before. I could never tell these movies apart, but I remember this one because of the girl. There weren't a lot of girls in Westerns.

I curl up against him as he dozes off, while the girl plots her revenge. My head rests on his arm and I tell myself he can sense me, that he knows I'm here when he wraps his arm around where I would be. I pretend he's not just hugging himself to stay warm.

I pretend it's a normal night.

I pretend I'm really sixteen.

I suppose I should feel grateful. In retrospect, I was happy. Well, I wasn't happy exactly, but I did have a happy life. I had my father. Fred. Three days in New York City. Summers and winters and the times in between. I had stories and hope in my life and, for a moment, I even felt what it was like to fall in love with someone. Sure, it was a lie and it wasn't real love and it was the wrong person, but I suppose that's just part of living, too.

The things I miss aren't the things I would've expected to miss. I remember a night, not so long ago, but that feels so far away now. A night when I remembered gum. When I missed it and its simplicity. I miss biting down into a new piece, miss feeling the sharp newness of it. I miss complaining that it's raining, miss how my shoes and socks would get wet and my shirt would stick to my back. I miss waking up for school and wishing I was dreaming, wishing that the alarm hadn't gone off yet.

I don't miss the big things we think are important; I miss the things that filled all the other minutes of the time I was here.

I don't want to know this. I don't want this knowledge. Not

as the clock ticks down what's left of my sixteenth birthday. Not as my body is opened up somewhere. Opened again to see where they've already opened me.

I just want to be a girl. All the parts of me that made me real. Maybe a lot of things make a girl, but I think being alive is the one I miss the most.

chapter forty-one

A re you sure you want to do this?" Thompson leads, and Malik and Gomes come up behind my dad. They're in front of the door to the house. Waiting. They know what's inside. Know he'll never be able to shake the image of it. They know he'll wake in the middle of the night sometimes and see that carpet, the furnace, the cobwebs in the corners by the room where I died.

"I am." He's not, but he needs this. He needs to make it real.

They don't spend time taking it all in, don't notice how the kitchen wallpaper is already starting to peel again. Some places just don't want to be fixed.

Instead, they bring him down to the basement. All the boxes are moved now. A pile on the other side of the concrete square. The door to the room is wide-open.

"Can I . . ." He pauses, looks around the basement. It's so normal. Average. It could be anyone's house. I could have been anyone. This could happen anywhere.

"I'd like a moment," he says. "By myself. I won't touch anything."

They nod and my dad walks into the room. There's the small

table, the lamp, and the bed. Nothing else to look at it. Nothing but the parts of the room that make it a room. Carpet. Closet. Beige walls.

I wish they'd painted it another color. Wish they'd prettied the place at least.

My dad reaches his hand out but he doesn't touch the bed. There are police markers on the few items of furniture. It's a crime scene. It should have been someone's room, and now it's something they'll show on CNN. Something strangers will look at and try to imagine what they did. *Why* they did.

"We still aren't sure what happened," Gomes says from behind my dad. His voice echoes in the basement. "We're waiting on some tests and we haven't been able to confirm anything. But we think it's likely it happened here."

"This was the last thing she saw, wasn't it?" my dad asks.

"I really am sorry," Gomes tells him.

My father waits, breathing in the musty basement. Seeing the carpet and walls. Trying not to look at the bed. I don't know if he'd be happier knowing I never made it that far.

"It's too quiet," he says finally, and he rejoins the officers. Malik closes the door behind them as Gomes leads my dad back upstairs. Thompson waits until they're all gone before turning out the light.

I wonder about her daughter. How old is she? We never would've met if I'd lived, but I still try to picture it. I could've been her babysitter. There doesn't need to be a Heaven; I can fill endless time with the could-haves and what-ifs.

Outside, it's torn up. The backyard is all holes. The spot where I was is one of many, although it's easy to notice now with the square of yellow tape around it. It's more of a memorial than Caleb gave me.

233

I don't know why my dad wants to see it. It's a hole, and now he'll know exactly where I was. For all that time. Did he drive by here? Does he remember fishing with me on this same lake? Will he be able to pass this way anymore, knowing my body was waiting for him? Knowing how much time passed while I longed to be found?

"They deserve to die," he says. It's a fact. There's no anger in his voice. No subjective, emotional response. He says it and the police agree and everyone knows it's fact. It's truth because that's what a person deserves after what they did. They deserve to be wrapped in blue plastic, to have a tarp stick to the backs of their legs where the jeans ripped. They deserve to wait and remember and relive it over and over while someone does it to other girls. They deserve every last minute of what I've experienced. But I don't want them here. I don't want to share this space with them. Their lives are a blessing. It means I'm safe.

My father stands with his legs pressing against the tape, the yellow against his jeans. Staring into the hole, into my grave. "When can I have the funeral?" he asks.

"That's up to you," Gomes says. "We can arrange it without the body, or once we're done . . ."

"She's not here anymore. That body. That's not Ellie. It doesn't matter what's in the casket. My daughter's gone."

He walks away, toward the front yard, down the driveway, and he keeps going. I follow him, my silent footsteps keeping time with his.

"I'm not gone, Dad," I whisper. "Turn around."

But he doesn't. It's not that kind of story.

chapter forty-two

Inside the courthouse, people rush from place to place. The media sets up to cover anything that happens during the arraignment. Caleb and Noah are brought in from wherever they've been kept. Neither of them seems nervous. Caleb's confidence hasn't been shaken at all.

In a dark room at the end of the hall, a woman stands in the corner, copying something. Gretchen and Kailey sit at the long conference room table, each of them cocooned inside themselves at either end of the giant oval.

She's called an advocate, but Gretchen can't stand the concept of her. She's too well dressed. Too professional. Too together to be the voice of girls who've been raped. While she copies, her suit nearly squeaks from its perfectness. It was pressed just last night, and her hair pulls the corners of her skin back. She takes the papers and passes them out to the two girls. Neither looks at them.

"I understand you may not want to speak," the woman says, "and we would generally suggest you don't. You don't need to. I'm here to speak for you. I'll be the liaison between their attorneys and you."

"I can speak for myself," Gretchen says. "Were you there?"

"I understand you don't feel I can appreciate your situation, but we're also trying to protect you. The media can be quite tough in these circumstances. And now, given what's happened with the Ellie Frias case, this isn't going away. I hate to say it, but it's probably only just getting started."

Gretchen looks down the long table at Kailey, who's looking outside. There isn't enough room in our small courthouse. It's supposed to serve six towns, but that's not enough space for the reporters. The ones who got here late, those who couldn't get in, have filled the parking lot and crossed over onto the lawn. One of them works for a big station, but her car wouldn't start this morning and now she's standing on the lawn, fighting with the mud that's swallowed her heels.

"I don't want to talk to anyone," Kailey says. She doesn't turn around to address the people in the room.

The advocate smiles. She sits by Kailey, already giving up on Gretchen, pressing her skirt with her hand as she sits. Gretchen sighs and looks at the paper, a list of resources for rape victims. She crumples it up and tosses it toward the wastebasket. It misses and lands by a stack of folding chairs.

"You don't have to," the woman says, reaching toward Kailey. She puts a hand on Kailey's shoulder and Kailey jumps. "We all handle things differently. I'm here to help you tell your story in a way in which you're comfortable."

"What's to be comfortable about?" Gretchen asks. "It wasn't comfortable for either of us. Why should it be comfortable for anyone else?"

"Gretchen, I won't take away your voice, but for Kailey's sake, let's try to figure out how we can get everyone on our side."

"Yeah, what side is that? The 'hey, it sucks to be raped' side?"

Gretchen asks. "This isn't a debate. Those assholes raped us. How is there a side?"

Kailey turns around and looks between Gretchen and the advocate. She runs a hand down the sheet of paper and sighs. "Let Beth talk. Please."

"Fine. Go ahead, Beth," Gretchen says. She puts her head down on the table, her hands in fists. Beth, the advocate, looks between the girls again, and turns to Kailey. She takes Kailey's hand. This time, Kailey doesn't jump.

"I do want you both to understand that the tactics they'll use may be troublesome. However, we can try to remember that they're nothing but tactics, okay? It will feel personal, but let's try to avoid taking it personally."

Gretchen doesn't look up, but she laughs. "They've called me a whore. People I've never met—people online—they say I asked for it. Guys have been threatening to rape me since, well, before this happened. Now they're saying I thrive on it. Yeah, it's personal, but let the media do their worst."

Kailey takes her hand away from Beth and turns back to the window. Beth stands and walks over to Gretchen. She tries to whisper, but her voice echoes in the dark room.

"I understand you feel like this is a sadly common experience for you," she says. "But we can't get anywhere if you resist help."

"Please stop saying you understand. You don't."

Beth nods. "I'll be right back. I'm going to see if I can find out where things stand. See if they're making any progress."

I can't decide how I feel about Beth. I sympathize with the fact that she's trying. It's not an easy job, and I suppose she's doing it with the right intentions. But Gretchen is right. Beth doesn't know. She wasn't there. She's not even from Hollow Oaks or the surrounding area. She was shipped in from Albany or something because this has become a big case. After it's all over, she'll probably write a paper on us. And everyone will think she's some kind of hero. The savior of the girls the Breward boys raped. Or at least two of them. Maybe three. Because the others . . . well, everyone forgets.

"You shouldn't be so defensive," Kailey says to Gretchen once they're alone, still looking outside. Still wishing she wasn't a part of all this.

"Don't tell me what I should be," Gretchen replies.

I leave the room. They're not getting anywhere. Meanwhile, Caleb and Noah are being read charges and people are building alibis and narratives to turn it back on us. Beth will come back and coach Gretchen and Kailey on how to say the right things. I don't know if anyone is coaching the boys, but it seems unfair. Why do Gretchen and Kailey have to learn how to be the right kind of victims?

And what about me? Beth can't speak for the dead girl. There's no advocate for me.

It seems backward. It seems pointless and hopeless. They've been trying to get more girls to come forward. But I can't imagine why anyone would. The system is set up to make you want to be quiet.

Outside, in the hallway, people flitter. I don't know if Caleb and Noah have been through the arraignment yet. I don't want to go in there. I hate looking at him. I hate remembering how much I used to want to look at him.

Gina Lynn came today. I don't know who she's here for. I don't know if she's here to defend him or if she's going to tell the truth. I see her cross the hall into the bathroom and I follow her. She interests me. They found me because she said something. They listened because Gina Lynn spoke.

She stands at the sink, her hands gripping the coldness of it, looking at herself in the mirror. Her makeup is perfect. Everything is perfect, except she doesn't feel perfect. She's still golden, but as I watch her, I see how her eyes fill up. How she bites her lip. Not hard enough to make a mark. Always balancing. What they see with what she feels.

"I can't do this," she says to no one but herself. "I can't."

She was so sure. She wasn't nice, but she was sure. She knew who she was, what she wanted. Did Caleb break her? Or was the girl I thought I knew, the one I assumed had all the answers, just as lost as the rest of us all along?

The door opens. Gina Lynn looks up, and Officer Thompson comes in.

"Oh. I can—" She turns to leave.

Gina Lynn looks at her, and the girl she was, the one who was better than us all, disappears. "Help me," she says. "I can't do this."

"Do what? How can I help?" Officer Thompson closes the door, but she doesn't move.

"He doesn't know. I came to you, but he doesn't know. He expects me to be here. He's called. I'm supposed to lie when the time comes. I don't know what to do. I'm so scared."

"He's under arrest. He can't hurt you while he's in jail," Officer Thompson says.

"How long will that last? Do you really think he'll lose?"

Thompson goes over to Gina Lynn, puts her arm around her. She's not a hugger and Gina Lynn isn't used to being weak. Neither of them knows what to do.

"Do you really think he'll hurt you?" she asks. It's a ridiculous question. He's being arraigned on murder and sexual assault charges. His record isn't great for not hurting girls. Gina Lynn doesn't bother to respond.

The two of them are reflected in the courthouse bathroom mirror, not much different on the outside. But Gina Lynn shines, even when she doesn't want to. Thompson just looks tired. They wait for something to reveal itself. Something to make sense. The mirror of a girls' bathroom is always being stared at by women who wish it could become a window.

"Let me see what I can do," Thompson says. "Just go in there. Do what you can. We'll figure it out as we go, but I promise, I *will* fix this."

"People always say that when they can't fix things, you know."

Thompson nods. "Yeah, I know."

"I'm sorry," Gina Lynn says. "I've made so many mistakes. I don't want to make this one, but I don't know how to change. It's important, though. I need it to be important."

"It is."

"I . . ." Gina Lynn pauses. A girl who always knew what to say. Knew how to make people listen. And now she's just another girl. Another broken girl with secrets, who can't figure out how to say the right thing. "My sister lives with my dad. Most of the time. She's ten. I'm not there. But maybe . . . I don't want my sister to be better off the farther away I go. I don't want her to need to be apart from me to be safe."

"I get it," Thompson says, "I do. Because I have a daughter. She just turned four, you know? She's only four years old and I don't know how to keep her safe, either. I don't know how to make sure she's okay. It's what I do, and I have no idea how to do it."

They continue looking at each other through the mirror, taking reflection as reality. Thompson sighs. "I need my daughter to grow up someplace different."

"You could move," Gina Lynn says.

"I don't mean scenery different. I need her to grow up and not be standing here in ten or fifteen years. When I said I promised, I wasn't just promising you. I was talking to her. To myself. To Ellie. I need my daughter to have a chance at growing up and surviving. Isn't that ridiculous? That it's not something I can promise?"

"I don't know," Gina Lynn says.

"Look, I'll figure it out, okay? I have to. There's too much counting on it."

"I can't stand the thought of him touching me." Gina Lynn still doesn't cry. She doesn't have her purse with her and she can't cry; her mascara will run. "I'm so afraid he'll get out. Every night, I want to be sick. I can't stop wondering. What happened that night? I let him in. I kissed him. He was in my bed. Was she . . . ?"

If I could speak now, I would say something. I spent a lot of time blending. Being quiet. Being good. But I want her to know that, despite all the cruel things she's done, despite her videos and forgetting my name and being with him when I wanted to, despite all that, I know she didn't know. I know she couldn't have known, because in a dark room at the other end of the hall, Kailey Howe sits. I didn't know about her, and I let him kiss me, too.

"He won't be able to touch you," Thompson says. "Not now.

They'll keep him locked up. At least until the trial and hopefully for much longer."

She turns on the water and washes her hands. Gina Lynn looks to her side. "What if he's found not guilty?"

"I told you. I can't let that happen."

"What about his family?"

"What about them?" Thompson asks.

Gina Lynn shakes her head. "I don't know. But someone had to know, right? Why not them? I can't explain it. I don't know, but there's something wrong with all of them."

Their moment is interrupted when Cassie comes in. Three very different women—all strangely connected to me. She looks at them, sees the way they're talking, and she turns to leave.

"Wait," Gina Lynn says.

"I don't want to intrude."

"Can you help me?"

Thompson shakes her head. "Not them. They don't care, as long as they get a story."

"For someone who let six months pass while a teenage girl waited in the ground, you seem pretty confident about deciding who cares," Cassie says. She puts her bag down and takes out a small wallet. A business card holder, I guess. She passes a small white card to Gina Lynn. "I'd be happy to talk to you. On or off the record."

"I need people to know," Gina Lynn says. "People have to know. I just can't be the one who tells them. I can't. I'm so sorry." I didn't like her, but I didn't know her well enough to hate her. I don't want her life to be full of my pain. I wish she wasn't a part of it, but we aren't that different. Not really. We both want to be noticed in the right ways. We both want to belong.

"I do care," Cassie says to Thompson. "You could have asked.

We all have our reasons for being here. Don't assume you know mine."

"I'm sorry," Thompson says. "You're right."

"Yeah, well, a hell of a lot of good sorry does. This town is full of sorry people. Ellie Frias is still dead, isn't she?"

It's funny the people who remember you. I suppose we all have our reasons for caring about what happens, for choosing which parts of the world count, which lives we let shape it. I don't know Cassie's reasons, but I know she's right. She's been here from the beginning. She cared.

She's also right about Hollow Oaks. Everyone is always sorry when it's too late. When it was too late for the factories and people's jobs. Too late for the families who had to leave their homes behind. And too late for all the girls who've been hurt in this town.

She's right. What good is sorry?

chapter forty-three

After the arraignment is over, Caleb and Noah stand to the side while Adrien and their father talk to the press. Guards stand by them, not just to make sure they don't run, but to protect them. From being harassed. Because they deserve to be protected, I guess.

A reporter calls Caleb's name. He smiles at her. Not a happy smile. Not a smirk. The smile of someone who's been stuck in an awkward situation that he doesn't understand. He charms them by being sorry. By pretending. He always loved pretending.

The words they're saying should not be in my vocabulary. Murder. Sexual assault. Premeditation. That's the worst one. Premeditation. Planning. Deliberate. Every conversation. Every afternoon. Every time he kissed me. Which ones were true? Which ones were deliberate? Which were part of the premeditation?

I watch it all and none of it truly surprises me. I was nobody. Gretchen and Kailey are nobodies, too. They aren't even remembered now that my body was found. They're just extra. Bonus points for the DA. And none of it matters as Wayne Breward jokes with the press.

Gina Lynn waits. She smiles at Caleb, waving to him when he looks at her. She lets Wayne Breward hug her after he's done giving his speech. The media takes her picture while she stands beside them. Some will use her to compare us. What motivation would Caleb Breward have to hurt me, when she was so pretty?

When my dad leaves the courtroom, when he enters the hall with his head down, the media focuses on him instead. They don't see how Adrien and Wayne Breward walk away, laughing about something unrelated, unconcerned about us. The media follows my father and he appeals to the humanity that might be left in the people at home.

"My daughter, Ellie Frias, was my best friend. Maybe that sounds odd, but it's true. When I came home every night, she was there and I knew she would always be there. I loved my daughter and suddenly she wasn't there." His lip shakes but he doesn't cry. "Someone took her away from me, and I don't know how or why. All I want is answers. I'm not looking for revenge, but someone should be brought to justice for this hole they left in my life." He pauses and looks at the sea of reporters. "To the people who have children, I beg you. Hug your kids tonight. Tell them you love them. Please just tell them you care. I loved my daughter. I wish I'd told her that more."

"Were Caleb and Ellie in a relationship?" someone asks. They're not interested in his regrets.

"I don't know," he says. "The police believe there was an existing relationship, yes, so I imagine there was."

"How do you not know?" another reporter asks.

My dad swallows. The DA is standing nearby, ready to intervene. Gomes watches from the side, but my father wants to speak for himself. For me. He looks at the guy who asked, the one who doesn't have children of his own yet questions my father's parenting. "I'm sorry. I loved my daughter. Unconditionally. But that doesn't mean I knew everything about her. And if I had, it doesn't mean I always would have agreed with her choices. I loved her. Whether she was or was not dating Caleb Breward is irrelevant. No matter what, she should be here today. Their relationship isn't a correlation to her being gone."

"Could it be a misunderstanding? Do you believe the charges against Caleb?"

My dad shakes his head. "You know what? I don't care. I don't give a damn who did it. I don't care about all the reasons or rationalizations people may have. She's gone. Tonight and tomorrow and every goddamn day from here on out, I have to go home to an empty house. They threw her in the fucking ground." He starts to cry and pushes through the crowd, needing air. Escape.

Gomes meets him outside and silently hands him a cup of coffee. They stand on the steps to the courthouse while the media below and behind them are kept apart by police officers. The questions are white noise, yelled to both men. Neither answers; each sips his coffee instead. My dad cries, breathing slowly, and tries to find small solace in the midst of it all.

"How is it at home?" Gomes asks. "Do you want to go somewhere else for a bit?"

He shakes his head. "No, I've got Fred there. My dog. Plus, it's . . . Jesus, I miss her so much."

"We should have the tests back soon. That'll give us something to work with." He drinks his coffee, crushing the cup in his hand. "I want to see them pay, Alex. I've never wanted something so badly." Gomes shouldn't tell him this. He knows it, but he never expected to handle a case like this. These things just don't happen here.

"I just want my daughter back."

They don't say good-bye. My dad finishes his coffee, too, and then they both walk away—Gomes inside to face the media there, my dad in the direction of the press congregating at the foot of the stairs. Gomes answers questions, but my dad walks past. Walks home.

It starts to rain while he walks.

chapter forty-four

Gina Lynn meets with Officer Thompson in a diner out of town a few days later. She waits, flipping the menu over, pretending she's here to eat. The waitress comes back a few times, but gives up when Gina Lynn can't decide. She just flips the plastic page over and back, looking for something on the list that isn't there. Looking for something to fulfill her.

"I'm sorry I'm late," Thompson says as she slides into the booth.

The waitress returns almost immediately.

"I'll have a coffee and . . . um . . ." Gina Lynn hands the menu over, and Thompson skims it. "Egg salad. On wheat."

"Anything for you?" the waitress asks, looking at Gina Lynn.

"Water. And vanilla ice cream."

Once the waitress leaves, Thompson takes out a notepad and Gina Lynn sinks deeper into the seat. The windows beside the booth are large—diner windows—and she can't be unnoticed enough. The irony. The girl who's always noticed wants to disappear, while the one who faded so easily just wants someone to remember.

"Is there anywhere you can go? Even for a little while?" Thompson asks.

"I don't know. I asked my dad if I could go there, but. . . . my mom . . . she says it's all ridiculous. She says I'm overreacting. She loves Caleb."

"You're her daughter."

Gina Lynn pulls a napkin from the dispenser, tearing it apart strip by strip. "There are things my mom cares about. And there are things she doesn't. Some people matter more to her."

"Ellie Frias wasn't one of them, I'm guessing?"

"She doesn't believe it. She says it's a misunderstanding. That Caleb wouldn't . . . How does someone misunderstand finding a body in a backyard?"

Thompson shakes her head. "People have a hard time believing what they don't want to believe. What makes them look inward."

"My mom says girls like that, like Ellie, you know? Well, she says these things happen to girls who put themselves in situations because they're desperate. But . . . I'm one of those girls, right?"

"What do you mean?" Thompson asks.

"I was with him. I had a relationship with him. I slept with him. We had sex the same night he probably killed her. Did they . . . ?" She pauses, trying to find the words. "When you found her body, was she . . . Had they . . . ?" She can't say it.

"We're still investigating, but yes, we do think . . ." Thompson can't say it, either.

Gina Lynn piles the strips of napkin into a snowbank. She blows on it, letting it drift away from her. "I'll never get that off of me. I feel dirty all the time. That night. I feel . . . he was there, you know? With her still on him."

The waitress comes back and gives them their food. Gina Lynn stirs her ice cream and they're both quiet. Thompson eats while the ice cream turns to liquid.

"We can certainly keep an eye on you, protect you, but it's bigger than that, isn't it?" Thompson asks.

Gina Lynn nods. "I have to get away from here. I have to get rid of this."

"Get rid of what?"

"I don't know. There's no word for it. *This.* All of it. Of this being who I am. Who I was." She looks out the window. "I have to get out. I'm going to California. To my dad's. My mom doesn't understand, but I need to get away from here."

"Have you talked to anyone?"

"Anyone who?"

"A professional?"

"You mean a therapist or whatever?" Gina Lynn asks.

"I suppose. Someone who can help you with the things you're dealing with."

"Why?" She gathers the napkin strips and dips them in her ice cream. It's noise. Activity to take her mind away from the thoughts. "What can I say? I feel guilty because I slept with a guy the same night he raped and murdered his ex-girlfriend? Poor me for feeling dirty? She was literally in the dirt. I don't have a right to that."

"You have a right to whatever you're feeling," Thompson says.

"I need to leave. I need so badly to go away."

"You know we need you, right?" Thompson asks. "Without anything tying Caleb to that house, without being able to prove there are hours missing in his story when Ellie went missing, there's a good chance we lose. You said you wanted to help.

You can focus on that. You can have that to pass the time, right?"

"How long is it going to last? How long do these things take?"

The waitress comes back, glaring at Gina Lynn as she removes the ice cream filled with napkin pieces.

Thompson sighs, stirring her coffee and filling it halfway with sugar. "Too long. I can't say for sure, but I promise, it will be far longer than you think you can handle."

"At least you're honest."

"We can assign someone to your house. Someone to stay with you as long as you need them with you. We'll figure out the best way for you to testify. Try to make it easy on you. I can get you a referral for someone to talk to. I'll be here. Whatever you need, Gina Lynn. But we need you, too. Ellie Frias needs you."

It isn't fair how she invokes my name. That I can't say what I need. I don't like being a symbol. I don't like being the dead girl who unites people in Hollow Oaks, or the dead girl who helps the police take apart a family that should've been taken apart a long time ago. I don't like any of these things, but most of all, I don't like that it's true. If Gina Lynn decides it's too much, that her life is more valuable than mine, this could end. If she decides to lie for him, Caleb and his family and their lawyer will bury it. Will bury me and Gretchen and Kailey Howe and the girl with the gum on her shoe and every single girl they've hurt. We will be as ubiquitous as the empty houses, and our ghosts will fade into this town.

"I don't know how to do this," Gina Lynn admits. "I want to help. I really do, but . . . I want to live, too, you know."

"I know," Thompson says. "I do."

Because that's how it goes. Gina Lynn's life for mine. Or mine for hers. Mine for Gretchen. Kailey for me. One girl always a sacrifice for another.

chapter forty-five

They hold the funeral without my body. While I'm still evidence. I guess that's what I always wanted. To be something. To leave behind a record that I existed.

I'm surprised how many people show up. I never talked to any of them. My dad and our priest are the only people here I actually knew. The whole church is full of strangers. Crying. Sharing their grief. Standing by a board my dad put together with pictures of me. Including the yearbook photo. These people I never met, never spoke to, stand there, hugging each other, talking about how much they miss me. People who never even said hello while I was alive.

If I'd been hit by a car, would this many people have come? Do they merely feel invested in the tragedy of it all?

It hurts that Kate's not here. I don't know if her parents told her. Maybe she can't get home from Ohio. My mom's not here, either, but that doesn't hurt. She probably wasn't invited. She probably doesn't even know I'm dead.

My dad sits up front, trying not to cry.

Right before Father O'Connell starts speaking, I see her. She sneaks in at the last second and sits in the back. The pink is obliterated now, but it's still there. The gum that can't be removed.

I would have thrown the shoes away.

Father O'Connell reads from the Bible. It's the same service we used to go to on Sunday, but every so often, he somehow links it to me. He works my name into the same script he reads every weekend.

I hate how cold it is. This isn't remembrance of me; it's functional closure. I feel selfish, wanting to be more important than Jesus in church, but right now, I do. I want to have an hour for me. He has an entire religion.

The hour is just another Mass, though. Another empty gathering of words that doesn't say anything about the space I held.

Until my father speaks.

"This is hard for me," he says. "It's hard to stand here and miss her. It's hard to say the things she was and all the things she wasn't or that I didn't know about. In the last few years, something happened with me and Ellie. I don't know what it was. We were close, but then, we weren't, and neither of us really tried to fix it."

He pauses and looks to where there should be a casket. To where there isn't a casket, because I'm being taken apart and studied so that my killers can be found guilty. So that I can serve as a testament to all the ways we die.

"I tried my best," my dad says. "I know I wasn't always what she needed. She should've had her mom. She didn't, though, and I had to deal with that. I tried to be both. I tried to make up for it. When her mom left, I was still young. I didn't know if I could be a father, never mind try to raise her by myself. We don't really get those choices, though, do we? She needed me, and I had to figure it out. For Ellie.

"Standing here is impossible," he continues. "It just doesn't make sense. I'll never know why. No matter how many tests they run, how many things they tell me, I'll never really know what she thought. I hate that I'll never know if she was scared. My daughter . . . Ellie . . . she died somewhere, alone. She was put in the ground carelessly, and I wasn't there for her. I can't live with that, but just like loving her, I don't have a choice."

He breaks down and Father O'Connell moves toward him, ready to lead the rest of the Mass, but my father puts his hand up.

"I want to be honest. It's really hard to believe in God today. I know I shouldn't say that. Not here, of all places. But I'm struggling to have faith in anything. Yet I hang on to the idea of Him because I need to. I need to know somebody is watching after Ellie. I tell myself someone will help me, will help all of us here today, will help us get through this. Someone will make sure those boys are punished. For Ellie and for everything else they've done."

He looks out at the full church, at all these people who weren't part of our lives but are now forever a part of his. Who now share his grief whether reluctantly or willingly. "I wish I could tell you that forgiveness is more important than revenge," he says. "But I can't say that. I don't believe it, but I don't want that kind of hate in me. So I'm here, hanging on to the idea that there's something out there with a plan. That God needed Ellie more than I did. That He had to have her beside Him. She was that kind of person, you know? She was the kind of person you just need. I only wish God hadn't needed her yet."

There's a lifetime of things I wish I could say. I wish I could tell him I loved him as much as he loved me. That I needed him the same way.

He sits down. Father O'Connell is quiet for a moment, letting it all sink in, letting everyone process before he begins a prayer.

While they pray, my father mouths pleas to God. I wish I could tell him God had nothing to do with this, but then I realize he needs to believe it. He needs to hope. To imagine me somewhere else. I want to tell him I'm here, but I would rather have him believe I'm happy.

As people filter out when it's over, the girl with the gum waits. She waits until it's only my father left.

"Excuse me?" she says.

My father looks at the people beyond the doors. People waiting to offer support, grief, kindness. Things we offer because what else can we do when someone's gone? But they're all things that sit on the edge of what we're really missing, and that hole still grows inside us.

"Were you a friend of Ellie's?" he asks. She's close to my age, so he assumes we could have been friends. I wonder what it would've taken to have made it true.

She shakes her head and pulls the sleeves of her hoodie down over her hands, clutching at the edges of the fabric while she tries to find the words. She's wearing a hoodie, but probably not because she's clueless about how funerals work; it's probably the only black thing she owns. When you're fourteen, you're not supposed to make a lot of funeral appearances.

"My name's Hannah." She says it as if she's unsure. As if, in the weeks or months that have passed since I watched her in the room with Caleb, she's forgotten everything she used to be.

Hannah is something related to the girl she was. This isn't Hannah, because Hannah was never with him. Hannah is still safe.

"Thanks for coming, Hannah."

I thought it was Rebecca or Rachel. Even our names are forgettable.

"I wanted to tell you. To tell someone . . ." She stops speaking, waiting for him to fill in the words. Waiting for someone else to hear what she can't say.

He sits at the end of the pew across from where she is. She hasn't moved out of hers yet. Not fully.

"What is it?" he asks.

"He hurt me," she says. "In the place they showed on TV."

"Caleb?"

My dad has become resigned to the way stories unfold now. Every day, something in the case changes, evolves, mutates until what was a guy who maybe accidentally killed his girlfriend turns into something nobody believes is possible. Except it's always possible. There's both a strange attraction to the awfulness of it and a weary acceptance of it being almost common now.

Hannah sits at the end of her pew and they look to each other across the aisle of the church. She should be with her parents, and he should be with his daughter. But when the world breaks you into pieces, sometimes you find what's left scattered among other people's broken parts.

"Yes."

"Do you want me to get one of the officers?" he asks.

She sighs and pulls her hood over her head so he can't see her cry. She's afraid of crying now. Afraid that it reminds her of how useless it really is.

"Hannah?"

She nods, and my dad goes outside to find Officer Thompson.

Thompson isn't supposed to be responsible for all the girls in this town. She's not supposed to carry the weight of everything that's happened, but she doesn't have a choice anymore. She sits in the pew next to Hannah, the two of them across from my dad, finding quiet in the church. She holds Hannah's hand, comforts her in silence, while mentally adding her to a growing list of girls who need help, who need a place, who need justice.

"Do you want to talk about it?" she asks.

Hannah shakes her head in response. The three of them sit—at my funeral—trying to put the world back together.

"I have an idea," Thompson says. "If I found somewhere we could go—all of you—could I count on you to try to come?"

"I don't know," Hannah admits. "I don't want people to look at me. To know what I am. To see all my flaws."

"You're beautiful. You're kind. And you're hurting. That's what you are. Those aren't flaws, Hannah," my father says. Officer Thompson smiles weakly at him.

Hannah thinks it over. "When would we meet?"

"I'm going to get your number. And I'll call you, okay? I promise. I'm going to fix this. All of it," Thompson says again. To another girl. To another person who needs the world fixed.

If I accomplished nothing in my life, I accomplished this by dying. I brought together the girls of Hollow Oaks, the ones who were hurt like me. I made them stronger by being part of something. Or at least I helped Officer Thompson do that.

They targeted us because they thought we were weak. But even the weakest girl has power inside her. She maybe just needs a little guidance to find it.

chapter forty-six

nside the church basement, a circle of girls sits. Officer Thompson coordinated it, but she hasn't figured out what it's supposed to be yet. Beth is here, too, although Gretchen won't look at her.

"It's nice having so many of you here," Officer Thompson says. *Nice* isn't the right word, but there's no word for what this is.

Gretchen, Kailey, Hannah, and four others surround her. There's a small girl and one blond girl I don't recognize. The other blonde I remember. She was the first. After I died and realized where I was. Three days later. They hadn't vacuumed the carpet yet, but she got the bed anyway.

The fourth girl doesn't look weak. I don't know how they picked her, and I don't know why it worked. She's tall and athletic, her dark hair a soft flow down her back. She seems confident, the only one here sitting proud.

The first blonde is Abby and the other is Julia. I like giving her a name. Julia. Not a timeline. Not the girl who came after me.

"I met Noah through my brother," Abby says. "They played on the same basketball team. He had a party one weekend and

Noah . . . He was cute. They were only sophomores, but I was thirteen."

"Did he bring you to that house?" Thompson asks.

Abby bites her nails. "No. He didn't bring me anywhere. It was in my room. He covered my screams with my teddy bear."

Julia doesn't say anything. She simply nods while the other girls talk.

The small girl, Kim, doesn't know the Brewards. "I just needed a place to go," she says. "My brother . . . he's in a program now. But it doesn't make it better not seeing him. I still do. I still lie awake at night and can hear him in the hallway. Every time the door creaks, I'm sure it'll happen again. Even though he's not really there. Even though they promised he couldn't hurt me anymore."

When they get to the other girl, the one who seems too strong to be here, she shrugs. "I tried to tell someone. Nobody believed me."

"We believe you," Thompson says. "I didn't get your name, though."

"Taylor. I filed a report. They told me they'd call me. That was a year ago. Nobody's calling."

Thompson sighs, frustrated that Taylor's here. Frustrated there are seven girls plus me plus however many didn't come. Didn't see the website. Didn't see it on the news. She's frustrated that it takes so long for anyone to listen.

"Do you remember the officer's name? I can—"

Taylor cuts her off. "I'm not from here. I came up here to meet him. I met him online and came to see him. I thought he was sweet. When I told them that after I reported it, they rolled their eyes. I knew they weren't calling. It was my fault that I came up here."

"I wish I was as brave as all of you," Hannah whispers. That's what it is. A whisper. She's almost missed as she speaks.

The other girls all look at one another, but no one has anything to say in response.

"I wish I could have come forward. Could have told someone. I didn't tell anyone. I didn't do anything. You're all so much stronger than me."

"It's not that," Gretchen says. "Everyone has their own—"

"No, you are," Hannah argues. "All of you. And Ellie. I admire Ellie so much."

Thompson looks to Beth, who shifts in her seat. "Why do you admire Ellie?" she asks.

"Because she got away. I wish I got away, too," Hannah replies. She pulls her sleeves up and there are red lines screaming from her pale skin. "I can't get free of it."

Beth reaches out and takes Hannah's hand. "You need someone else to help you, Hannah. We're not qualified—"

"I don't know who else to ask. Who to tell. You're all so much braver than I am. Than I was. I wish I was like Ellie. She wouldn't let them win. She's not ruined like I am."

"No," Julia says. "No, you're wrong. I know how you feel, but you're wrong. Ellie's dead. She's *dead*, Hannah."

"I know," Hannah says.

Thompson leans into the circle. "Hannah . . . Ellie wouldn't want this for you. No one wants this for you. I know she can't tell us what she thinks or what she would want, but I can tell you this. If I asked Ellie's dad, do you think he'd say he was glad? That Ellie was brave? That there was a victory there?"

Hannah shakes her head. "I don't know. I just can't get away from it."

"You can," Kailey says. "We all can."

"No one will ever love me now." Hannah starts to cry. Taylor joins her. Abby just nods.

"Do you all think that?" Thompson asks.

Gretchen shrugs. "What do you think?"

"Someone will love each and every one of you," Thompson argues. "I promise you they will. You're all young. I know it seems impossible today, but someone will love you and will care and will hurt for you in the way you're hurting now. They'll want to make that pain stop."

"Your parents love you," Beth says to Hannah.

"They don't care," she says.

Thompson shakes her head. "No. No, that's not true. I don't know what they've said or done to make you think they don't care. I don't even know if they're any good at being your parents. Maybe they are and maybe they're not. But I can absolutely tell you this. No matter what they're like, no matter what you think you've done, you deserve to be alive. Someone wants you to be alive."

I do, I think. I want every single one of these girls to be alive. Not because I don't want to share my space with them, but because I do. Because I want to come here, too, and feel like I belong somewhere. I want to remember living—in all the beautiful parts, but also in all the pain. I want them to live because I want Caleb and Noah to fail. They can't have everything. Not if these girls are still here.

"He still   " Hannah says. "Nothing's changed for him. Nothing will change. He'll probably be allowed to get away with it. Even his girlfriend . . ."

Officer Thompson shifts in her seat and I can see how she's

trying to decide what the right thing to do is here. Should she tell Hannah what she knows about Gina Lynn? Should she let Hannah be angry?

"Sometimes," Thompson says, "things aren't always what they seem. I think Gina Lynn might surprise you."

I watch Hannah remember. All the times she saw Gina Lynn at school. Saw them kissing. Saw the way Caleb smiled and passed her in the hall, knowing what he'd done. All the times she was forced to relive it. To remember.

Hannah connects Gina Lynn with everything Caleb is.

"No," Hannah says.

"Maybe—" Beth starts.

"No," Hannah says again, more forcefully this time. A word she's given up hope on, but not here. She needs the word to mean something here. "I can't find a way to understand. Not with her. He was her boyfriend."

"He was Ellie's boyfriend, too," Gretchen says.

"I understand how you're all feeling right now," Beth interrupts, "but neither Officer Thompson or I is a therapist. Perhaps we can—"

"Seriously. Shut the fuck up, Beth," Gretchen says.

"Well, this wasn't what I'd had in mind," Officer Thompson says, but nobody moves. They hate that they need to be here, but they do. They need to be a part of it and they wait. Wait for it to feel better because they're here. It doesn't happen, of course.

"We should keep doing this," Kailey says. "I want to. Even if . . . well, regardless of what happens with the trial."

"Me, too," a few of the girls reply.

"What about us?" Gretchen asks. "What happens to me and Kailey? What's going to happen if they're found guilty? Nobody's checked on our cases in a while."

"It's just that . . . with Ellie," Thompson explains, "it's a bigger case and they—"

"We aren't going to be remembered," Gretchen says. "If we're lucky, they'll tack on a couple of years because there were other charges. If we're lucky."

"We're not," Kailey whispers, and that shuts down the conversation for a while.

The guilt of being the reason they can't find safety, of preventing them from having their own stories heard, makes me get up. I go upstairs, into the church.

Father O'Connell left after letting the girls in. The early-evening light turns the mostly empty church into the innards of a kaleidoscope, the stories from the windows becoming shadow shows over the wood.

I think of Gina Lynn. How she looked at the diner. How she was in the bathroom at the courthouse, trying not to cry. She'll never know I forgive her.

I imagine tears and wish I could cry for Gina Lynn. I wish that I could express the hurt I feel for the last girl I would have imagined forgiving. I feel the ache of understanding as I watch the day die from the windows up ahead.

chapter forty-seven

The trial is a phenomenon. It's the biggest thing to happen in Hollow Oaks in maybe forever. They found DNA evidence to link both boys to my body. Something that might matter, although it's all just news and noise. Stories. Lawyers talking and experts saying things like they're writing an encyclopedia.

I should care more. Should go every day to hear the conversations, as late spring becomes summer and summer starts to die with the leaves. I should pay more attention, but I'm dead. Court isn't what I miss. This is all here for the living. Instead, I spend time at home, trying to make it real, and I let the rest of them worry about these things.

I heard, through the news, sitting with my dad each evening and following the story with him from our couch, that Wayne Breward was arrested and charged as well. It turns out Gina Lynn wasn't the only one who lied. But she was the only one who admitted it. Their father was charged with obstruction of justice. And then his DNA was also found on my body. Since he helped them cover me up. Now he can't buy Caleb and Noah a verdict. Now he'll sit in prison himself for a time—an accessory, they called him—and he'll finally know what it's like to lose.

I'd stopped going to the courthouse, but I go today because they're going to talk. Caleb and Noah are taking the stand today. I want to hear what they say. How they defend it. How Caleb pretends. I need to hear how he makes sense of it.

Nancy Breward sits on a bench outside the courtroom. With her husband in jail now, too, she's all that's left. Her face is thick with makeup, but she dabs at her eyes where she's been crying. The beige mask peels. It sheds onto her tissue, leaving the yellowed markings of the old and the newer blue-black. So many shades of bruising with their own timeline. At least they'll all have time to fade now. I wonder if she remembers the color of her own skin without them.

"Someone should be covering how three men can hurt so many women in one town," Cassie tells Gus while he unpacks his equipment. "Why isn't that the story?"

"People want this to be an anomaly," he tells her. "We can handle monsters. We can't handle our neighbors doing these things. We can't believe these are the same people we see at Christmas parties and basketball games."

"But they *are* their neighbors. Monsters, sure, but they live next door."

Gus shrugs. "You can't tell them that. That's not what they want to hear. They want to know that those three men are something else. That it can't happen again. That it won't happen again."

"That's ridiculous. Of course it's going to happen again. Especially if we ignore what's actually going on here," Cassie says.

"Yup. It is. It's absolutely absurd," Gus agrees. "But you know what Gwen said. Get the story people want. You can't change them."

The courtroom fills as the day starts. People, mostly press, stand in rows along the back walls. Heat circulates through the room. They all tug at their clothes, and it's only ten in the morning. By lunchtime, the lawyers will be desperate to get to their offices and take off their ties. Just to breathe in space.

It's fall now, but it's warm. An unexpected warm, the kind only late September brings. You expect it to be fall. It looks like autumn. But the weather doesn't care.

I look at Nancy Breward again. She reapplies her lies to her face. I think of the bruises she's hiding. It's easy to make her a victim. It's also easy to be angry at her for staying, for letting her sons grow up just like their father. I guess, though, when you love and hate the same person, your mind has trouble choosing.

I understand when they bring them out. Caleb sits beside Noah, both of them dressed like they're on a job interview. Noah smiles at the jury, but Caleb's somber. Sad. His mouth curls up awkwardly and he looks empty. He looks at the jury and then around the courtroom and I hate myself all over again. I hate myself because I hurt for him. I almost believe, for a moment, there was a mistake. That he's here by accident.

I remember loving him when he looks like this. I remember kissing him a year ago. I remember feeling happy when he held me.

I wonder how many eternities you have to live through before you can let go of that part of yourself. How many times would I need to die to be able to separate Caleb before and after?

They start with Noah. Maybe because he's older. Maybe because it's easier to convince them that there's no reason for him to be a part of this. I'm curious how he can defend himself. I didn't even know him.

Adrien brings him to the stand and they chat like old friends. Noah is the boy you bring home for dinner. He's charming and sweet and he laughs at the right times and looks serious when he should. I know what's true, but even I start to wonder how it's possible. How this could be true when he's so clearly a nice guy. Just a regular guy whose life has been turned upside down because of me.

Finally, Adrien says my name. "How did you and Ellie Frias meet?" he asks.

"She was Caleb's girlfriend."

"But how did you actually meet?"

Noah looks around the courtroom. His girlfriend—I think her name is Leah—sits with Nancy. She smiles at him and I want to be sick.

"I didn't really know her. I only met her once."

"Did anything stand out? That one time you met her?" Adrien asks.

"She was . . . she was something."

"Care to elaborate?"

"She was just wild. I don't know. You'd really need to ask Caleb. I barely knew her."

They chat about Noah's college goals, about his basketball games and records. They talk about everything that's not me, and I almost forget what this trial is even about. Adrien makes Noah human. A person who wouldn't do these kinds of things. But he did, and no one remembers.

Until the DA comes up for the cross-examination. The DA, whose name I still don't know, isn't interested in playing games. He doesn't care if anyone on the jury likes Noah.

"Tell us about Ellie Frias," he says.

"Like I said, I didn't really know her," Noah replies.

"But you had sex with her?" the DA asks. "The one time you met her? You knew her well enough to sleep with her, am I right?"

Noah smiles. "You don't have to know much to . . ." He pauses and realizes this isn't really the place. "I met her once. I was doing some work for my dad at one of the houses. He fixes houses, you know? The ones everyone keeps abandoning?"

"Yes, we're all aware of what your father does. Was your father working on the house where Ellie Frias was found?"

"He worked on a lot of houses. He may have worked on that one."

"And was that where you met her?"

Noah shrugs. "It was so long ago. I don't really remember where it was. It was one of the houses, but there were a lot."

"What happened that night?" the DA asks.

"What night?"

"The night you met Ellie Frias."

"I was doing some work, like I said. I was upstairs. Caleb was with her in the basement. Sometimes we'd go out to the houses . . . for other stuff. Since they were private."

"You'd go there to assault women?" the DA asks. Adrien cries objection, but Noah responds anyway.

"I don't need to assault them," Noah argues. "I have no problem finding girls who want me."

"Do you normally share girls with your brother?"

"Not really. No. But I guess Ellie was into that kind of stuff. Caleb said she begged him to ask me to come downstairs. That she wanted us to pass her around. I mean, I thought it was kind of nuts, but whatever. You know what they say about the quiet ones, right?" He actually laughs. On trial for murder and with multiple charges of rape, he laughs.

"And you just went along with it."

"Well, yeah. I mean, why not? I was single back then. It was a Saturday night and I was stuck fixing a sink. You tell me if you were sitting around working on plumbing and some girl showed up, asking you to do these kinds of things with her, you'd say no? Bullshit."

"Were you at the house on Pilot Lake, the one where Ellie's body was found? Did this happen during the weekend she went missing? Was that the Saturday night you're referring to?"

"I don't remember. I doubt it. That was in, what? November? I probably had a game. It would have been the beginning of the season."

The conversation becomes logistical. Circular. Boring. I'm just a body. Just a girl. Someone Noah's brother dated. Someone who asked for it. He reminds everyone and then they're done. The jury is left with that memory at the end of it all. That my body may have been found in that house, but I went there by choice. I asked for it. They didn't need to force me to do anything, because this is who I was. And somehow, I ended up dead, but it had nothing to do with these boys who were just being boys.

Nobody even cares that I'm dead. No one talks about how I cried. How they threw me into the dirt. They just make sure everyone knows that I was a slut. That I wanted it. They remind the jury repeatedly that this was the natural consequence of having a boyfriend, of going somewhere with the intention of having sex with him.

chapter forty-eight

After they're done with Noah, they break for lunch. I hate how normal that is—that there's a break in things. That everything goes on. I feel like the day should mean more. That there should be a bigger sense of it all, but it's a day and people need to eat.

My father goes with the DA to an office across the hall from the courtroom. As the DA closes the door, I see the anger in my dad's face.

"Why is my daughter the one on trial right now?" he asks. "She's dead. She doesn't get to tell her side of things. How can you let them sit there and say those things?"

"They have nothing. There's no way they can prove they didn't do it, so they're hoping the jury likes them enough to wish they didn't. They're trying to make them doubt that they could have."

"By making Ellie look like that? That's how they make those boys likable?"

The DA microwaves a meal wrapped in plastic. The green beans look radioactive. All three of us watch the meal spin inside the microwave, trying to process everything Noah said.

All the things Caleb has likely been coached to say. Trying to think like a juror who might pity the poor kids who will lose out on college and basketball championships and getting married and having kids because of the inconvenient dead girl.

"You said it yourself," the DA says. "Ellie's not here. She's an idea. Noah and Caleb are kids. Either of them could be their son. If they can make them likable, some of the jurors might prefer to let them move on with their lives. They don't want to ruin their lives if they don't have to."

"I feel like I'm going to be sick."

The microwave dings and the DA sits with the meal, poking at it with a spork. He invites my dad to sit, too, but he keeps pacing. My dad stands by the door, watching the DA eat his lunch.

"Ellie was my best friend," he says. "She was smart. Funny. People keep saying she was a little weird. Quiet. But she wasn't. She was perfect just the way she was." He breaks down, trying not to look at the DA and his nuclear lunch and the case file on the desk. "I love my daughter. Someone needs to be responsible for what happened to her."

"Someone will be," the DA says. "I promise."

There seems to be a lot of promising happening these days. People just toss promises around when they don't know what else to say, but hey, maybe one of them is true.

———

CALEB LOOKS LIKE he's in study hall or posing for his yearbook photo. He's clean-shaven and his hair is trimmed neatly. I wonder what the negotiations are for maintaining your appearance in prison.

He sits on the stand, running his hand through his hair and

looking uncomfortable. Not guilty—just like he somehow ended up here by mistake.

Adrien starts out like he did with Noah. Friendly. They're buddies, and this is just a chat.

"How did you and Ellie Frias meet?" he asks.

"She flirted with me in the halls."

"The prosecution has been trying to argue that you somehow targeted her. When you met this flirtatious girl in the hallway two years ago, would you say you were planning to target her?"

"No, nothing like that. I could barely pass my classes. I don't think I'm smart enough for all that. To see two years into the future."

They both laugh. The idea is funny. Absurd.

The word *target* echoes in my head, though. I didn't realize that was what they'd been saying during the days I wasn't here, but is it true? Did Caleb target me? Did he see me that first day, the new girl, quiet and alone, and wonder what it would take to hurt me? I don't know. I probably won't ever know.

I think that's what keeps me here sometimes. The not knowing. The wondering if there was anything I could have done. If I was just expected to end up like this.

"Let's talk about Ellie," Adrien continues. "You were in a relationship?"

"We were," Caleb replies. "She thought it was more serious than it was, though."

"I take it she didn't have a lot of boyfriends?"

"I don't know. I really doubt it. Guys didn't really pay much attention to her. She was odd. At first, I liked it. It was kind of cute how awkward she was all the time. But it got old fast. And I got bored. It wasn't a big deal, but she had a hard time getting over it."

"You have admitted that you slept with her later. Although you'd broken up."

Caleb shrugs. "Look, I'm a guy. I've been with a lot of girls. She wanted to, and I liked her enough to think she was still cute. It didn't mean anything. I was just bored."

"Would you say this was something Ellie did often?" Adrien asks.

"No. Definitely not." Caleb laughs. "I think that's why it was such a big deal for her. I should've known better. I should've, but she was so desperate. You should have heard the things she'd say. It was kind of sad, but kind of hot in a way, too. I don't know. She was obsessed with me."

"You've also admitted you weren't totally honest about your relationship with Ellie when she went missing. Why was that again?"

Caleb sighs. "It was a mistake, but . . . after Ellie and I broke up . . ." He pauses and looks at the jury. "I broke up with her because I'd started seeing someone else. Ellie and I weren't really working. I liked her and all, but we were in different places. Plus, we were moving really slow." He pauses again and looks back to Adrien. It's rehearsed, but it's so much like all the times we talked. The pretending. I wonder if I'll ever know where the truth was in the things Caleb said.

He looks embarrassed and shakes his head. "There were things I could get with my new girlfriend that I wasn't getting with Ellie. It was a pretty easy decision. These things . . . they matter, okay? You know what I mean. You're a guy. You were young once."

"I understand," Adrien says. "But Ellie wouldn't let it go, right?"

"No, she just kept showing up places, asking me to sleep with her. Things had been going well with my new girlfriend, but every time I'd turn around, Ellie would be there, telling me I'd change my mind. Telling me she was sorry she hadn't been ready. And I'm not gonna lie . . . I was flattered. I liked her, and yeah, it would have made a difference before we'd broken up. But I'm not the kind of guy who cheats on girls. I kept telling her no, because I don't cheat. That's so shady."

"In the end, though, you decided to sleep with her after all?" Adrien asks.

"One time. There was one time and it was a mistake. She was into it. She wanted me to get my brother involved. She wanted to do all kinds of things, and I felt bad about my girlfriend, but I don't know. It was stupid. It was a huge mistake and I felt really bad about it all, but I don't deserve to be here. I didn't want to tell anyone, because I knew it looked bad, but nothing happened. We were only having fun," Caleb says.

Adrien lets him sit quietly on the stand for a few minutes, softly sobbing. Everyone's eyes are on him. On the good boy who got mixed up with the wrong girl. I watch it and I'm impressed. Disgusted but impressed. Thankfully, the DA isn't.

"We understand Ellie was your girlfriend, and then you broke up. You continued the relationship on the side, though," the DA reiterates. "So tell us. What else happened that ended with her dead?"

The DA knows the media. He knows the jury. He makes sure they remember what he says. It doesn't matter when Adrien objects and the judge tells the jury to disregard it. You can't disregard what you've already heard.

"I didn't kill anyone," Caleb says. "It wasn't even that serious."

"Okay." The DA pauses and looks through some papers he's holding. "Can you explain how Ellie ended up in the backyard of the house on Pilot Lake?"

Caleb shrugs. "I was with my girlfriend that night."

"I didn't say what night," the DA points out. "I asked how she got there. How did she know about that house?"

"I don't know. I mean, we'd been there before. She and I had gone to a bunch of different houses. I just assumed—"

The DA cuts him off. "We have DNA evidence that links you to her body. People at school say the relationship was serious. Your alibi is flawed. Hours are missing from your story. There are a lot of questions here. Let's start with the big one." He pauses. The effect works. The jury is listening closely. "How did Ellie Frias end up dead?"

"Look," Caleb says, "I made a mistake."

"A mistake?"

"I didn't kill anyone. Yeah, fine, I was with Ellie that night. Yes, we were all at that house, but I didn't kill her."

The courtroom freezes. He realizes it as soon as he says it. He's not supposed to admit it. His alibi has been to swear he wasn't there. Not at the house. Not that night. Even if he wasn't with Gina Lynn, there was nothing putting him at the house that weekend. Everything is counting on him not being there.

Caleb smiles, nervous, and looks up. Out into the courtroom. He looks right at me and he has no idea. Not that he ever did.

"Are you saying you were with Ellie Frias the night she died?" the DA repeats.

"I lied. I lied, all right? I didn't tell anyone about being with her that night. I lied to my girlfriend. I told her I was going home for something. That I had to help my dad with something. But yeah, I was with her."

"Why did you lie?"

"I didn't want to ruin what I had with my girlfriend. I made a mistake. I'm not the kind of guy who cheats. I didn't want her to know."

"So now, to clarify, you definitely were there? That's the truth?" the DA asks.

Caleb nods. "Yeah, okay? Ellie and I met up that night because she wanted to have sex with me. And I . . . Gina Lynn—my girlfriend—she was being moody. I figured, why not? It was dumb, but hey, I'm a guy. Ellie was desperate for it and I was pissed at Gina Lynn. It didn't mean anything. I made a mistake. We went to the house. It was a good place to be alone. We went there so we could have sex. I felt like shit after, all right? I left. I rushed home, took a shower, and went back to Gina Lynn's. I didn't want her to find out."

"Okay, to clarify, you cheated on your girlfriend," the DA confirms, "then left your ex-girlfriend, the one you'd just had sex with, in an abandoned house, and then surprise, she just turned up dead. And at no point did you think to come forward with this information when she was missing for six months."

"I said it was a mistake," Caleb says, but his voice cracks. He messed up. His perfect story, his excuses, his lies. They'd been built around him by everyone else, and he couldn't even hold them together.

"In fact, you insisted you absolutely were not there that night. That the night you slept with Ellie was a different night and at a different house. And now you're saying that you were there, at that house, on that night?"

Adrien is furious, but it's too late.

"I knew how it looked, okay?" He turns to the jury again. "I'm just a kid. I'm a guy and I made some mistakes. I did something I'm not proud of. I hurt my girlfriend by cheating on her, and I'm going to have a lot of making up to do. But I'm supposed to go to college. I have all these plans and I was just . . . I couldn't help myself. I screwed up, okay? But I didn't kill anyone. I swear, I don't know what happened to Ellie. I wasn't even thinking about her after, because I knew how mad Gina Lynn would be if she found out. Maybe that makes me a bad person, but it doesn't make me a murderer."

"Do you even care what happened to her?" the DA asks.

"Sure, but it's not really my problem. It's not my job to go around looking for missing girls. To figure out what happens to them when they're stupid. She was there that night, too, you know. She showed up and I don't know where she went, but it wasn't my job to go looking for her. That's on them," Caleb says, and he points to Officers Thompson and Malik, along with Detective Gomes.

I can't stay. I can't sit here and listen to the case they make against me. There's no proof Caleb didn't kill me, so they turn it on me. They make it my fault. They remind everyone I was pathetic and weak.

I don't get to speak for myself. I have no voice here, and I can't fight back. The frustration tears away what's left of me and I leave the courtroom because I would rather not know what else they think. I don't want to be humiliated. I'm already dead; I'd like to spend the rest of forever not feeling this ashamed.

I decide I'm not going back. Not until they make a decision. I can't listen to any more of it. Can't listen to them try to make it okay. I can't have this be the way I'm remembered. I'm angry, but it's useless.

I run when I get outside, although it's only air moving faster. Part of what they said was true, and that's hard to accept. I stood in my room that night thinking about him. I got dressed up and I planned it. I put on makeup and purple silk and I told myself I would come home different after. I went there willingly.

That part of the story runs alongside me, another ghost. All my wants, all my stupid needs, they stay with me and I can't shake them no matter how fast I run or how far I get.

chapter forty-nine

t takes forever for them to deliberate. I don't go back, just like I promised myself. I spend my days at home. Watching Fred. Watching my dad. Pretending I'm a junior. Pretending there's a reason I'm still here.

One night, Gomes comes to our door. The porch light burned out, but it's another dead light, and my dad gave up on saving them.

"Am I interrupting?" he asks my dad.

"No, I'm not . . . No. Do you want to come in?"

Gomes shakes his head. It's grown cold. That's how long it all took. The leaves are nothing but shattered, dry bodies strewn along the road now. It's barely after five and it's dark. My dad and Detective Gomes stand in the darkness and neither says anything. It's winter now. I've been gone more than a year.

"I just—" Gomes starts and then he looks up at the Christmas lights. "Do you want some help with those?"

My dad shakes his head. "I don't think my dog cares if we have a tree."

"Yeah," Gomes says.

"So, did you need something?" my dad asks.

"I just wanted to let you know they're saying they have an answer. That they're going to decide tomorrow. In case you want to be ready."

"Okay."

"Do you need anything else, Alex?"

"Not anymore. Have a good night," my dad says, and he shuts the door.

Gomes stands on the porch for a moment, wishing he had something else to say, and then he turns and leaves. Winter broke the trees and now it's breaking all the people, too.

In the morning, I walk. My dad takes the car in, but I don't feel the cold anymore and I like seeing the things I didn't see when I was alive. All the things I didn't notice. It's another gray day and the grass is coated with frost as I head to the courthouse.

I want to hear what they decide. I want to know what kind of person they think I was.

When I get there, the media is gathering. They review what they've learned. All the things that have been said. I try not to listen. I don't want to know. Don't want to relive all my own failings as people look for reasons to prove I should be dead.

I stop when I see Cassie, though. She's been here since the beginning, and she wants to be here when—and if—it ends. I know that, even if the jury decides today like they're supposed to, there still has to be a sentencing. If anyone remembers to bother, they'll still have Gretchen's and Kailey's cases, too. Very few of them will stay for that part of it, but Cassie will. She'll be here until there's nothing left.

Not that it matters. It's all show. None of it changes anything.

"Do you have it?" Cassie asks Gus. She's setting up for a recap and she wants the courthouse behind her. I never noticed it before, but she wears a wedding band. It's odd. She's this whole person beyond a reporter, beyond the one who came here when very few people were asking. I don't know if it's new. Maybe she got married during all this. I try to imagine her wedding. Try to imagine how you separate these parts of yourself.

"We're expecting the jury to finish deliberations anytime now," she says once Gus confirms they're ready. "Noah and Caleb Breward have been charged with murder and sexual assault. It's been a long and complex trial . . ."

I walk away, leaving her to her story. To why she's here. She cares more than the rest of them, but at the end of it all, Gus is right. She can only tell the story people want to hear.

Each of the reporters is saying the same things. I walk among the crowd of them. Some are here for television, some for the press, but they're all preparing their statements. Waiting for an answer. Then, regardless of the outcome, they'll move on. It doesn't change for them if Caleb gets to go free or if he spends his life in jail.

At the top of the steps to the courthouse, one of the court employees holds the door open. He doesn't even need to speak before one, and then two, and then the rest of the reporters rush up the stairs. The crowded lawn and lot are grass and pavement within minutes, the last of the media running inside.

It's crowded inside again. Everyone's tired. The judge's already graying hair has turned nearly white since the case started. There are things people in these jobs expect to see during their careers, and then there are cases like this one.

When everyone settles, the judge looks at Caleb and Noah. At my father. At the jury. He turns to them.

"Have you reached a verdict?" he asks.

"We have, Your Honor." The jury is mostly old. Normal

people. People who maybe understand. It's half women. "For the charges of first degree murder, we find the defendants guilty."

The word echoes. My ex-boyfriend and his brother are guilty. They killed me and these twelve people confirm it.

Noah smirks as they say it and flips them off. Nancy breaks down, forgetting her makeup, burying her face in her hands. Leah's not here today; I don't know if she gave up on Noah after hearing the things he said or if she just decided not to be here. Gina Lynn left for California after she told them what she knew. I don't think she'll ever be back.

I turn to look at Caleb. I need to see him. I need to know he's surprised. Scared. I need to feel vindicated.

Nothing's changed in him, though. He's not smiling, but he's still sitting, that same confidence he always wore wrapping him up in all the things he knows he is.

"She didn't even matter," he says to Adrien. "All this for a nobody."

I don't know what I imagined. I don't know if I believed he'd cry. If I thought something would happen and he'd admit he loved me and he'd screwed up and something in him was wrong. Whatever I thought, I still hung on to that. I believed all the words he said. Even after all of it, inside of me were those words. All those beautifuls. All the things I will never hear anyone else say. The things nobody but Caleb will ever call me.

And I was a nobody to him.

"We can appeal," Adrien says. "And there's a chance the sentencing can be reduced. Don't let her ruin your life."

"And the other charges?" the judge asks, as the courtroom settles. Reminding them that there's more. That I'm dead, but that wasn't the end of the hurt they caused.

"For the charges of rape, we find the defendants not guilty."

Not guilty.

It's chaos in the room, but it's empty sounds. It's hollow.

The trial is over. I see people moving around. Caleb and Noah are taken somewhere. Nancy is led out into the hall. My dad stands, his hands in his pockets, with the DA and the cops. Motion fills the space. Time passes, but it's a haze. The world keeps moving around me but I'm swallowed up by the vacuum of those two words.

Not.

Guilty.

Caleb and Noah will serve time in prison for my death. Probably the better part of their lives. They'll always be remembered for it. The media has plastered their faces across the Internet, across everyone's television sets, and Sunday morning breakfast tables on the front page of the newspaper.

They didn't win. I should be happy. I'm hurt by what Caleb said, but I should be happy. They'll pay. They're guilty. My father has closure. They won't walk past him on the street. He won't see Wayne Breward's face on an ad somewhere or on campaign posters for the next election. He'll be allowed to heal. I'll be avenged.

Except . . .

The words again.

Not guilty.

Not.

Not.

Not.

Not.

It's a drumbeat. A metronome of denial. Twelve people heard it all. Or at least enough. They heard enough not to trust them. Not to believe their stories, but they still couldn't be convinced that it wasn't my fault.

"Just drop my case," Gretchen says to Officer Thompson as the crowd disperses. "It's a waste of time."

"Not necessarily," she argues. "Ellie wasn't here to give her side. She—"

"She's dead—and they still don't believe her. Drop my case. I don't know what Kailey's going to do, although I doubt she'll continue, either. If they have a body, and they have DNA, and they have proof, but it's still impossible to prove to a jury that Ellie didn't go there hoping for that to happen, just let it go. Please."

Thompson nods. She has nothing else to offer. "I want you all to still meet. It's something, isn't it?"

"Yeah. Sure. It's something," Gretchen says.

chapter fifty

A fter it's all over, around Christmas, Kate comes to see my
dad. I don't know where she's been or how much she's
heard about the trial, but she shows up one night with a
tin of cookies her mom made. They didn't want to acknowledge
me. To even use my name. But they can't not send cookies.

Kate stands on the porch, looking at the broken screens. The
Christmas lights hang down by her forehead, blown free during a recent storm. Her hair is shorter now. A pixie cut, I guess
it's called. She dyed it pink. A color that doesn't work with
how dark her eyes have gotten. A color I always hated, but she
wouldn't know that.

"I'm Kate," she says when my dad opens the door. "I live
behind you. I knew Ellie. I brought you cookies."

"Come in." He holds the door open and lets her cross inside.

"My parents didn't want me to know," she tells him while he
pours her a glass of lemonade in the kitchen. The glass is an old
one with a giraffe on it; he bought it for me at the zoo once when
I was little. "About the trial. About what was happening. They still
don't want me to mention it."

"I wondered why you didn't get involved," he says.

Kate takes the lemonade but doesn't drink it. Instead, she traces patterns on the glass in the little water droplets as they form. Erasing them before they exist.

"I don't know if I could've helped anyway. There's not much I know that wasn't in the news. Ellie liked Caleb. She was scared about starting school. She didn't know many people. It's all pretty much true."

"He said she begged him," my dad says. "During the trial. He said that she was desperate to hang on to him." He wants her to deny it. He wants to hold on to the girl I was.

Kate shrugs. "She was too nice. Too trusting. I remember when we first met . . . that summer when I took her to the mall. For the clothes and stuff?" My dad nods. "She was just . . . she wanted so badly to be part of something. There was this group of kids. They were standing below us at the mall. We were in the food court and we could see them. The guys kept trying to grab the girls and the girls were flirting with them, playing hard to get. I remember Ellie said to me, 'It must be nice to be able to say no.' I had no idea what she meant by that. But I feel so bad I didn't."

"Was she happy?" my dad asks.

"She really liked him. By the time she disappeared, I was gone. I don't know how it was for her then. But that summer? Yeah, she was happy. She was sure he felt the same way."

My dad nods and paces the kitchen. He tidies the bills on the counter and starts the dishwasher. Anything to keep himself from thinking.

Kate's parents' kitchen is bright. Sunny. Ours is cold. It feels like the kind of place that's dirty no matter how much you clean it. The table is old. Jagged holes and scars cover the top of it. My dad tried to add stain to make them less obvious, but now they're just gaping sores. None of our appliances match.

"I wanted to help," Kate says. "I did. I don't know what I could have said, but I did want to help. I talked to one of those cops a few times on the phone. It's just . . . my parents . . . they didn't want me involved. They found me things to do this summer after school got out. They tried to keep me out of it."

"They came by once. After they found it. Found *her*. Your mom made me banana bread."

Kate starts to cry. "I'm really sorry, Mr. Frias. I did like her. I liked Ellie a lot. I wish I knew more. More about what happened. More about who she was. I wish I could go back, could figure out what I could've said. I wish I'd tried harder. Stayed in touch. I wish there had been something I could have done. I wish I could've saved her."

"I know," my dad says.

"Sometimes I think it's my fault."

"Why's that?" My dad sits and waits. Kate sips the lemonade, taking in the way our kitchen doesn't shine; she sees how everything here feels old, even if it isn't.

"Ellie and I weren't close. But we should have been. When she came to me, I had a lot going on and I thought it was fun. She was just a kid. She wanted help with clothes. Maybe with high school. I had so much happening in my own head and it was a distraction. But I never . . . I should have been her friend."

She drinks the whole glass of lemonade and pushes it across the table to my father. He wraps his hands around it and spins it back and forth.

"Caleb and Noah Breward are assholes," Kate continues. "I never liked Noah when I was in school with him, and I figured

Caleb couldn't have been much better. But even then, she liked him. I warned her what they were like, but I didn't know. I only knew they were jerks. They were rude. They thought they were better than everyone. I told her what they were like, but I didn't even know what they were like."

"I know the Brewards," my dad says. "Everyone does."

Kate nods. "When I was in high school, Noah and his friends were horrible to me. They made up rumors. Nothing that mattered, but it made high school pretty miserable. And on top of it, I missed a lot of school. I hated them. But I didn't know. And Ellie . . . she liked Caleb so much. She insisted she saw something in him and the way she talked about him, I believed her. I knew what it was like to have someone make you feel like you didn't deserve to be happy, but he did the opposite for her. I tried, but I didn't want to argue. I didn't tell her no, because I thought she was right. I should've said no."

My dad sighs. "She needed someone. She was lonely. I don't think I understood how lonely she was, but it was hard. Without her mom. I loved her more than I ever thought possible, but I was only one person. I was just her dad."

"I should have been a better friend," Kate says. "I should have been better. The whole time, I was just wrapped up in me."

"Yeah, well, we all kind of are, aren't we?"

They consider that over the streaks of condensation from the lemonade that now tie them together across the table. Kate feels guilty, but I didn't know her, either. I was just as wrapped up in myself. I wish they could know. I wish I could tell them. I wish I could tell them it's not their fault. That they did everything they could have done.

"Your parents said you were sick," my dad says. "Are you doing okay now?"

He gets up and puts the glass in the sink, wiping the table dry with his sleeve when he sits down.

Kate leans back in her chair and looks outside. From the window, under the shade that never goes all the way up, her house peeks over the rock wall. It's at the bottom of a hill, but the shingles are visible when you're sitting at the table.

"They worry too much," she says. "I was sick. Well, I guess I'm still sick, but I function. I have seizures. They're random. They don't seem to be triggered by anything specific, and they worry that I'll have one and I won't be close by and nobody will know what to do. It took so long to convince them to let me leave, to let me go away for school. By the time I did, it was too late. I had to take a year off."

"Ellie said you were taking a year to figure things out," my dad says.

Kate smiles. "It sounded a lot better to say I was discovering myself. Reinventing myself. That's what I told Ellie. Because I didn't want to say that sometimes I freak out and my parents were afraid I'd scare people. That I'd been in and out of hospitals and nobody could find a reason for it. That we never knew if I'd get better or worse. We were so afraid of the possibilities."

"How have you been? Especially after everything that's happened?"

"I'm good. My parents were so careful. They wanted me to start over. I knew I had to be somewhere else, and they made sure nothing from this town came with me." She pauses, debating. She wants to say she's sorry. To apologize again for running away. For taking care of her and leaving me here, but she doesn't need to, and my dad shakes his head. He knows. It's over now anyway.

"It's better," Kate says. "Ohio is nothing special, but it's not here. This town does something to people."

"You're telling me."

They sit at the table, silently remembering me, trying to find anything to say. They both have a missing piece now, but the pieces look different. The holes aren't the same. The edges of what I was to Kate don't line up with where the missing part is for my dad. They try to connect anyway. To find solace in knowing someone else gets it. But it's not the right fit for what's missing.

Fred starts to bark from outside. It's late and he needs a walk. My dad stands up to get the leash.

"Thanks for coming by, Kate. I think Ellie would've been glad you came."

She gets up and hugs him. It's awkward and uncomfortable like it should be, but it also makes me long to be a part of it. To be there between them as he wraps his arms around her. Trying to remember what it feels like to hold a daughter in his arms.

chapter fifty-one

What are the things that make a girl? Are they the things she does? The people she knows? The clothes she wears?

Kate goes back to Ohio after Christmas. Gina Lynn stays in California. And Cassie heads back to wherever she came from after the sentencing, when Caleb and Noah were told they'll likely never see the outside again.

Detective Gomes retires. He suggests Thompson get his position. They give it to a man from another town instead.

Hollow Oaks tries to go back to normal. As normal as it can be. There's more sadness here now, though. Sometimes people see me in the places that are left behind. They remember the house where I died. The bank decided to have it demolished, but it was only one house. And without the Brewards, more and more houses stay abandoned. They don't get cleaned up, and the whole town starts to look like a memory. It's the image from a faded postcard you find in a general store in another broken town on your way to somewhere living.

My dad has been trying to move on. He goes to meetings for parents like him. Parents who've lost someone. Nobody understands exactly what he's been through, understands his kind of loss, but he goes because it's the closest thing he has to sympathy.

There's a woman there. Tonight, she's coming over for dinner. He cleaned all afternoon and then I watched him sitting on the couch, waiting, trying to get Fred to stay on the floor.

She's pretty. When she stands on the porch waiting for him, her hair doesn't shine in two colors. It does sparkle, though. It looks a little like sunlight. I like that; my dad needs some light in his life again.

He lets her in, and I leave them alone for tonight. I most likely have eternity to watch out for him, so I leave him his moment. An opportunity. All the things that were put on hold for him while I was alive.

I don't begrudge him this. He loved me. I loved him, too, and I want there to be a place in the world where that love still springs. We all deserve to know that we've carved a place out, a place that is noticeably empty after us, but there's plenty of space for us each to have that. Plenty of space for me and for the woman with the shiny hair.

I head to the church basement, where the group of girls waits. Kailey stopped coming right after the trial. She couldn't handle it. She'd been the one who said she wanted the group to continue, no matter what, but after she heard, after she spent a few days under the weight of *not guilty*, she realized she couldn't do it anymore. Couldn't sit there and face the reminder that the group was for girls who weren't heard. That she'd been raped by someone twelve strangers declared not guilty. While they were punished for my dying, Kailey never got that kind of justice. She left, but new girls started coming.

Officer Thompson talks quietly. There are sixteen girls now.

One or two knew Caleb or Noah, but most are like Kim. I don't know what happened to some of the girls I saw in that room, but now there are girls who have nothing to do with me here. More girls who found this place. Not because of me, but because of their own stories. Because Caleb and Noah Breward can spend the rest of their lives in prison, but there will still be a need for places like this. A place where someone might finally listen.

One night, after the trial, I followed Officer Thompson home. I watched her with her daughter. Malik was there, making them waffles for dinner, their relationship evolving into something else. Something new because of me, and I think I like that. I saw Thompson lying on the floor, listening to Rana tell her stories with her stuffed animals.

I wonder how she keeps that safe. How she can survive, knowing that her daughter is at home with her stuffed animals while sixteen girls—plus Kailey and me and however many Thompson hasn't heard from—wait every week in a church basement. I don't know how she does it, but she does, because it's her job. Because she has to. Because *someone* has to.

The girls talk about what happened, what they hope for next. What they wish for.

You know what I wish? I wish my dad called my mom after they found me and that she flew back and they fell in love again. I wish she cried over my grave and that she regretted every minute we could've had but didn't.

That didn't happen. She never returned his call when he left a message. Had to say on voice mail that their daughter was dead. Maybe she doesn't even know. Maybe the message somehow missed her and the next card will come. When I should've been seventeen, my dad will go to get the mail and he'll see that envelope. Always the wrong date. He'll start to heal, but then he'll open the mailbox and the card will be there, mixed among the bills he still can't pay, and he'll have to relive it every year until my mom finally forgets. Until she realizes I'm gone.

The things we wish for don't happen. This is how things really go. That's who my mom is.

I listen to the girls talk, and I don't take my dad's moment tonight. Because maybe if I don't, next year when he gets that card, the woman with sunlight in her hair will be inside making coffee. Maybe he'll tuck the card away and head back into the kitchen, tossing it aside with the rest of the mail and then he'll wrap his arms around her. Maybe he'll sob against her back, but it will be harder for him to reach all the way around her because her stomach is just a bit bigger than it was last month. Maybe they'll live and there will be life and things will keep happening. Maybe they'll have a girl.

Maybe in this ghost town, with all these empty houses, there's a chance for that.

So while these girls sit and try to heal and talk about what they wish for, I join them, sitting here with my own ghosts. I sit with all my memories and all the things I didn't say and won't ever get to say. I unload my own wishes and regrets, even though nobody hears me.

A room full of girls holding on to each other's hopes and stories. They're not the same story, but that's okay. Because all the things that make us different are also what we need to believe in when they try to break us.

You can break a girl. You can destroy several parts of her, but a girl is made up of so many things.

There aren't nursery rhymes this complicated. When you ask what makes a girl, they tell you it's sugar and spice and everything nice, but it's not. It's regret and wishing and summer kisses and falling in love and being hurt and heart-break and fear and fishing with your father and wearing the wrong clothes and getting drunk because you feel so bad you want to die. It's hoping and the memory of sunlight and how you can't stop lightbulbs from burning out. It's all the big things and the little things in between. It's living and it's dying.

A girl is everything I was and wasn't and all the things I thought I'd be and all the things I didn't know I was until later. It's all the things that died when Caleb put me in the dirt that night.

These are all the things that make a girl—and it starts with just that one piece to put her back together again.

chapter fifty-two

One time, one evening similar to this one, although warmer, my dad found a tent in our attic. He'd been looking for something of his from school—I don't remember what it was—but he'd found an old tent instead. From before I was born. He said he and my mom had loved camping, especially on warm nights.

We brought it outside and sat in front of it, under the stars. The store's lights spilled across the sky throughout the town, but there were some breaks in it. Breaks that came from the trees by the lake on one end. The darkness overhead was milky, but there were strips of full dark inside it, so I could see a few stars. Never enough for a constellation, but pieces of a story. Of a person.

"Your mom used to love the stars," my dad said as I looked for them.

"I wish I remembered her."

"She was the kind of girl you meet only once in your life." He looked at me. "Unless you're lucky enough to meet her daughter."

"Did you love her?" I asked.

"I did. I loved her too much to stop her when she didn't want me to love her anymore."

"I wonder if anyone will ever love me."

"I love you, Ellie," he said.

I laughed. "Ew. Not like a dad. I mean, I wonder if anyone will ever want to camp with me under the stars or will remember the things I liked even after I'm gone."

"Of course someone will, Ellie. You're too special to be forgotten."

"I hope so," I told him.

A streak came across the dark patch of sky and I wished on it. Shooting stars were supposed to be good luck.

I wished on that star that someone would remember me someday. That someone would love me enough to make sure I wasn't forgotten.

I don't know how long I'll be here. I don't know what comes next. I go back and forth through the places I loved. Spend time with my father. With Fred. I treasure the moments, even if they don't know I'm a part of them.

Time changes when you're dead, but I'm more aware of it now. Since I don't know for sure how much I have left, I try to pay attention to the things I want to remember. Just in case.

I could be angry. I am, sometimes, but then I remember.

I don't know a lot. I was fifteen when I died, and it's hard to know much when you're fifteen. But when I sit in my living room and watch Fred sleeping, when I watch my dad as he laughs at something on TV—a laugh that he's had on pause for more than a year now—I can't be angry. Because in those moments, this is what I do know.

I know that after everything that happened, after all that I lost . . .

I know that I was lucky. I know that I was loved.

I know that I *was*.

Author's Note

THE TRUTH IS I started writing this book because I was angry. I was angry at seeing the same kinds of stories in the news. I was also angry for personal reasons, for the girl I was when I was fourteen and seventeen. Maybe it's that girl—that part of me—that makes me notice these stories more. This anger drove the creation of the story, but as I began to see the world through Ellie, I discovered something else.

Toward the end of the book, Ellie sits in a room with girls who've survived being sexually assaulted. She could be angry. She could be mad that these girls were given the one thing she was denied—life. They were granted a chance to continue. But Ellie isn't angry. Instead, she chooses to focus on what's beautiful in the world.

Some days, especially after surviving assault, it's really hard to see what's beautiful. Some days, it feels like there's nothing in front of you but creeping darkness, but it's not true. Because at the end of darkness, there's always light. Maybe it's filtered. Maybe it's dimmed because of the darkness that led you to it, but the light still exists.

Anger is easy, but hope can feel impossible. I don't want that to be the case. I started writing this book angry, but I ended it with hope. Ellie realizes, too late unfortunately, that she mattered. She realizes she was real and that she affected people around her. She changed the world, even if the ripples were hard to see. I ended the book hoping that those ripples extended past the fictional characters on the page. I hoped that Ellie's story would reach girls like Ellie, girls like the rest of the survivors in the book, girls like me when I was younger.

I hope you know that you matter. Your life matters. Every day, you count and you change the world by existing. You affect the people and the places around you with the ripples you send out into the universe. And when it's hard to hold on to hope, when the light feels like it can't keep burning, there's a world of people behind you whom you've affected. They're there and they have your back, even if you can't see them.

I promise you—we're behind you. I promise there's light at the end.

Acknowledgments

OBVIOUSLY, I NEED to start by thanking my agent, Mandy Hubbard, because without her, there'd be no book. There was a late night in February 2016 when I happened across her Twitter and she was tweeting about a manuscript she was reading. Since she had only just requested mine days earlier, I was sure it couldn't be mine she was talking about. A few hours later, after she announced to the world how heartbroken and wrecked she was, she e-mailed me. So thank you to Mandy for being wrecked! And I'm sorry for ruining your night, but I hope it was worth it.

Thanks also to Lindsay Mealing and Linda Epstein at Emerald City Literary Agency (ECLA) and Taryn Fagerness in foreign rights for supporting the story—and me—right alongside Mandy.

Of course, there's my editor, Anna Roberto, who loved Ellie and felt her pain from the beginning. Thank you for helping me make those adjustments to strengthen her story and thank you for believing in this book. (And, also, you are so right—Angela Chase for life!)

To everyone else at Feiwel and Friends, thank you for giving

Ellie a voice. She—and I—appreciate it more than I could ever put into words.

To my critique partner and friend Erin Callahan, for being the person I never knew I was missing until I met you. I wish we'd met years ago. Thank you for writing such great stuff that I walk away from our exchanges inspired to work harder on my own writing (and admittedly, absurdly jealous of your talent). Also, thank you for giving me last-minute advice and input on court procedures.

To my friend and fellow author Bree Barton for being there. I'm not sure if you can thank someone for simply existing, but if so, thank you. It's been a roller coaster, that's for sure, but I can't wait to go through the next stages of the journey with you.

To all the people I met through debut groups and social media and Camp ECLA. There are too many to name individually, but it was so nice to finally feel like there was a place I belonged. Thanks as well for the emotional support, including being there on Facebook and Twitter during that flight to Seattle that WOULD. NOT. END.

On a personal level, thank you to Jamison for always being supportive and listening to every little worry while still pretending to be interested. I owe you many dinners that don't involve talking about books to make up for all the ones that have!

To Karen, because even though we don't talk much anymore, for years you told me that you were positive there would be a book with my name on it in a store somewhere. Thanks for having faith when I didn't.

To my parents, friends, family, in-laws, and English teachers in high school and college for not thinking something was wrong with me when I'd walk out of a room to go read somewhere. Thanks especially to my dad, for never missing a night of reading when I was a kid and for instilling the love of books and stories in me.

To my kitties, including the ones I've lost, because I don't care if people say it's silly to recognize your pets. I love you and you're my favorites. And finally, to my husband . . .

When I was writing this section and I asked for your feedback, I hadn't written your part yet. You told me I should thank you for nothing, because it would be funny, but I can't. Without you, without you pushing me to fight for what I loved, without all the long nights and tears and "I'm done with this" conversations, there would be no acknowledgments page, because there'd be no book. My life would be so different in so many ways without you and there's simply no paragraph in the world that can capture everything. Thank you for encouraging me, for knowing when to be supportive and when to challenge me, and for making me laugh when it was all too much. I love you. You deserve five thousand and one candles in the wind.

Resources

RAINN: Rape, Abuse & Incest National Network
https://www.rainn.org

National Sexual Assault Hotline
1-800-656-HOPE or https://hotline.rainn.org

National Alliance to End Sexual Violence
http://endsexualviolence.org/forsurvivors

National Sexual Violence Resource Center (NSVRC)
1-877-739-3895 or http://www.nsvrc.org

Victim Rights Law Center
http://www.victimrights.org

End Rape on Campus (EROC)
http://endrapeoncampus.org

It's on Us
http://www.itsonus.org

SVYALit Project (Teen Librarian Toolbox)
http://www.teenlibrariantoolbox.com/2014/02/svyalit
-project-index

I STOP SOMEWHERE

DISCUSSION GUIDE

1. Throughout the novel, Ellie talks about what makes a girl. At one point, she references a nursery rhyme that says girls are made of "sugar and spice and everything nice." In that same nursery rhyme, it's stated that boys are made of "snips and snails and puppy dogs' tails." Discuss the differences this nursery rhyme points out about perceptions of gender. What difference does it make that this is something we teach young children? How do you think knowing this nursery rhyme affects your perception of gender as you get older? Does this way of thinking seep into how we generally treat people based on gender? How so?

2. In trying to determine what makes a girl, Ellie also wonders if the things she saved in a box in her bedroom are what truly define her. She considers the mementos to be the only real mark that she ever existed. What do you think makes a person who they are? What do we leave behind that proves we were alive? If these things are material, as Ellie wonders in the scene in her room, what does that say about the things that were left behind in the abandoned houses in the town? What mark was left by the people who used to live in those houses?

3. Ellie says at one point that for most people, Kailey is easier to believe than Gretchen. What makes Kailey easier to believe?

What does this say about our social expectations of behavior based on gender?

4. Discuss the other girls and women of the novel. How are these characters connected? Officer Thompson, Kate, Gina Lynn, Cassie, Gretchen, Kailey, Hannah, and the other girls who attend the survivors' group, as well as the girls who were assaulted but never came forward, all play a role in Ellie's life—and death. A recurring theme is trying to define what makes a girl. Given the diversity of these women, what do you think truly makes a girl?

5. In many ways, Gina Lynn starts out as representative of the mean-girl trope. However, she eventually shows us a different side of herself. Why do you think she denied for so long that Caleb was involved? What do you think made her decide to come forward?

6. After Ellie goes missing, her picture is posted on the Internet along with articles asking for people to share any information they have. Most of the comments that follow are crude and heartless. How does social media impact Ellie's life, as well as her case? Why do you think people act this way in the face of the tragedy and pain of others?

7. Ellie witnesses Gina Lynn, Caleb, and their friends taking part in what they call "loser baiting," where they make YouTube videos that throw a spotlight on people's pain. Ellie says that it was easy to excuse hurting others because "they weren't us," but when the spotlight is turned on her own father, she still remains quiet. Why do you think people find

it funny and entertaining to see others humiliated? Why do you think some people who do not find these kinds of videos and images funny still choose to stay silent about them?

8. As the case unfolds, it's revealed that Caleb and Noah sexually assaulted other young women in the town. Most of these young women didn't report their assaults as soon as they happened and some never did, due to fear. What does that say about our society and how we view sexual assault? Ellie almost addresses this directly when she says that she's both a rape and murder victim, but unlike rape, there's never a debate about murder and whether she asked for it. Later, Caleb and Noah are found guilty only of the murder and not Ellie's assault. What do you think the significance of this is? What other aspects of the novel address our social attitudes and assumptions about sexual assault? In what ways can we change these attitudes?

9. At one point, a local man interviewed on the news says, "These boys have their entire futures ahead of them. It's concerning that they're being forced to take from their college savings to defend themselves against baseless accusations." Why do you think some people, whether they know those involved or not, are so quick to write off the victims and their futures, focusing only on what the boys may lose if they're found guilty? How does this tie into the previously discussed gender roles and expectations in our culture?

10. What role does status and wealth play in Ellie's story? Within the town, Caleb and Noah are held in high regard. Ellie was essentially deemed a runaway, and the search for her was

limited, mostly because of where she lived and her family's status. How do we view one another based on where we live, who we're related to, what we look like, how we dress, etc.? Ellie says that Wayne Breward took out TV ads for his campaigns because he could, and later, she states that she and Caleb walked through Gina Lynn's party with the "privilege of [could]." What privileges are allotted to people based on their perceived rank? Discuss how the assumptions we hold of others based on their class status affect society as a whole.

11. How do the empty houses—the zombies, as they are called—play a role in what happens to Ellie? Beyond being a physical location for the crimes to occur, how else do they affect the power given to the Breward family? Why does Caleb's status matter, and how is that connected specifically to these abandoned houses? There are rumors in the town about Caleb and Noah, as Kate mentions. Why do you think the people of Hollow Oaks are willing to ignore these rumors? Later, Ellie says that people in other towns around the country, seeing the story on the news, pretend that this couldn't happen in their towns. Could it?

12. Ellie's closest relationship was with her father. She loved him, but she admits she was embarrassed about his job and she sometimes blamed herself for his staying in Hollow Oaks. Alex Frias admits to Detective Gomes that he resented Ellie at times, too, and was ashamed that he had. What does this say about the love between parents and children? Ellie isn't angry that her father resented her sometimes; in fact, she's relieved. Why?

13. There were many things Ellie didn't tell her father, which come to light as her case unfolds. Later, in the scene with Kate's parents, they refer to their daughter as Katie, even though Ellie knew her as Kate. In what ways are we different people around our friends than we are around our parents and other family members?

14. Ellie says she and Kate weren't really friends, although during her freshman year, Kate was the person Ellie trusted most. What makes someone a friend? Ellie knows that she remembers only her version of the times she spent with Kate and that Kate may remember those times differently. Is this selfish or just human nature?

15. At several points in the novel, Ellie references light and light dying. Whether talking about a burned-out or dying lightbulb or a shooting star, this comes up quite a bit. She even says that lights always seemed to be burning out. How do these images connect to Ellie's story?

16. The title of the novel comes from the poem "Song of Myself" by Walt Whitman. How does the title answer any questions about where Ellie may actually go? Considering the last line of the poem, "I stop somewhere waiting for you," who might be the *you* that Ellie is waiting for?

Thank you for reading this Feiwel and Friends book.
The friends who made I STOP SOMEWHERE possible are:

Jean Feiwel, *Publisher*

Liz Szabla, *Associate Publisher*

Rich Deas, *Senior Creative Director*

Holly West, *Editor*

Anna Roberto, *Editor*

Christine Barcellona, *Editor*

Kat Brzozowski, *Editor*

Alexei Esikoff, *Senior Managing Editor*

Kim Waymer, *Senior Production Manager*

Anna Poon, *Assistant Editor*

Emily Settle, *Administrative Assistant*

Danielle Mazzella di Bosco, *Senior Designer*

Starr Baer, *Production Editor*

————

Follow us on Facebook or visit us online at **mackids.com**.
Our books are friends for life.